FATAL

FLAW

Fatal Flaw by Susan Murphy
Copyright Susan Murphy 2022

First published in 2022 by Susan Murphy

Version: 1 December 2022

The moral right of the author has been asserted.

FATAL

FLAW

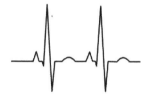

SP MURPHY

Acknowledgement

So many people helped with the writing of this book. From ideas and reading sections to offering their time and feedback, I thank every one of you who came along on this long journey with me. In particular, Yasmin, Karen and Adam who read and gave feedback and Louise who workshopped titles.

To my dad who persevered, critiqued and listened, and to Jeremy who did so much work to get it ready for the world, I am eternally grateful to you both.

CHAPTER

1

Jayda Crane panted in response to the 500-metre sprint she'd challenged herself to at the end of her morning run. Despite her exceptional physical fitness and lean frame, her lungs still gasped for breath and filled with the cool morning air. She smiled, enjoying the burning sensation which also served as a reminder to stay on track with her training. She had one month to be ready for her first marathon and nothing was going to get in the way of crossing the finish line.

She slid the key into the lock of her front door and twisted, listening for the familiar click before turning the knob. The house still had a faint aroma of the chicken she had cooked for dinner the night before. The smell made her stomach groan.

In her bedroom she sat on the edge of the bed, kicked off her sneakers and wriggled out of her running pants, pulling the spandex down to her aching feet. When she stood, her mind, already subconsciously aware that something was wrong, abandoned the to-do list she had been mentally penning. Instead, it began to wander through a montage of previously recorded smiles, birthdays, loves and losses, as if the mere second it took for her body to fall to the bed had lasted hours.

Jayda's chest constricted and her breath caught in her throat. By the time her head hit the soft, imitation mink bed cover, her mind had traced every memory it had collected. For not more than a millisecond, as the last cells of her brain seized and ceased to function, she wondered why she was dying.

Dominic Santino woke with a start. There was a rapping at his front door, loud enough to wake every one of the neighbours in his modest apartment complex. He checked his alarm clock. 1AM. He threw on a t-shirt and went to see who was making the racket at such an ungodly hour. Through the peephole he could see his captain, Harry Bryant, leaning against the wall. His face looked red and his eyes heavy.

Harry rarely made house calls, especially in the middle of the night. Santino unlatched the chain and opened the door. 'Harry? is everything…'

Harry Bryant shook his head, causing his straggly, sweat-dampened hair to fall across his forehead. He dismissed the concern with a wave of his hand and staggered past Santino, a strong smell of alcohol wafting behind him. At the kitchen table, he slumped into a chair, letting his large, loose frame fill the seat.

Santino followed, collecting some glasses and a bottle of scotch. Harry probably didn't need any more alcohol at this point, but Santino knew his captain well enough to know that offering him a coffee or water was not going to fly.

'Want to tell me what's going on, Harry?' he asked. He slipped into a chair at the other side of the table.

His usually rock-solid captain appeared to be coming undone before his eyes. He had good reason. Everyone who knew Harry was feeling for him, but seeing him in such bad shape, the shadows moving behind his eyes, black and crow-like, and his vulnerability, unnerved Santino. Harry was the man you turned to when everything fell to shit. Not the man who fell to shit himself. Ever. But this was different.

Harry looked up, allowing Santino to see the wiry red lines that were streaking the whites of his eyes. The skin on his face was ruddy and sagging, pulling his features down with it. 'I wish I could answer that, Santino, I really do. I don't know what's going on, but I want to find out.' The words came out in a rasp through chapped, raw lips.

Harry shook his head and poured almost half a glass of the scotch. 'My mind feels like it's going a million miles an hour all the time, coming up with different scenarios. Things that I know are stupid, but still, possible. That's why I came here, Santino. I didn't want to have this conversation at the station.'

Santino wondered what he meant by *have this conversation*. He was clearly there to get something off his chest, but what it was remained a mystery. 'Harry, you just lost your nephew. Who wouldn't be upset and confused? You know that better than anyone. You've seen families in the same situation. Hell, you've been the one to go in and tell them bad news more times than you can probably count. The shoe might be on the other foot now, but these are still really hard times for anyone. It's not lessened just because of the work you do.'

Harry stared at the amber liquid in his glass. 'I wish that was all it was. Something's not right here, Santino, I can feel it.'

Santino nodded to reassure him. Harry was suffering and, when grief was raw, it was easy to create theories. They allowed the brain to bring sense to what was happening. It reminded Santino of a woman he had comforted some years earlier at an accident scene. She had hit a young boy, a seven-year-old, who had run onto the road in front of her car while chasing a ball. Santino had sat with her for some time, listening and watching her wild eyes dart back and forth while she came up with at least a dozen different theories about why it had happened. They ranged from the child being pushed, to her having accidentally taken a muscle relaxant instead of a pain killer earlier in the day. She was so desperate to find a reason to hang onto. In her mind, there had to be something, but the reality was that she was simply driving down that road at the exact moment the boy's ball got away from him. It rolled onto the road and their worlds violently collided. Sometimes there were just accidents.

'I feel like there might be something more to Jason's death, Santino,' Harry said.

Santino crossed his bare arms over his chest and listened to his friend and mentor with sadness and dread. He wanted to offer Harry support and reassurance, but he knew there were rarely any words that could offer real comfort. 'It's been less than a week, Harry. That's not enough time to really know anything, especially from an evidence or medical point of view.'

From what Santino knew of the case, there had been no indication of anything suspicious reported by others who attended the scene. Harry's nephew, Jason, had some kind of medical episode at the wheel causing a car accident, and he had died. Santino hadn't checked on the details since the initial report, but as far as he knew, there had been no decision about the cause of death, nor any suspicion of foul play. If there had been, he would have heard about it by now.

The last thing he wanted was to come across as condescending or dismissive to a man he respected and admired, but at the same time, Santino wanted to be careful not to feed Harry's suspicions about the possibility of something bigger going on. 'Something might turn up, Harry, but you also have to accept the fact that it may well have just been a medical episode that led to Jason's accident. Nothing sinister.'

Harry was again staring into his glass as if it was willing him to dive in and drown his sorrows. 'I thought that at first, I did. This shit happens every day, right? I've seen it my whole career, we both have, and I know that families always want something or someone to blame, but that's not what this is. I went to identify his body with my sister and something wasn't right, I'm telling you. They can't even explain what happened to him for Christ's sake. Before I left, I spoke to one of the autopsy technicians at the morgue.'

'You didn't speak to Robert?' Santino asked.

Robert James was the Chief Medical Examiner and a long-time friend of them both.

'Robert wasn't there, he's away, but this other guy said they've had four others just like Jason in the last eight days.'

'Just like Jason? I thought they hadn't formally determined the cause of death.'

'They haven't, but that's the whole damn point,' Harry said. His eyes were wide and filled with a fiery determination. 'They're just like Jason in that they had some kind of brain haemorrhage that was listed as inconclusive or unexplained or something. They all had some kind of medical episode, but they have no clue what that episode was or why it occurred.'

Santino could see how much it was eating Harry up, but a passing comment made by a junior in the Medical Examiner's office was no better than speculative gossip.

'I'm not dismissing what you're saying, but surely that's fairly normal, Harry. People die. This is LA.'

Harry shook his head. He closed his eyes, placing his forefinger on one eyelid and his thumb on the other. He rubbed hard, pulling them together so tightly in the middle that Santino thought he might have to pry them loose before Harry did himself an injury. 'I know you think I'm making something of this because he's one of my own and I'm upset or grieving or whatever. Hell, I would too, but I've been a cop a long time, Santino, and standing in that autopsy suite, there was something in my gut that was churning.' He looked at Santino with conviction in his eyes. 'That feeling, you know what I'm talking about.'

Santino did know. He'd felt it many times throughout his career. It was like a knowing that wouldn't leave you. A bad smell that would weave itself into the fabric of your clothing, and eventually into your skin. There was no washing it away, no matter how hard you tried.

'Jason is dead, I accept that', Harry said. His voice sounded almost pleading. 'But five people, barely middle aged, all dead for no good reason and showing the same kinds of organ and tissue damage? What the hell is that? Jason wasn't sick. He was the strongest lad I'd seen in a long time and to just go like that…'

Harry's voice trailed off. Santino could almost see the lump in his throat bulging at the front of his neck as he gulped another mouthful of scotch to relieve it.

'Okay, Harry. I hear you and I agree that it sounds a bit off, but what exactly are you getting at? If you want me to say that there might be more than a coincidence here, I can't. I have no idea. A feeling isn't really enough to go on, no matter how good your instincts are. I don't have to tell you that. If this was a family you were talking to, what would you be saying to them?'

Harry was shaking his head. 'Damn it, Santino, I know! Under different circumstances I'd say the same thing, but you weren't there.' Droplets of sweat slicked his hair to his forehead and ran down his face as he moved.

Santino took a drink and stayed silent. There was no point going back and forth over it while Harry was in this state. 'I'm assuming you intend to look into it further then? Is that what this is about?' Santino asked.

'I have to. I can't just let it go, not yet anyway,' Harry shrugged.

Santino pushed his dark hair back from his face and made circles with his fingertips at his temples. He could feel a headache brewing behind his eyes. He tried to think of a way to measure what he was about to say so that it didn't come out as if he was dismissing Harry's claims, because he wasn't. But Harry needed a reality check before he fell too far down this rabbit hole.

'I know this is hard to hear, but it's just not enough, Harry. In fact, it's barely anything at all. It's your gut instinct, and I'm not dismissing that because I know you have a sixth sense for this stuff, but what can I do to help with any of this? There's nothing to go on at this point.'

'There's more though.' Harry sat up straighter, the fire returning to his eyes. 'One of my sister's friends, an acquaintance really, her daughter died suddenly yesterday. My sister first met her when they were pregnant with the kids and now her daughter is in the morgue next to Jason. Same age. No signs of being sick or having a disease. I'm waiting on more information, but you can't tell me that's a coincidence too, because if it is, it's a damn big one.'

Santino bit down on the inside of his cheek. It was a habit of his whenever something piqued his interest. Sometimes he bit so hard it bled. The death of the friend's daughter raised some questions. It was, at the very least, a possible connecting factor. 'Okay, I'm listening. Are you thinking there could be some kind of virus or something that people can catch, given that they knew each other? Centre for Disease Control would be all over it if it was.'

'That's just it, the mothers still kept in touch, but the kids hadn't seen each other for years. And screw CDC. You know what they're like,' he snapped.

Santino raked his fingers through the waves of his thick hair. It was still damp from his earlier shower and left moisture on the inner sides of his fingers. He rubbed them together, thinking over what Harry had just said. He wasn't convinced. Grief, particularly in the early hours and days after losing a loved one, had the keen ability to skew normal thought processes. It made people hear, see and feel things that they thought were signs from their lost loved one trying to tell them something, or lead them toward some kind of message. It also kept deep and restful sleep at bay, making wild and emotionally charged thoughts feel like reality. Even so, the hairs on Santino's arms stood up slightly when Harry told the story. 'I admit, it's concerning, Harry, but if the kids hadn't seen each other, maybe it is just a horrible coincidence. Either way, I still don't know what it is you want me to do with this? What can I do?'

'I trust you Santino and I need someone that I know will be discreet and keep it quiet, just while we check it out. There may be nothing to find and hell, my judgement might be way off with all this. God knows, I'm so close to retirement I can taste it, but I can't rest until I've done all I can to make sure, for Jason. You would too if it was your family.'

Santino poured them both another whiskey, even though he knew he shouldn't. He could feel his shoulders tensing and his head felt like it was being tightened in a vice. Whiskey would only make it worse. But Harry was right. If it was someone Santino loved, he would be at it like a dog with a fresh meaty bone. Nothing would get in his way, no matter how far-fetched it seemed. He would turn over every stone and go down every path, no matter how obscure, to make sure there was nothing left to find.

Harry Bryant was a good man and Santino owed him a lot. Whether to help him wasn't even in question. What was in question was whether or not that help would just buy into a delusion most likely brought about by grief. And if it did, then he wasn't helping Harry at all. It could actually cause more harm.

He studied Harry again, taking in how ravaged he looked. There were deep lines across his forehead, permanent reminders of the weight of all he had seen in his long career. It was sad to see it coming to a close like this. Harry deserved to end his career with a celebration of the blood, sweat and tears he had put into his work, but instead he risked killing himself with drink and stress before even reaching retirement.

'Can you speak to Robert and see what he thinks?' Santino asked. 'He'd be the one who would know if there was any possibility of a connection. Regardless of your personal feelings, what about someone at Disease Control? You must have a CDC contact.'

'Yeah, I've left a message for Robert to call me back, but I haven't heard from him yet. I don't want any other agencies getting involved right now if we can help it, especially not that mob.' He sighed and shook his unsteady head. 'I'm not so foolish as to think there's going to be some miraculous discovery here that will explain everything and tie the reason for Jason's death up in a nice little bow, Santino. All I want is for you to keep your eyes and ears open, that's all. Make a few calls.'

Santino could make some calls. There was no harm in at least asking a few questions to put Harry at ease.

Harry continued. 'I've told the guy at the Medical Examiner's office to alert me to anything similar and I'll be keeping watch myself. I've got feelers out with my contacts in other departments and if anything comes up, just go take a look for me, discreetly, that's all I'm asking. See if anything stands out or if there's any possible link between any of them. I trust your judgement. And if there's not, I'll accept that. I'll have to, I guess.'

Harry leaned down and pulled a bundle of papers from his bag, placing them on the table between them. 'This is what I've managed to put together so far. These are the ME's notes and the notes in our system. I know this is a longshot, Santino, but as far-fetched as it might sound, I've always trusted my gut instinct and right now, it's telling me there's something here, something is off with these.' He tapped his finger on top of the pile. 'Just take a look, please.'

Santino nodded. 'Go home and get some rest, Harry. You look like you haven't slept in days. I'll take a look, you have my word. I'll text Robert and see what he thinks first and we can go from there. Do you know when he's back?'

'Tomorrow or the next, I think.' Harry downed the rest of his drink and stood up on unsteady legs that threatened to buckle beneath him. He grabbed the edge of the table to balance himself before taking a step. 'It means a lot, Santino. I just need to be sure about this before I walk away. Keep me updated.'

Harry reached out and waited for Santino's hand. As they shook, Santino could sense the weight of grief in Harry's grasp. Why did bad things happen to good people? There were so many scumbags who were deserving of a quick and unpleasant end, and yet good young men like Jason took the hit.

When Harry was gone, Santino collected the notes and spread them out on the living room coffee table. Five faces, including Harry's nephew, Jason, who was a beat cop downtown. Five people, six if he included the friend of Harry's sister, who were dead for apparently no good reason. The problem was, most times, death didn't need a good reason. Death was one of those things that took without warning and left a hurricane in its wake. Families, questions and heartbreak. Perhaps Harry too was just a piece being flung around in the force of it. Either way, he'd keep his word and take a look, even if he wasn't convinced.

Santino woke to the sound of his ringing phone. He squinted and rubbed at his eyes while feeling around in the bed covers to find it.

He pushed aside the files and photos of the deceased that Harry had left him and just managed to get to it before the call went to his voicemail. 'Hello?' he answered.

'Santino, how can I help?' Robert James bellowed down the line. His upbeat tone hurt Santino's pounding head. He pulled the phone away to alleviate the pain before bringing it back to his ear.

'Robert, thanks for calling me back so soon.'

'Are you still sleeping, you lazy bastard? I've been at work since six,' Robert teased.

'Lucky you. You've also been away on holidays, I hear. When was the last time I took any time off?'

'Fair call,' Robert said, 'but you're an idiot. Life is short, believe me. I'm currently opening up a 43-year-old guy. Take time off, go and do something that's actually fun for once in your life, or hey, here's an idea, find a good woman and…'

'You're the last person I'm taking life advice from, Robert,' he laughed. 'I actually need to ask you about something.'

'Well maybe you *should* call me for life advice, but I'll leave that for another day. What do you need?'

'Harry Bryant came by here two nights ago and was in a bit of a state,' Santino said. 'You've heard that he recently lost his nephew, Jason?'

'Yeah, I only got back yesterday, but I heard about it this morning when I got in. Harry left me a message, but I haven't called him back yet. My assistant mentioned something to me about a car accident with the nephew. I haven't had a chance to scratch myself, let alone review any cases. Is there something I need to know?'

'Sort of.' Santino hesitated, unsure where to start. 'Jason was behind the wheel at the time, but that's not what caused his death. Someone at your office told Harry that the cause was some kind of brain haemorrhage, but that it's still unclear what caused it. It's hard to explain, but I was hoping to run a few things by you and get your opinion, off the record of course.'

'Off the record? Okay, now you've got my attention.'

Santino didn't explain the *off the record* comment. That could wait. 'Harry seems to think there might be a bit more to Jason's death than first thought and he wants me to quietly follow up on a few things.'

'What sort of *more* are we talking about here, Santino?'

'He thinks there might be others, deaths that are similar to Jason's and that there could be something to it, maybe a link.'

'I haven't been here for three weeks, so I'm not up to speed, but I'll talk to the others and check out the case load. Did he say what he was thinking in terms of a link?'

'No, he doesn't know and he's not even sure there is something. Neither am I to be honest, but it's got him a bit rattled so I'm checking into it for him.'

'Come by and see me later, I'm here all day, and all night probably,' Robert joked.

Santino laughed. 'I will. And tell the 43-year-old I'm sorry he's been left in your hands.'

'Yeah, yeah, go away now, some of us have to actually work,' Robert said.

Santino hung up and packed the files into his satchel. He showered, hoping the beating water and heat might clear his mind and his headache, but the quiet only complicated his thoughts.

Was he wasting his time with this? Looking into Jason's death and getting Robert and God knows who else involved could end up wasting everyone's time and prolonging Harry's pain. The whole thing made him uneasy. He was being pulled into investigating this out of a sense of loyalty to Harry, but if it turned out there was no evidence to suggest anything other than a tragic accident in Jason's death, he would have to convince Harry of that. Something like this could force Harry to end his career on a sour note, rather than the high he deserved after so many years of dedicated service to the people of LA.

He dressed and grabbed one of the bran muffins his elderly neighbour, Mrs Dawson, liked to bake for him and leave at his door. He had told her on numerous occasions that it was too much, but she insisted that the comfort of living next door to a detective was worth all the baking in the world. And he didn't mind. She reminded him a little of his mother and to have Mrs Dawson occasionally visiting eased his guilt about not seeing his family nearly enough. He made a mental note to book some leave days and take a trip to Manhattan to visit his mum and sister. He hadn't seen his nieces and nephew for months.

He hadn't even started his car when a text message came from Robert.

> *Don't bother coming here, I have to head to a scene, I'll explain later. Had a quick glance at the case lists and it is looking a bit, shall we say, interesting. Can you meet me at the scene instead? This one might even fit the bill of what we were talking about. Female, name is Jayda Crane, 79 Carling Lane, Culver City.*

Santino started the car and headed straight to the address Robert had given him. The faces and scenes in the photos Harry had left him consumed his thoughts on the drive. Heartbroken families that would want answers. They deserved to know why, but hoping for an answer that might never come was a terrible thing to cling to. It only led to dealing with the reality all over again when hopes were dashed. He wondered what Robert had meant about the latest death fitting the bill. Maybe he was seeing something there too, just as Harry had.

Pulling up out front, the stone-fronted cottage appeared clean from the outside. Neat garden, manicured lawn and a seemingly nice neighbourhood filled with what he guessed were middle-class families, most of whom were currently gathered on the other side of the road watching on.

Stepping out of his black Lexus, Santino took in the sound of the gravel-laden driveway that crunched beneath his leather shoes. He stopped at the porch, noticing pools of water that had gathered on the red concrete, most likely caused by the bright yellow watering can on a table nearby.

He turned at the sound of a vehicle pulling up. Robert smiled at him from the driver's seat of the Medical Examiner's van. 'You got here fast, did you fly?' Robert joked as he hopped out.

Santino went over to the van. 'I was already in the car when I got your message. Have you got something for me?'

Robert took his bag from the back and moved closer to Santino. He kept his voice low. 'I managed to get a quick look at the case load over the last few weeks and I'll admit it's a bit unusual – at least without some kind of event as a catalyst.'

Santino wasn't sure what he was getting at, but he had known Robert long enough to know he would eventually explain himself properly.

'I don't think we've ever had so many cases listed as undetermined in all my years in the job. I'll know more once I've had the chance to properly review a few, but this one inside might be something similar, based on her age and the info I was given over the phone. That's why I've come myself. They said it looks like a natural death from the outset, but we'll see.'

Robert pulled out a package of white coveralls and threw it at Santino. 'Get that on and we'll go in and have a look.'

Inside, there were no obvious smells, other than the scent from a vase of roses on a stand by the front door, their petals still fresh and full of a perfect red hue. They looked hand-picked and were probably from the bush in the front garden that he had passed on the way in.

The walls were adorned with wallpaper from an earlier era, its paisley swirls dressed the entrance hall and a matching orange and brown carpet covered the floor. Santino guessed that it was most likely a rental property.

Two local LA County Sherriff's Department officers leaned against the wall of the long hallway that led to the bedroom. They were already whispering about Santino's arrival, their voices travelling along the space, alerting the officer in the bedroom. Santino knew why but cared little for their questions about the presence of a Homicide detective at what appeared to be a natural death. He too was wondering why the hell he was there. There was also the fact that Santino wasn't very popular in law enforcement circles thanks to the widely publicised Fitzgerald case. He had given up, or in their words, 'ratted out' several of his peers and others in positions of importance. Either way, today he was with Robert, so none of them would dare say a word.

In the bedroom, the dead woman was face-up across the middle of the bed, her legs draped over the edge. Jayda Crane's right foot, still partially stuck inside a pair of black pants, indicated to him that she had been in the middle of changing when she died. Santino moved closer as the local officers continued their muttering.

Jayda's eyes were open. She was looking at the ceiling, a pained expression contorting what had been a beautiful face. She was wearing only a singlet and briefs, her running shoes on the floor in front of her. Santino whispered a Catholic prayer for the dead. He thought of his mother and the image of her kneeling at the side of the bed where his dead father lay. Tears were streaming from her red eyes and falling onto her cheeks as she recited the rosary again and again. He had stood behind her, listening and studying his father's face, the skin already waxy.

Santino could sense that the eyes in the room were on him. Their burning questions and judgement were burrowing into his back as he bent over Jayda and looked closely at her. She too had already taken on the waxy sheen. He turned his attention to Robert who had slipped on gloves and was gently lifting her left arm. At first glance, there didn't seem to be anything that was ringing alarm bells.

Surveying the room, Santino looked for any clue that would tell Jada's story, or at least tell him something about what had happened to her. The dead always had a story to tell if you knew where to look, but Jayda gave nothing away at this point.

'Pity, she was a real looker.' The words came from somewhere behind him.

Santino turned, anger surging through him. The voice had come from one of the young officers who had previously been in the hall. He was now standing in the doorway of the bedroom. Santino shot him a warning glare causing him to snort and shift nervously from one foot to the other. Santino left Robert to his work, pushing past the officer with a stiff elbow jab, causing the man to lurch forward clutching his stomach.

Santino ignored the abuse that followed and made his way down the hall to the other rooms. In the small kitchen, the stone benchtops were clean, except for a few items left out from the previous evening's dinner. She had eaten alone, one plate and one glass, rinsed and drying on the sink. She had showered, the bathroom floor still slightly damp and the towel, not yet fully dry, slung over the top of the door the same way that he did at home. Every window was shut and locked and the rear door was still secured with a dead lock. No sign of forced entry.

His thoughts went back to Harry. Harry was convinced that Jason's death was more than just an accident and Robert had, at the very least, confirmed that there had been some strange cases lately. If there was a connection of some kind, could Jayda be another to add to the list? He shook off the thoughts and reminded himself that all of this was nothing but theories and possibilities.

Robert appeared in the hall. 'Anything?'

Santino shook his head. 'Nothing that stands out.'

'I'm nearly done here. Do you want to wait?'

'I've got the files that Harry gave me in my car,' Santino said. 'Can you meet me at the bar around the corner on Pitt Street when you're finished here? I want you to have a quick look over what I've got, but I don't want to waste too much time on this if there's nothing in it.'

Robert checked his watch. 'Sure, but I've literally only got half an hour, we're swamped back there. And there better be food. Order me something. Something with meat and none of that green crap.'

Santino laughed, shaking his head as he went back to the car. It always amazed him that in spite of the fact that Robert spent his days looking at the insides of people who had ruined their bodies through bad habits, he continued to drink, smoke and eat copious amounts of bad food.

When Robert arrived at the bar half an hour later, his face was flushed and his brow furrowed causing it to crease into a series of uneven grooves. 'I don't know who is recruiting these idiots, but the standard of these young cops is seriously at an all-time low. One of them was actually on the phone having an argument with his girlfriend – inside the house. Not outside, not quietly either. In the house, without giving a shit about who had to listen to it. Is my food coming?'

'It's ordered and coming,' Santino assured him.

'Good. I'm on a tight timeframe so you'll have to catch me up on all the details later, just give me the short version for now and tell me whatever you think I need to know right now.'

Robert patted his forehead with a handkerchief. 'I'm sweating like a pig here.' He leaned back and eyed Santino from head to toe. 'How is it that you, no matter what the circumstances, always look as if you stepped straight off one of those designer men's mags with your pressed suit, crisp white shirt and slicked back hair? It's bloody ridiculous. While I'm over here looking like I've come from Hobo magazine as their man-of-the-month.'

'I do my best,' Santino laughed. He pulled the case files from his satchel and handed them to Robert. 'This is what Harry gave me, but there could be more. I'll explain what Harry said later, but basically, there doesn't seem to be any real explanation for Jason's death and someone at your office told him there had been several cases just like it. The thing that did make me take notice though was that Harry mentioned a friend of Jason's mother who had a daughter the same age as Jason, and she also died this week with no definitive reasons listed. You gotta admit, it's odd.'

Robert was nodding while looking through the files. 'There have been a higher than usual number of cases in the last few weeks overall, but we have a staff meeting this afternoon to go through each one in more detail. That should hopefully make things a bit clearer and give me a better insight into whether or not there are signs of a link between them.'

'But there is a higher number overall?' Santino pushed.

'Yeah, that's my understanding, although no red flags seem to have been raised at this point, so don't get your hopes up just on that. We can get spikes when there's a full moon, I shit you not. I'll talk to the team and see if anyone has concerns.'

'And what about this friend of Jason's mother? Her daughter's death?' Santino asked.

Robert shrugged. 'What about it? The mothers know each other, so what? It's not uncommon for people who know each other to lose loved ones or die, you know that. If we can determine that there is a link based on their tox-screens or something else, then that could give us a starting point, but right now, I wouldn't go making assumptions. You don't want to end up under a microscope again with the LAPD and the media.'

Santino watched as Robert cut into the steak and chips that had arrived. He was scoffing it like a man who hadn't seen food for a month.

'I know that,' Santino said. He didn't need to be reminded. 'But it could be something they had in common, or passed to each other, couldn't it?'

'No way to know.' Robert was talking while moving a large piece of meat from one side of his mouth to the other. 'Were they intimate? Did they go out and eat together or spend time together?'

'Harry said the kids hadn't, but the mothers had been in fairly recent contact,' Santino explained.

'There are too many variables here, Santino. Without looking too much into it, the cause of death in each of these looks like something from within rather than external factors. Now, that's only a guess, I haven't seen all of the info, but it doesn't look like any common disease or illness that we'd usually see. Once I've had the chance to look inside the Crane woman, I'll be able to tell you more. You can't always rely on some of the juniors in my office.'

'Well, that's good to know. Jesus, it's a pretty important job,' Santino sneered.

Robert waved his hand at Santino, dismissing his concerns. 'No, not like that. Don't get on your high horse. They're good at what they do, but they haven't been around long enough to spot everything. Not like those of us who have been doing it since the dawn of time. You know what I mean, you see things others don't see. That's why I'm the boss.' He grinned and slopped the last of his steak in the gravy before filling his mouth.

'Still not comforting,' Santino told him.

Robert's phone chimed. He took it from the holder at his waist and answered. Santino could hear that it was a male on the other end. He stood up and turned away from Santino. The conversation was brief but seemed to leave Robert unsettled.

'I have to get back,' Robert said. 'If you can bring me copies of these notes tomorrow, I'll compare them to what we have, but I want to know exactly what Harry's thoughts are on this before I give it any real time. If there's any link, I'll hopefully see it in the notes, but if not, you might want to seek out a genetics specialist to take a look as well.'

'Genetics?' Santino was thrown by the suggestion.

'It would be worth seeing if you can get the cases reviewed to look for some kind of genetic condition or something along those lines as well. Keep in mind that if there's any hint of there being a connection to anything viral or bacterial, the CDC will be in like a shot.'

'What does that even mean?' Santino held his hands palms up at Robert and shook them as he spoke. 'In layman's terms for God's sake.'

Robert smiled understanding his frustration. 'As I said, I'm not convinced from what I've read that this is about something viral or external. I'm thinking that it's more likely something within the person themselves. A defect or congenital abnormality. It might not help in terms of linking them, but it's worth checking out even to exclude something from being a possible link, especially in Jason's case, so that Harry can be satisfied.'

'And where do I find someone to do that?' Santino asked.

Robert wiped his face with a napkin before tossing the crumpled paper onto his empty plate. 'I do know of someone, but… ah…'

'But what?' Santino pushed.

'She's the best, brilliant actually, but I'm not sure she's doing this kind of work anymore. I haven't been in contact with her for a few years.'

'I'll find her, don't worry. Just give me the details you have.'

Robert pulled a piece of paper from his bag and wrote down the information. He slid it across the table to Santino. 'Tell her I send my regards.'

CHAPTER

2

The number three lit up above the elevator doors as they slid open. Santino stepped out into a deserted, white corridor, a stark contrast to the modern brick exterior of the building. There was only one department on this floor according to the lobby receptionist, and the lettering on the glass at the end of the corridor signalled he had come to the right place:

Department of Human Genetics
UCLA School of Medicine

The office waiting area was decorated in the same austere white, furnished in a minimalist style, with four chairs, a magazine table, television and an unusually high desk. It was awkwardly placed in front of the only visible window. The desk was bare except for a single tray marked 'in' and a computer with an over-sized monitor. Next to it was a small, round bell. He smacked it with an open palm and waited as the sound echoed off the bare walls.

'Can I help you?' A young woman appeared from behind one of the two doors that adjoined the reception area, her eyes appraising his well-cut suit and polished shoes.

'Good afternoon.' Santino smiled, flashing his open wallet. 'I called yesterday…'

'Detective Santino.' The young woman barely glanced at his badge. 'Professor Sloane is expecting you. Please, have a seat, she won't be long.'

Santino eyed the writing on the silver plate that was fixed to the tempered glass of the door the young woman disappeared behind. He grinned, imagining that the plate must have been specially made to accommodate the numerous acronyms and qualifications following the Professor's name.

Arnya, her name alone conjured numerous images in his mind of what a female Professor of Genetics might look like. Adding that to the string of letters after her name, he imagined grey hair and a European accent, although Robert's tone when he had given Santino the details, made him suspect he might be way off base.

While he waited, he replayed in his mind the anguished face of the dead woman, Jayda Crane. He thought about her family and the fact that by now they would likely be reeling from the news of her death. It had always been the worst part of the job. Seeing distraught parents, partners, children or siblings was something you could never desensitize to, or at least he couldn't. Reminding himself to update Harry, he pulled out his phone to send him a message. He only managed to type a few words before his attention was caught by an image on the television in the corner of the room. He walked over and stared at a familiar face, listening as the newsreader explained.

> *'Dogged by controversy after narrowly escaping a jail term over the death of his friend and employee, the late Maurice Stephens, we can today confirm that Parker Fitzgerald is now one of America's richest men following the death of his father, billionaire pharmaceutical tycoon, Rupert Fitzgerald.'*

Fitzgerald smiled at the camera, like a cat that had finally caught the elusive mouse, as he spoke of his sadness at his father's passing.

> *'My father was a brilliant man, a philanthropist who was years ahead of his time. My family are devastated by his passing and ask for privacy while we grieve. What I can say, is that I intend to continue my father's legacy and I will be sitting down with the board to discuss an exciting new direction for Alpha Pharmaceuticals.'*

Santino's lips turned in and tightened. He was about to curse when the name-plated door opened. 'Detective Santino?' The receptionist called to him from the doorway. 'The Professor will see you now.' She ushered him into a large office.

Professor Sloane had risen from her orderly desk. She came around to greet him, holding out her hand. Santino tried not to smile, remembering the image he had conjured in the waiting room. He couldn't have been further from the truth.

Adjusting his jacket, he extended his hand to hers. 'Thank you for seeing me, Professor Sloane.' Her skin was soft and cool, but her grip firm. He wondered how Robert knew her.

'I'm not really sure I can help you, Detective. Perhaps if you explain a little more about what it is that you need exactly.'

The Professor slipped her arms from her lab coat, revealing a tall, sleek frame. Hanging the coat on the back of the door, she gestured for Santino to take a seat on the black leather sofa, while she took the maroon armchair.

At a short distance he had thought she was attractive, but now, close enough for him to see the details of her face, she was actually quite intriguing. Slightly olive skin, high cheekbones and full lips gave her face symmetry that some might say equalled beauty, but her eyes; her eyes were what intrigued him. Soft and oval in shape, they were deep and penetrating, one hazel and the other green. The slight imperfection didn't detract from her symmetry, in fact, it enhanced it, adding interest and a uniqueness to her.

The Professor's attention moved to the solid marble coffee table between them and the files Santino had placed on it. Santino realised he had been staring at her and quickly moved on. 'I'm investigating a series of,' he paused momentarily carefully choosing the right words, 'strange deaths that have occurred recently. I was referred to you because, Professor Sloane, I was told that you're the best geneticist in the country.'

He shifted his eyes about the room as he spoke, taking in his surroundings and making mental notes, a habit he had engaged in for as long as he could remember, even well before he had become a police officer. His school friends used to tease him about it, telling him he'd make a good cop one day since nothing ever got passed him without being noticed and mentally documented.

Arnya rubbed her hands together and shifted in her seat. 'And may I ask who would be so kind as to say that, Detective?'

It wasn't exactly the time or place to be charming, but he was good at charm and he needed her help. 'I'm not usually in the habit of revealing my sources, Professor, but in this case, I'll make an exception given that I'm sure he wouldn't mind. In fact, he asked me to pass on his regards. It was Robert James, the Medical Examiner.'

Arnya nodded in recognition, a smile forming on her full lips. She looked back at the files and quickly moved on without further acknowledging the source.

Santino continued, pretending not to notice how Robert's name had caused a shift in her manner and a glint of something in her eyes, even if it was only for a second. 'I'm looking at a recent case, several in fact, which appear, at least from first glance, to be natural deaths. There were no signs of forced entry, no sexual assault and no indication of any kind of struggle, but each one, and there are now six in total, we think, is identical to the others. The deceased don't appear to have any clear or obvious link to one another, other than their age and the fact that the autopsies provided the same inconclusive results with little explanation. From what I've been able to ascertain, and that's not much at this stage, they didn't live in the same local area, eat at the same places, or attend the same functions. Yet, there's something that seems similar about their deaths. Robert is cautious and reluctant to make any call just yet, but he agrees that it's unusual.'

The Professor was listening intently. Getting up, she crossed to a small office refrigerator, poured some Perrier water and handed Santino a glass. 'Do experienced Homicide detectives usually investigate deaths that appear to be natural?'

Santino smiled nonchalantly. She had clearly done some research on her guest and wanted him to know it. It was no secret that he'd had a turbulent career. He never attempted to hide his past, although he hadn't expected to have it raised at this meeting.

'Clearly you know my background, given the media attention the Fitzgerald case attracted, and the fallout. I suppose people are being reminded of that now with the recent events and his father's death.'

Arnya smiled. 'What I mean to ask, Detective, and I mean no disrespect, is how you came to the conclusion that the deaths are unusual if they appear to be natural?'

'There are five so far, six if the young woman I was called to recently turns out to be the same. If they are indeed the same. I'm sorry to sound so unclear, but I don't have anything solid right now. What we do know is that they're all around the same age, are otherwise known to be healthy, yet each died suddenly without any indication as to why. According to Robert, who has only done a basic review of the files at this point and also attended the scene of the last death, their brain cells just spontaneously self-destructed. Non-Traumatic Intra-Cerebral Haemorrhage'. He read from the file. 'This was also the cause in the other cases as well, but there are no reasons given, or found.'

Arnya paced back and forth with her finger pressed to her lips. She walked around the entire room twice before Santino broke the silence. 'I'll be honest Professor, I'm not sure there even is a link, but there seems to be something that's not right here. People like to talk about coincidences, but in my experience, coincidences often lead to connections and I'm starting to see a few here, even if I can't explain them yet. It seems odd to me that there would be six cases, in a short space of time, of people all in the same age group who have died in the same manner with no apparent underlying cause.'

'And Robert is sure it's not viral or bacterial? Something airborne?' she asked.

'Like me, Robert isn't sure of anything at this early stage, but he doesn't think so. He's doing further investigations as we speak.'

Continuing to pace the room with slow strides, Arnya ran her fingers along the strands of dark hair that fell in waves around her face. She appeared to be a million miles away in thought. He took the opportunity to look around a little more, his eyes fixing on a second door, behind her meticulously organised desk, marked LABORATORY. That explained the lab coat. There were no pictures in her office, no photos, in fact there seemed to be a complete lack of anything personal in the room. She was either a minimalist who liked to keep work and personal life completely separate, or she was a workaholic.

The only sign that she had a life outside the room was a pair of sneakers under the desk and three takeaway coffee cups in the trash can.

He turned back to the Professor and placed the file on the coffee table. He wondered what someone might think if they were surveying him in the same manner. They might come to the same conclusion that he barely existed outside of his work.

Arnya pulled her chair around and sat beside him. She spread the photos and statements from the files across the glass top and began to read. Santino watched as her body appeared to relax into a familiar position of study. She read quickly and moved fluidly as she turned pages, sitting still in the chair between bursts of paper shuffling. Without knowing anything about her, other than the obvious, he found her interesting.

The intercom made a high-pitched noise and a voice boomed from the tiny box. 'Professor Sloane, I have your conference call with Germany on hold on line one for you. Would you like me to reschedule?'

Arnya looked at her watch. 'I didn't realise the time,' she said. Her cheeks flushed.

Santino touched the watch on his arm instinctively. He noticed that she wore hers on her right wrist as he did, the opposite of most people who were right-handed.

'I'm sorry, Detective, but I must take the call. Can you leave these with me and I'll get back to you?'

'That would be great, these copies are for you, Professor. I trust that we can keep this between ourselves for now?'

Arnya hesitated before answering. 'Of course.' She agreed, but seemed unsure. Santino had the feeling that had she not been in a hurry she may have questioned him on the secrecy of the information, but for now it would have to wait.

'Thank you for your time, Professor. I look forward to hearing from you.' He placed his card on top of the files that still lay strewn across the table and closed the door behind him. A visit to Robert was next on his list.

Dreading the peak hour traffic, Santino headed to the freeway. His mind was running back and forth over the cases and his conversation with the Professor, not the least of which was how Robert knew her. He had the feeling that the details were not going to be shared with him, at least not willingly. As he pulled into the parking lot of the ME's office, he wondered if he could push Robert to be a little more forthcoming with the story.

He stepped out of the car, taking a moment to admire the beauty and heritage of the building that housed the Office of the LA County Medical Examiner. Its magnificence was lost on those required to enter it. The people who worked there no longer noticed its charm or the detailed work that had gone into crafting every stone that was clad to the original red brickwork. And those who came for other reasons were often in no frame of mind to consider its elegance, caring only for their breaking hearts while their loved one lay still and lifeless inside its walls.

Santino wondered if he was the only person who actually stopped to admire it. His love of buildings, especially old ones, had been passed down to him by his father who was long gone from life now, but who came alive in his memory when he looked at places like this. He could almost hear his voice, quietly explaining the intricacies of the structure. When Santino was young, they would take long family drives in and around the city, stopping to look closely at the stonework and touch the different textures of the walls. The old churches had been Santino's favourite. He and his father would talk about the precision in the building, while his sister moaned about going home and his brother played hangman on squares of paper. His father had a deep appreciation for things that were well designed and well built, making it his life's work. It was the sole reason he had packed up his family, leaving his hometown of Torrecuso, 30 miles northeast of Naples in southern Italy, to 'build the best buildings in the world'. He stayed true to his word, starting a construction business that grew substantially and had made a small fortune, and right up to his last breath, he still loved to drive his grandchildren around the city to show them his masterpieces.

Santino touched the stone as he entered, feeling the roughness against his fingers. Sometimes he wondered if he should have gone into the building industry instead of the LAPD. His father would have loved for him to have followed in his footsteps. But being a cop had pulled Santino from an early age. The badge, and the ability to do the hard stuff, appealed to his nature. Even if he had tried something else, he was sure that he would have ended up on the force at some stage.

He entered the autopsy suite where the receptionist had told him Robert was working. It never got easier to come into these places, even after years of it.

Inside, the air was cool and filled with the smell of harsh chemicals that penetrated Santino's senses and burned his nostrils. It caused his nose to twitch. Robert didn't look up as the grinder worked to separate skull from the flesh of a young man who had been killed by what looked like a gunshot to the face. The sound made Santino's skin feel like it had ants crawling all over it.

The metal autopsy table with the body of Jayda Crane had been pushed to the far side of the room while she waited her turn. In his memory, she looked different, but that was often the case with the dead. Santino noticed early on in his career that when a person hadn't been dead for long, they still had a presence of life about them as if they hadn't yet moved away from their physical bodies. Sometimes, if the death wasn't traumatic, they looked as if they were just sleeping peacefully. But here, after time had passed, Jayda was long gone, merely dying flesh and bones.

Santino instinctively made the sign of the cross and touched the crucifix that hung beneath his pressed white shirt. He rarely went to church anymore, but he was a product of a strict Catholic upbringing, parts of which often still found their place in his life, particularly in circumstances like this.

'Long time, no see,' Robert joked. He peeled off his gloves and patted Santino's shoulder.

'Anything on Jayda Crane yet?' Santino asked.

'Nothing yet. The family's here to ID her now, flown in from Florida because they wanted to do it themselves. Did you get anywhere with the genetics stuff?'

Santino nodded. 'Maybe, not sure yet. I've just come from the university now.'

Robert flashed Santino a wide smile. 'And how is Professor Arnya Sloane?'

Santino caught the same tone in Robert's voice that he had heard the last time he mentioned her name. 'The Professor appeared fine to me. She seemed interested to look at the cases, if that's what you're asking?'

Robert looked up at him and raised an eyebrow. 'I guess that is what I'm asking. And maybe a bit more.'

Santino was about to dig a little deeper when the intercom crackled. 'Dr James, the family are in the waiting area,' the receptionist announced.

Robert shook his head. 'Duty calls. How about if I give you a call later when I'm finished up here and we can meet for a drink and go over the details and your visit with the Professor? I want to hear more.' He made air quotation marks, "off the record" of course, as you said.'

Robert had always been a live wire. He liked a joke, a drink and a bet and had a dry sense of humour that could sometimes be interpreted as a bit *off-centre*. He claimed the dead never laughed at his jokes, so he made extra effort to be funny when he was around the living.

Santino agreed. 'I'll see you later,' he called back. He left Robert to his work and was still smiling when he entered the corridor, coming face to face with a couple sitting uncomfortably, side by side on a long bench seat. The man's pleading eyes met Santino's causing the smile to fade quickly. He swallowed hard against the familiar look of overwhelming grief that consumed the man's round, red face. Letting go of his wife's hand, the man stood up.

'Please, can we see her now?' His voice caught in his throat on *her* as the word and all of its meaning seemed to settle heavily on his chest and escape in a choked mumble.

Santino took his shaking hand, cupping it between both of his to steady him. 'I'm Detective Santino. Dr James will be with you in just a minute, please sit.' He gestured for the man to return to the seat beside his sobbing wife. 'I'm sorry for your loss,' he said. He pulled up a chair to sit beside them.

'She was our only child, she was everything.' The woman sobbed into her patterned handkerchief.

Her husband touched her knee affectionately and took over for her. 'We never thought we'd have children. We'd all but given up, so when we got a little help and Jayda came along, we couldn't believe it. She was like our own little miracle. We just don't understand. It makes no sense, she's healthy. Our girl is healthy. She runs.' His voice trailed off as his eyes moved toward the doors of the autopsy suite. He straightened his back and met Santino's eyes. 'That girl in there, my daughter, she was everything to us and I could not have been more proud to be her father.'

'Mr and Mrs Crane, please come in.' Robert's voice was soft now as he appeared at the door. There was no hint of his usual humour and playfulness as he held the door open for the shattered couple who would soon be burying their only child.

Santino wondered if his search would lead to finding an answer that might give them some understanding and closure about what happened to her. If there was one.

CHAPTER

3

The aroma of the 2000 Shiraz immediately calmed Santino's wired senses. Wine, red in particular, always had that effect on him. His parents often drank it with their evening meal and the smell, even all these years later, still brought comforting images for him. Memories of sitting at the family table, laughing and babbling with his siblings as the smell of home-cooked Italian food filled the air and their father recounted the events of his day. There was always some crazy story or catastrophe to laugh about. He longed to feel that again, just one last time.

Robert was late as usual. Santino had already been at the bar for 30 minutes. It was almost Robert's signature move to arrive at least half an hour late to any meeting or catch-up. Santino picked up his glass, swirling the liquid. The memory he had been enjoying of his childhood was still lingering when his mind began to wander to a new place, a place that once again stimulated his senses. The intriguing Professor Sloane.

Like a scene from an old movie, the slow melodic tune casting out from the jukebox in the corner of the dimly lit bar filled the spaces between the chatter around him. Every detail of his meeting with her played over in his mind. She was smart, but that wasn't her strongest quality. Even in the short time he'd spent with her, he could see that she was intuitive and focussed. The way she had paced, considering the aspects of the cases and feeling her way through them rather than just reading the lines of notes in the files as others might have done. And she was right about the fact that these weren't the kind of cases he was usually called on to investigate. She had done her homework and made sure she knew who it was that had requested a meeting with her.

'Hey, glad you could make it,' Robert said with a grin. He planted himself on a stool beside Santino at the bar. 'Scotch and Coke,' he told the barman who had managed to momentarily tear himself away from a group of young women at the other end.

'How did it go today, with the family?' Santino asked.

'As well as it always goes. They were devastated and struggling to understand. I'm not a religious man, Santino, but sometimes you have to believe that there must be a reason or logic for a beautiful woman like that, with so much of her life still ahead of her, to just cease to exist. Her poor bloody parents.' Robert shook his head. 'They were lovely and just shattered.'

'What's gotten into you with all this deep and meaningful talk?' Santino said.

'I don't know, it just feels harder some days. Maybe I took too much time off.'

Santino knew what he meant. It did feel harder some days, especially when dealing with grieving families. 'Robert, sometimes there's no logic or reason and that's exactly what makes it so damn hard. Sometimes things just are the way they are. Accidents happen and people do things that are unimaginable and at times, even they don't understand why. Life and death are just mysteries beyond our understanding and always will be.'

Robert downed his drink and clanked his glass on the bar for another. 'Well, I don't completely agree with that, but I get what you mean. Anyway, I'm not here to contemplate the complexities of man, science or religion or whatever the hell it is we're talking about. Give me the full story on all this, from the start. What exactly did Harry have to say when he came to see you and what have you come up with since we spoke?'

Santino put his glass down and turned his body to face Robert. He folded his arms across his chest and went back to the start in his mind. 'As I told you, Harry showed up at my door, pretty much in the middle of the night, and he'd been drinking heavily.'

'That's understandable, given the situation', Robert said. 'I wish I'd worked on him, Jason I mean. For Harry, you know? Poor bastard. My assistant told me that when they came in the mother was an absolute mess, almost hysterical. She was angry of course and demanding answers, but once he spoke to her, she calmed down a bit. People need someone to blame, you know? It seems to help if there's someone to blame.'

Santino agreed. 'I know. But I don't think any of this stuff with Harry is about blame. Harry's been on the force a long time and he's got a good head for things that don't sit right. It's like a sixth sense, and even if it wasn't his nephew, I would trust that instinct 100 percent. I am still worried that he's being driven by his own need for answers, but you know Harry. He's tough, no bullshit and he wouldn't ask a favour lightly. The kid's death has really got him tied up in knots and he's sure there's something more to it. Jason idolised Harry. Hell, he only joined the force to be like him.'

Robert seemed to weigh up Santino's remarks before he answered. 'So, basically Harry thinks there's something we should be looking at here and even though you know he's emotionally driven right now, you trust him enough to think there might be something in it, is that the gist of it?'

It wasn't solely that Santino trusted Harry. He trusted himself and his own instincts and something was niggling at him. 'Yes and no. It may have started with Jason's death, but surely even you can now see that there's some strange crap going on.'

Robert shifted on his stool, not quite nodding in agreement, but not dismissing Santino either.

'When Harry came to my place that night he stank of booze and cigarettes, and he practically stumbled in the door. But he was coherent and convinced that there was something more to Jason's death, and the daughter of the mother's friend I told you about. He had the files with him of similar cases, the ones you saw the other day, and hell, I'm sceptical but there could be something here, couldn't there?'

Robert shrugged. 'Sure, there's a few more than usual, I'll give you that, but other than the mother's friend, what exactly is it that's got him, and you by the sounds of it, so convinced there's something bigger? That's what I don't get. Are you thinking murder or something else? Harry hasn't called me back since I left him the message, by the way.'

Robert was a man of science. He needed more than thoughts and gut feelings. 'You've seen the notes,' Santino said. 'Jason died suddenly at the wheel of his squad car with no explanation, at least none that your office found. He had signalled to a driver to pull over and as the cruiser drew in behind, it didn't stop, colliding with the rear of the parked car. Jason was found gripping the steering wheel, staring straight ahead. The cause of death as you know was…'

'Non-Traumatic Intra-Cerebral Haemorrhage,' Robert finished. 'The same as what was noted in the other cases. Gary said that when he opened the skulls expecting to find a normal brain within the Dura, what he found was pretty much like a lump of Jell-o. And I hate to say it, but it was the same with the Crane woman as well. I did it late this afternoon.'

Santino gave him a questioning look. 'Plain English please, Robert.'

Robert smiled and dropped his shoulders. 'Okay. Right now, I still honestly have no idea. After an initial infection, viruses and bacteria take time to incubate, the person would become ill and gradually deteriorate, but this happened suddenly, like boom! But then again, thinking about it, how could it be genetic? One of the deceased was African American and another had a Greek background. It would have to be an acquired syndrome, but acquired from where? I'm really just guessing at this point. We don't know. A gene mutation perhaps… could be any number of things.'

Santino's mind was struggling to keep up. If Robert couldn't come up with a plausible explanation, then would there be any hope of finding one? 'I honestly don't know, Robert. I was hoping that Jayda Crane's autopsy might have provided a bit more insight, but I assume there wasn't much else?'

'Well, not at this point, but there's still tox-screens and bloods to come back, that takes time. We won't know anything for a while. The thing is, you're assuming that there actually is something to find. What if this turns out to be just a string of coincidental deaths? Sometimes that happens when you're looking for patterns, you know that. It's like buying a green car and then suddenly noticing every other green car on the road. Now that you've got me looking too, we might be leading each other up the garden path.'

There was a loud crash behind Santino that made him leap from his stool. His hand went to his gun before he realised it was a tipsy young woman who had tripped over the strap of her dangling handbag. He helped her up and returned to his stool, sharing a relieved exchange with Robert.

He picked up his glass and took a drink to settle the adrenaline coursing through him. 'Look, I know at this stage it's just a hunch, but I've been a cop a long time, Robert, and I've learnt to trust my gut. If you'd seen Harry's face when he asked… I'm worried about him.'

Robert pointed at his glass. 'Yeah, well he comes from a long line of Irish cops who all loved a good whiskey, doesn't he? I've had to open a few of them up myself. Their livers ain't pretty, I can tell you that.'

Santino cut in. 'But he doesn't abuse alcohol, at least he didn't in the past. I need to do this for him. You know how much he's done for me.'

Robert sighed heavily. 'You were lucky when Harry was brought in. God knows what might have happened if it had been someone else.'

'Lucky's an understatement,' Santino scoffed. 'My career was over. If it wasn't for Harry replacing Thiele after the Fitzgerald case, I would have been gone for good and not just from the LAPD either.'

Robert agreed. 'Thiele was rotten through and through. He was in everyone's pocket, anyone who was willing to pay that is, and let's face it, Fitzgerald was an endless money pit.'

Thiele had been pulling the strings for Fitzgerald, doing all of his dirty work and covering his tracks for the right price. And that included trying to ruin Santino. 'Harry is, and always has been, absolutely honest and fair. He was the only one willing to judge me on my merits, as a person and as a detective, instead of the bullshit in the media. I owe him a lot.'

Santino hadn't realised that he was almost shouting. Robert held up his hands to settle him.

'I know, I know, Santino, you don't have to sell it to me,' Robert agreed.

Santino dropped his shoulders. It was a technique he had learnt from the police psychologist he was ordered to see after the Fitzgerald case. 'Harry's been keeping detailed notes since Jason died, looking for similarities and possible links and he's given me full authority to check on every lead and possibility. So, for now, I'm going to put my own feelings about it aside and just focus on what the information is telling me. Jason was only 36 and he had a really promising career. His family deserve to at least have the assurance that what happened to him was no one's fault, especially for his mother. I want to give that to them, to Harry.'

'I know that, Santino, and I commend you for it, but it could be risky for your career. Chasing ghosts and possibly wasting department time and resources.'

Santino shrugged. 'It wouldn't be the first time, would it? But if there's something that ties them, I have to find it. Could it be something common to each of the deceased, something they were given, like a medicine or an antibiotic or something that might have reacted in each of them for some reason? Immunisation shots, that kind of thing. It couldn't be anything like that, right?'

Robert leaned forward resting his arms on the bar. He shook his head with slow, steady, side to side movements. 'All of those sorts of things are highly unlikely. Although, in my line of work, you never quite know what might roll in the door next. We get some really bizarre stuff and it gets worse every year, so who knows. I'm not willing to agree at this point that there is evidence of a connection, other than the ages and the autopsy findings, because there's just no obvious link. But to be honest, after being brought up to speed by the others about how many have come through in the time I've been away, it could be a concern.'

'So, it's possible, right?' Santino asked.

'Yeah, it's possible. But if there was a drug that was causing this, we would have more dead by now. And there wasn't anything that stood out in the toxicology reports for the previous cases, that I know of, that would make me think it was drug-related.'

Santino tapped his fingers on the bar as he thought about what Robert had said. 'Just answer me one thing. Do you think there's enough here for me to keep looking? When Harry asked, I said I would, but I want to be sure that it isn't a wild goose chase, that hurts Harry more in the long run.'

Robert tilted his head back and stared at the ceiling. 'Look, if we get more at the rate we have been, this could be real trouble, especially if we can't give these families any answers, other than the generic one we've been providing. Even though I'm not going to commit to saying that I think they're linked, the answer is yes, I think it warrants a look. But it's going to be hard going to find something concrete to grab on to.'

Santino could feel the mixture of adrenaline and dread sink to the bottom of his stomach and then surge high into his chest and throat. 'Well, I'll just have to find something to grab on to as you say.'

'I'll do what I can, but a word to the wise: think long and hard about whether you want to be doing this.'

Santino already knew the answer. There was no walking away now, even if he wanted to. It wasn't in his nature to give up.

Robert caught sight of the television behind the bar. 'Speak of the Devil. And this Muppet, Fitzgerald? I suppose you've seen what's going on with him?'

Santino ordered a refill and stared at the screen. 'He's a piece of work, isn't he?' he said through clenched teeth.

'And now he's a billionaire piece of work,' Robert added. 'How does that even happen? Essentially, he gets away with murder and then inherits a fortune. We should be so lucky!'

Santino felt his pulse quicken. 'That son-of-a-bitch should have had the book thrown at him. We only touched the tip of the iceberg when we pinned him for Maurice Stephens' murder. If only I'd been able to...'

'You did what you could and at least you got him, even if he didn't do any actual time. What else could you have done? Don't go dredging all that up again. It only does your head in.'

'Self-defense? It still kills me. What a steaming load of absolute horse shit. He murdered his best friend in cold blood and his money bought him the get-out-of-jail-free card. That's the truth,' Santino spat. 'If I'd just taken my time instead of rushing to expose them all, I could have gotten more, found out what was really behind it. There was more, I know it. And so did everyone else. If I could just do it over again...' He stopped, rubbing his hands over his face. Even mentally going back to that time was enough to bring a wave of anxiety and stress. 'The only reason he killed Maurice was to shut him up and stop him talking because Maurice knew everything about the Fitzgerald empire. He may have been an out of control drunk, but there was a reason he ended up like that and all roads led back to Fitzgerald.'

'There's no denying that you're a bloody good detective, Santino,' Robert assured him, 'and you've got a reputation for being, shall we say, relentless. But that's also your downfall sometimes, and with him.' He pointed at the screen. 'It almost cost you everything, you stupid son of a bitch. Sometimes you have to protect yourself and let things go.'

Santino knew what Robert was saying was true, even if he wasn't very diplomatic about it. 'He was hiding a lot more, that's all I'm saying. Alpha Pharmaceuticals was rotten to the core, and still is.'

'Anyway, it's history now,' Robert added, 'so just let it go, for your own sake. Take my advice now and move on. Once and for all. Families were torn apart, hell, the entire city changed after that, and it'll never be the same. But people will slowly forgive and forget.'

'Yeah, point taken, but it pisses me off. You say forgive, but that's exactly what shits me. There were so many rotten eggs taking money and doing the dirty, and yeah, their families were hurt when it all came out, but it should be about people forgiving *them* for their wrongdoing, not forgiving *me* for being the person who exposed it all. And now I've gotta look at Fitzgerald there on the TV, gloating and acting like he's the king of the world. He's scum, plain and simple. It's bullshit.'

'I get it, and don't get hung up on my poor choice of words, you know I'm shit at this stuff. But I'm just trying to say that you did the right thing and while there's still some bad blood around, just keep moving forward, that's all. Anyway, about this Harry situation. Tell me more about how it went with Arnya Sloane.'

Santino shook his head, trying to push away the blinding anger that came with talking about the Fitzgerald case. It made his head pound and his eyes burn. 'Yeah, it went well.

She's agreed to take a look at the files. I appreciate the referral, so thanks.'

'Did you tell her who referred you?' he asked. There was a hint of caution in his tone.

'As a matter of fact, I did.' He left it there and waited for Robert to push. It didn't take long.

'And? Did she say anything or ask about me?'

He could tell that Robert was hoping to hear that she had been interested or pleased.

Santino gave him a questioning look. 'Like what? What's the story there? Did you two have a thing?'

Robert grinned. 'Something like that. But it was centuries ago, another life. She's still beautiful though, isn't she? She's one of a kind.'

Santino agreed, although he didn't say it. The Professor had certainly impressed him. 'She's a striking woman,' he said. 'I'm surprised she ever had anything to do with the likes of you.'

Robert laughed. 'Touché. Did she seem happy?'

'How the hell should I know?' he laughed. 'I wasn't there for a personal interview or to find out how her life was going.'

'Is she married? Kids?' Robert persisted.

'Jesus, Robert, I didn't take her on a date. Did you send me there for help or to spy on your ex?'

He didn't deny that she was his ex. 'No, I just wondered, that's all. I haven't seen her for quite a while.'

'Well, I didn't notice anything like that, but there was something so different about her. I found her really interesting. She seemed to have this intense focus and she moved about the room as if she was somewhere else, like in a trance of concentration. It was really unusual. She definitely intrigued me.'

'Okay, okay, that's enough. Is there anything else you can tell me about all this that might help?' Robert asked, changing the subject. 'Anything I should look out for?'

Santino shrugged. 'Not that I'm aware of at this point. Just let me know if anything turns up with the tox-screening for Jayda Crane and if anything else comes in that might be connected.'

'Tox won't be back for a while yet. Just a caution though, we both want to help Harry, but we also need to keep in mind that thousands of people die of natural causes every day. Some in really bizarre circumstances. The most important thing is that we keep our wits about us. While the age and overall health in these cases are common factors, that's not exactly cause for alarm. I'll keep my eyes and ears open though and let's just hope that the bodies don't keep coming the way they have been. If they do, it won't be long before every agency is swarming over this stuff, and your files.'

Santino had turned back to the TV screen, oblivious to what Robert was saying. Robert followed his gaze. The vision of a local shopping centre filled the screen, the words, *two dead*, rolling across the bottom.

'Buddy, can you turn up the volume?' Robert called to the bartender. The man was clearly annoyed by the request and snatched the remote to lift the volume.

The newsreader was delivering a breaking item.

'In separate, but strangely similar incidents, a 38-year-old man collapsed and died at the checkout of a Safeway supermarket today, while a woman, also aged in her late thirties, was

pronounced dead after collapsing while filling up her car with gas just two blocks away. So far, no other details have been released.'

'Shit, where's my phone?' Robert frantically patted his pockets and checked his bag. 'I've left it in the damn car. I better go, they've probably sent out a search party for me.'

'Thanks Robert,' Santino called as the Medical Examiner disappeared out the doors. He had a feeling that by the morning Robert would be calling to tell him they had two more possible links. If he did, any doubt Santino still had would be gone.

Santino stared down at the ruby-red liquid in his glass. Maybe any doubt he had was already gone.

CHAPTER

4

Arnya Sloane packed the case files into her bag and headed home. Her pounding head longed for a hot bath, some pain killers and a decent night's sleep. The bouts of insomnia always worsened when she was stressed, and lately, she had barely been sleeping at all. Her anxiety levels had reached an all-time high due to diminishing funding for a research project she had dedicated the past two years of her life to. She drew in a long, deep breath refusing to let her thoughts be consumed by her mounting anxiety. Right now, she just needed to get rid of the pounding.

At her apartment, the bubbles of the overflowing bath water sparkled with a myriad of colours and popped effortlessly in her hand. The hot water, soothing her aching shoulders, helped her mind to go back over the events of the last few days and the case files in her satchel. Ever since the detective had brought them, she had thought of little else. It felt good, albeit a little irresponsible given her work situation, to finally have something other than the funding grant to sink her teeth into, even if it did mean she was using it as a distraction from everything else.

And then there was Robert James. It was a name she hadn't said aloud for a long time. It had surprised her that she'd felt a flutter when the detective said it. Not to mention the detective. Another interesting character. Well-dressed, well-mannered and not at all what she thought he would be. The media had at times made him out to be somewhat of a villain, even though he was largely cleared of any wrongdoing.

She splashed the warm water over her face, washing away the swarming thoughts. They would only lead to a continuation of the thudding inside her skull. Sinking lower into the water until her face was almost completely submerged, she cleared her mind and exhaled slowly, feeling some of the tension release.

As much as she wanted to wash it all away for a few short hours, the case files were back on her mind before her head emerged from the water. The deaths had piqued her interest and trying to push that aside was no use.

A strange but familiar sensation on her exposed hand made her jump. 'Kit Kat, stop that,' she laughed, gently pushing the cat from the side of the bathtub. He refused to be ignored, finding his way onto the sink beside her and purring loudly. 'I miss him too.'

Kit Kat had been her father's cat and he was accustomed to a certain amount of fussing and attention. When he came to live with Arnya after her father's death two years ago, it had taken some adjustment, but they'd grown very fond of each other. It was very much a give and take relationship, with her doing all of the give and him doing all of the take, but in spite of his completely selfish nature, he was great company and reminded her of her father and his gentleness.

Shrivelled and wrinkled from the water she had settled in for far too long, she swallowed pain killers with a mouthful of Pinot and spread the case files across the floor of her apartment.

Opening each one, removing the contents and placing them side by side with the others, she felt a spark. The case files represented something new and personal, a reminder of the kind of work she had hoped to do when she first chose this path; work that might make a difference that she could see and feel, not just more money to further ongoing research.

Moving through them, one by one, she studied the details. The first was Anton Berg. 37-years-old. IT consultant. No known health issues. Married with two children. He had collapsed at work in front of colleagues. The notes indicated that he had been in good spirits and appeared to be well. At lunch time he was making a coffee in the lunchroom and had suddenly stopped what he was doing, turned to others with a vacant look and dropped to the ground without warning. His colleagues dialled an ambulance and began CPR, but he was completely unresponsive.

Arnya put the file down and picked up another. Taryn Graham. 34. Student and waitress. Vegetarian. No obvious illnesses. Died suddenly at the gym in the locker room. Taryn's notes indicated she was fit, a keen soccer player and had no known health issues. She had completed a weight training class and swim before entering the locker room.

She opened another. Jason Bryant. 36. Police officer. Fit. Medical done at the academy showed excellent overall health. No obvious illnesses. Died suddenly during a routine traffic stop. His police cruiser ploughed into the rear of a car that he had signalled to pull over.

As Arnya continued through the cases there were obvious similarities emerging, but they were common and non-specific, not the things you might usually find like shared workspaces, visiting the same coffee shop, buying from the same store or a mutual contact of some kind. The overall similarities in no way linked them. All were in their thirties, but they came from varying ethnic backgrounds. None of them, as far as was indicated, had been in contact with each other and there were no other specifics that appeared to be common to all of them. One was a vegetarian and another a vegan, while the rest were not. None of them had any significant health problems noted, except for Michaela Parsons who had Fibromyalgia, a non-degenerative pain condition. Arnya tapped her pen on the files. Despite the similarity of their ages and cause of death, they seemed un-linkable. And yet she could sense a connection between them. If there was one, it was there somewhere. She just had to find it.

Santino despised the bitter taste of the poison that spewed from the discoloured glass jug of the office coffee pot. Truly good coffee, according to his mother, could only come from a stainless-steel percolator, filled with freshly ground espresso beans. It had to be simmered on the stove top just long enough for the water to rise to the top, blending in perfect harmony with the coffee. Today the poison wasn't even hot.

His usually organised desk was piled high with case files, four more in the seven days since Jayda Crane's death, and his answering machine was full of messages from contacts and confidantes in other departments, all of whom had been asked, as a favour to Harry Bryant, to contact Santino in the event of any similar deaths or new information.

He swallowed hard against the black liquid as the smell burnt his nostrils. The cases now seemed to be spreading far and wide across not only the state, but the country. Yet there were still no clues and no indication as to why these people were dying. Robert too was inundated and only returning calls when he could, which was not often.

Santino sat down and flipped through a few pages of the top file. Based on the information he had, the geographic spread of the deaths was far enough that no formal links were being made by authorities, at least none that he knew of. He wondered if some other detective in some other place was looking at a pile just like this and asking what the hell was going on.

Santino checked his watch. His meeting with Professor Sloane in an hour would hopefully shed some light on it all, at least he hoped so because so far, no one else seemed to have a clue, including him. He was beginning to wonder if they were dealing with something completely new, something that would continue to be so random they would never be able to connect the dots. That prospect scared him.

Despite being well-dressed, he gathered up the case files and made a quick detour home to shower and freshen up. There was a smell that always seemed to linger on him and in his clothes when he left the station. It was as if the toxicity and negativity of the work created its own scent and attached itself to him.

When he arrived at the meeting, the Professor was already seated in one of the many booths that lined the walls of the dimly lit coffee shop where they had agreed to meet. He paused at the door, watching as Arnya smiled at one of the waitresses and took a purse from her case. She then had a brief but friendly exchange with a man, a waiter, and looked to the door, catching Santino's eye.

Santino entered and made his way over to her. 'Professor Sloane, thank you for meeting me.' He slid into the empty bench seat across from her.

Arnya reached into her case and took out the files, placing one hand on top of the pile. 'It's no problem. This is convenient actually, being so close to my office. I come here a lot.'

He had been deliberate about convenience to ensure that she wouldn't put him off. He wanted to hear what she had to say.

'I've had a good look through the cases Detective, and at this stage, I hate to be the bearer of bad news, but there doesn't appear to be anything that stands out in the written notes.'

'Nothing at all?' he questioned. The anticipation of getting some answers was quickly fading. He wondered if the possibility would soon be out of reach all together.

'Not yet, but that doesn't mean there's nothing to be found. In fact, the sheer randomness of the deceased persons, combined with the many similarities in the way they died, only serves to make this even more bizarre, and in my mind, more likely that they are somehow connected, but that's only my personal opinion at this stage.'

He appreciated it regardless. 'I'm interested to hear any theories you have, Professor Sloane.'

She smiled and explained. 'They all lived different lives in different places, with no connection to one another, and yet they died from exactly the same cause – under different circumstances. Then there are all of the more general things like, for example, the fact that they were in the same age group, yet have varying ethnicity.'

Santino was impressed. She had clearly spent time going over the cases.

'I'm happy to look into it further,' she said. 'But I would need access to samples taken from the deceased persons and complete medical histories of course.'

Santino nodded his agreement. 'I'm sure I can get you those things in time, but as I mentioned to you previously, this is something that needs to remain confidential right now, so I would need your assurance that you will keep it to yourself. And please, call me Dominic.'

'I'm sorry Detective… Dominic… but I'm sure you can understand when I say that I'm a little uncomfortable with the secrecy surrounding this. I hope this isn't something that's likely to come back to bite me later.' She gave him a questioning look. 'If I'm going to be involved, then I need to have some context. I need to at least know what the secrecy is about, I'm firm on that.'

Santino shifted in his seat. He needed her help, there was no doubt about it, but he had also given the Captain his word that he would keep it as quiet as possible, on a need-to-know basis only. The last thing any of them wanted was an unofficial investigation blowing up in their faces. However, he wasn't sure how much longer keeping it quiet was going to be possible. After seeing his crowded desk today, it was only a matter of time. 'I'm not officially investigating these deaths, Professor. I'm doing it as a favour to someone and so I'm quietly gathering information without triggering any other agencies until I know whether or not there's something actually here to be concerned about.'

He held her eyes, trying to interpret the look on her face, but she gave nothing away. If she was unimpressed to have her time wasted with what may well be a wild goose chase or personal vendetta, she wasn't showing it.

'Professor, there is something going on here, I'm sure of it now and I really do need your help. I'll be completely honest and say that this situation was originally brought to my attention through a personal friend, a cop, and I was sceptical at first, but there's more to it and I'm going to find out what that is. I've spoken again to Dr James... Robert... off the record, and he admits that this has him stumped too. There have been more deaths since we last met, many more, and my message bank is literally full. I'm not even sure how much longer I'll be looking into it because if things keep going the way they are, others will start wondering the same thing and far more important people than me will swiftly take over.'

He took four new case files from his satchel and placed them in front of her. 'I pulled a few from the pile, the ones I thought were the most similar based on the general criteria, but there are more. Robert is inundated too and I'm assuming that, pretty soon, people with loud voices are going to be jumping up and down for answers. We're past the point of wondering if something is going on here, there *is* something going on and whatever it is, it's increasing. And fast.'

Arnya kept her eyes on him, but he could see his words had unsettled her. 'How are these coming to you if this is being kept under the radar?' she asked.

'I still have some friends around the place and my Captain, Harry Bryant, called in a few favours with people he trusts. They're forwarding anything to me and keeping me in the loop. I can't imagine how many more calls... deaths... there might be if news of this becomes public. I've had calls coming in from far and wide in the last few days as it is.'

Arnya opened the files and looked at the notes. 'So, your captain is aware of this then and you have his support?'

Santino weighed up how much to tell her of Harry's connection. 'He is. One of the deceased, Jason Bryant, is his nephew. Harry is the one who brought it to me.'

Arnya remembered the case. The police officer who died in his squad car.

'I can get you whatever information you need,' Santino said, 'but I also need your help. Whatever the connection is, if it's an illness or some new disease, it's going to blow up fast, that's why I'm hoping it'll stay quiet for now so that I can make some headway. We want to try to work out what's happening before anyone else takes over.'

'But why?' Arnya asked. 'Won't the truth be uncovered faster with more eyes and ears and hands working on it?'

Santino scoffed. 'I hate to sound cynical, Professor, but the more eyes and ears and hands, the more likely it is that the truth will never come to light. You can trust me on that.'

Arnya appeared puzzled by the remark.

'As I said, my captain, Harry Bryant, is the one who asked me to look into it. He initially only wanted to keep it quiet because one of the deceased is his nephew. He didn't want it to look like he was doing it out of his own grief or using his position, but this has blown up into something much bigger, as you can see.' He pointed to the files. 'I'm mindful of the fact that people are dying here and we can't just sit on it, but I've also been around long enough to know that once whatever this is gets out, we may never find out the truth. As soon as we have something concrete, we'll make sure the right people know.'

The waiter arrived with Arnya's coffee. 'Anything for you, sir?' he asked, in a heavy French accent.

'A double-shot short black with a dash of milk, no sugar, thank you,' Santino said.

Arnya looked up from her cup.

'Ah, same as the Professor, you share her good taste, yes?' the waiter joked.

Santino smiled at Arnya. It was rare that anyone liked their coffee as strong as he did.

'I come here all the time,' Arnya said. 'The coffee is wonderful and the baristas know my order. They usually have it ready for me when I arrive, but I confused them today by arriving later.'

Santino listened to her unnecessary explanation about the coffee. He wondered why she was telling him these details. It was common for people to go off on tangents when they were nervous or uncomfortable and he wondered which one she might be.

He stared for a moment at her mismatched eyes. As the coffee machine grinded fresh beans loudly and the aroma wafted through the air, he wondered if she would help him. He was sure that despite her annoyance with the secrecy issue, the cases had already captured her interest enough to make her want to get involved.

When the grinding gave way to a quieter whirring, Arnya continued reading the new case files.

'I'm really not sure that it's a good idea to keep something like this quiet, Detective. Despite your misgivings with our system, the more people working on this will surely mean a quicker resolution. I really don't understand,' she said. 'Why aren't you calling in anyone and everyone to get this under control?'

Santino could see her point. 'When you've worked in law enforcement as long as I have, Professor, you learn quickly that getting all your research and background work done before anyone knows you are doing it is a great way to ensure that evidence remains intact. As soon as people know, particularly if they're guilty of something, the race is on for them to cover-up and get rid of anything they can. As I said, I know that sounds cynical, but I have seen evidence swept under the carpet and complete lies told in the media just to hide the truth from the public.'

Arnya hesitated. 'I understand, but I'm not sure it's the best approach. It's obvious that you've had a lot of experience with the media throughout your career, especially during the Fitzgerald case, but are you sure about this?'

Santino nodded. 'I have, and I can tell you that what you see in the media is not always what is actually happening. Powers much higher up the chain than us often make decisions that they decide are for the *greater good* regardless of what the truth is. This case is personal because my captain's nephew is dead. He wants to know what happened and he wants me to find out. With what has unfolded in the last few days, it's more important than ever that we stay silent until we've collected as much information as we can and before there is any chance of anyone or anything being hidden or eradicated.'

Arnya didn't react to what he had said. She sipped her coffee and took a moment before responding. 'I suppose I will have to take your word for it,' she said, 'but if what you say is true, then the increasing numbers are alarming. And if they are appearing over a much wider geographic span than first thought, then you know that this won't stay quiet for long. Regardless of your feelings on the matter, CDC will have to be notified, if they haven't already picked it up.' She met his steely gaze. 'I will help you, but only if you keep me 100 percent informed and give me the information I need.'

'Of course, anything you need,' he assured her.

'There is one other stipulation.' She was looking him squarely in the eyes, holding firm. He didn't doubt her determination for even a second. 'As you say, people's lives are clearly being lost here. These deaths may be related, or they may not, but if we do find that there is a common link between them, you must act swiftly to ensure that whatever it is, it's dealt with or contained by the proper authorities. Whatever is needed must be done, and quickly. I will not be a party to anything that delays saving lives or puts further lives in danger. Do I have your word on that, Detective?'

Santino, impressed by her once again, held up his hand like a Boy Scout pledging an oath. 'I absolutely give you my word. We're on the same side here, Professor, and as soon as I – we - get any indication that there's something concrete, some hard evidence of a link, then I'll be making sure that it goes straight to the highest authorities to deal with.'

Arnya remained quiet for several seconds before speaking. 'Okay, well I've been looking at a few things, but I'm going a bit further into the possibility of something called *apoptosis*.'

Santino hadn't heard the term before. He looked at her blankly, hoping that like Robert, she would lead into a simpler explanation. 'In English?' he smiled.

'Apoptosis is the process of programmed cell death that occurs naturally in the bodies of multicellular organisms. For example, a developing human embryo grows fingers and toes because cells between the digits die off or apoptose. Without apoptosis your nose could grow like Pinocchio's, even if you didn't tell lies'.

Santino laughed, appreciating her efforts to find a simple explanation and lighten the mood.

'It's estimated that in the average human adult, between 50 and 70 billion cells die each day due to apoptosis.'

Santino was still getting only a basic grasp. Science had never been his strong point. He preferred to leave that stuff to people like Robert who would then explain it to him in plain terms. 'Is it likely that… apoptosis… is what killed them then?'

'No, Detective, that's the rate at which humans lose cells, what you're losing as we speak.' She took another sip of her coffee and seemed to be considering the best way to explain. 'It's when something goes wrong that problems arise. Defective apoptotic processes have been implicated in an extensive variety of diseases. Excessive apoptosis can cause degenerative diseases, whereas an insufficient amount can result in uncontrolled abnormal cell reproduction, such as we find in cancer. In all of these cases, the possibility of a cell death phenomenon, and I'm not saying that is what this is, but if it is, then it appears to be concentrated in the pons varolii, a part of the brain stem responsible for respiration, among other things. In effect, severe damage to the pons would cause your body to forget how to breathe.'

The very thought of his brain forgetting to make him breathe terrified Santino. In situations like this, where nothing could be done if it happened, ignorance was preferable. 'This might sound basic and crude, but when Robert explained it to me, he said that it seemed like their brains had been reduced to Jell-o.'

'That's an interesting description, I suppose.' She smiled. 'Typical of Robert. There could also be…'

Santino's phone vibrated on the melamine tabletop as the screen lit up. He read the message:

> *Come down to the office as soon as you can, I may have something for you – Robert*

He looked up at Arnya who was watching him intently. 'Any chance you've got time for a quick trip to the ME's office? Robert has something he wants me to see in connection with the cases.' He held up the phone message for her to read. 'I'd appreciate your expertise.'

The Professor didn't answer straight away. Santino could see that she was unsure and considering the request.

'The information Robert has could prove to be important. It would be good if you had it prior to reviewing the new files.'

Arnya nodded. 'I'll need to check my diary and speak to my assistant. I didn't expect to be out of the office for more than an hour.'

Santino suspected that her hesitance might be more to do with Robert than the contents of her diary. Robert had said they hadn't seen one another for a long time. Perhaps she didn't want to see him again.

Santino politely pretended not to notice her delay in responding. 'I understand if you're too busy, Professor,' Santino offered. He could tell from her body language that she was thinking about whatever it was that was concerning her. 'I know I've already been taking up enough of your time with this.'

Again, there was a pause. He could see that she was chewing the inside of her lip and wrestling with her thoughts. He didn't dare ask what those thoughts were.

'It's fine, Detective, let me grab my jacket and bag from my office. I'll meet you outside in ten minutes.'

Santino stood up as she did. After days of mounting deaths and unanswered questions, he felt relieved that Arnya had agreed to help. Her scientific knowledge was reassuring, and, at a personal level, her presence continued to captivate him. He could certainly see why Robert had once had feelings for her.

More importantly, he hoped that Robert had something that might finally provide some answers

CHAPTER

5

Arnya took the new files Santino had given her. She left Santino in the coffee shop and headed back to her office. Breathing a sigh of relief at the sight of her clear afternoon schedule, she grabbed her jacket and put on some lip balm. She rubbed her lips together and then stopped, realising what she was doing. 'You broke it off with him, remember?' she said aloud. As much as she hated to admit it, human nature sometimes just won out over considered intelligent self-talk and the prospect of seeing Robert was making that very clear.

She wondered what it was about seeing an old flame that made people feel so vulnerable. Why did she even care if he saw her and thought that her lips looked like old boot leather and that she had aged terribly?

She headed back down to the front of the building where Detective Santino was already waiting at the side of the curb. She could see he was pressing the buttons on the radio and wondered what he liked to listen to. If she had to guess, it would be blues.

She hopped into the passenger seat and swapped her glasses for sunglasses. Santino turned the radio off.

'Thanks for doing this,' Santino said. He pulled out onto the road. 'I appreciate you taking the time away from your work. I'm sure it's an added pressure you don't need.'

Arnya smiled. 'The truth is, Detective, I appreciate the distraction. Grants and funding can be a tedious business and sometimes real life is a welcome relief. Not that this situation is welcomed.' She quickly corrected herself, realising how that might have sounded. 'Even if it is a terribly frustrating and sad situation, I'm glad to feel like I'm helping in some way.'

'I didn't realise it would be like that – the work you do, I mean. Human genetics research sounds like it would be interesting and complicated. What about family? Do you have any kids?'

Arnya was taken aback by the question and didn't answer immediately.

'I'm sorry,' Santino said, 'that was probably a bit personal. Comes with being a detective, unfortunately. We're always asking way too direct questions and pushing the limits. It doesn't cross over well into normal life. You should see me on a date. It's usually a train wreck.'

'No, it's fine, I'm just not used to people asking me something like that so directly, as you say. It's not that I mind talking about myself, it's more that I don't tend to socialise that much thanks to long work hours. And it's been a long time since I actually had a one-on-one conversation with someone about myself outside of a work context.' She realised how absolutely sad that sounded. She couldn't remember the last time she had said out loud to another human being just how unhappy and disconnected she had allowed herself to become.

Santino gave her a gentle smile. 'Well, if you don't mind, then I'd like to hear about it.'

Arnya smiled. 'Okay. Not married, no kids and generally no life. Unfortunately, that's it.'

Santino laughed. 'You can do better than that, surely. A corpse gives away more than that. What about siblings, or parents? A partner or a pet even?'

'A pet, yes. A cat. Now I sound like a sad cat lady, don't I?'

'No,' Santino lied, flashing her a grin.

'The cat was actually my father's, William Sloane. He was a fabulous family practitioner, loved by everyone and admired by his colleagues, but I didn't share his natural ability to put people at ease. I excelled at practicals and aced exams, but the people side of medicine, the emotion and the loss, was beyond me, unfortunately. I could never find the right words or ease a distraught family with just a touch the way my father could. He could connect with them on a level that was truly honest and sincere, even when beneath the surface his heart was breaking for them. That's why I chose this path instead.'

Santino nodded slowly. He didn't turn to look at her or say any of the usual things like, *I'm so sorry* or whatever it was that people usually said when someone poured their innermost thoughts out in a car ride with a virtual stranger.

Arnya decided that a short summary would end the conversation quickly and let them both off the hook. 'My parents are both deceased, and I never had any siblings. I always wanted some, but alas, I was an only child. For a long time my work was everything. No partner, no children, I just worked all the time.'

'But not now? You said that in the past tense.'

Arnya shrugged. 'I didn't know this ride was going to turn into a session on self-reflection and analysis. What about you, Detective? Who is Detective Santino when he's not in the news or arresting bad guys?'

'If only we had more time,' he said. There was a deliberate teasing in his voice. He pulled into a space and shut off the engine. 'That conversation will have to wait for another time.'

Arnya's stomach knotted at the sight of the Medical Examiner's building. She resisted the urge to check her reflection in the mirror and felt irritated that she even wanted to. *She* had been the one who had broken it off with Robert. *She* had broken *his* heart, yet here she was still behaving like a teenager who desperately wanted to impress a boy. She felt ridiculous. This was a professional visit.

'Are you okay?' Santino asked.

She knew she had hesitated a minute too long in the passenger seat. 'Yes, I'm fine. Just collecting my thoughts before we go in.'

When they entered the autopsy suite, Robert pivoted and turned from the table he was leaning over. He appeared stuck to the spot on which he stood. Arnya's unexpected presence seemed to throw him more than either of them had anticipated. When he finally moved, he bumped one of the rolling metal trays and fumbled clumsily like a silly character in a bad romance movie.

'It's wonderful to see you Arnya, it's been a long time.' He said the words earnestly with a slight croak in his voice as if his throat had tightened. He fixed up the tray and removed his gloves.

Arnya nodded, unsure how to interpret his reaction. She tried not to show that she was pleased at his awkwardness, but she was. 'It's good to see you too, Robert.'

Santino stepped closer and looked at Robert. He was sporting a dark shade of purple around his right eye and a small cut across the bridge of his nose. 'What the hell happened to you? Have you been starting fights in seedy bars again?'

Santino was teasing, but with Robert anything was possible. Santino had seen him when he was full of alcohol and ready to take on the world. It was his sense of humour and loud mouth that usually got him into trouble.

'You should see the other guy.' Robert was joking, but there was an uneasiness in the exchange. 'Fell off the golf cart,' he confessed. 'You know me, I can fall off of, or over, anything.'

Arnya grinned, remembering Robert's hopelessness when it came to anything that required coordination.

Robert saw the look and his face reddened.

'What have you got for us, Robert?' Santino interjected.

'Um, follow me,' Robert said.

Leading them to a nearby gurney, he uncovered a body. The young man, probably in his mid-thirties, looked much like the others had; eyes open and his face contorted into a pained expression.

'What exactly are we looking at?' Santino questioned. There was nothing that immediately stood out.

'It's not the body,' Robert said. There was an element of excitement in his voice. 'CoD is just the same as the others.

It's his name.' He picked up a file and turned it toward them to see.

Santino leaned forward to read it. 'Sydney Graham,' he read aloud.

The significance took Santino a moment to register, but Arnya made the connection immediately. 'He's related to Taryn Graham, the young woman who died two weeks ago?' she said. 'Brother?'

'Yep,' Robert said. 'And, there's one left.'

Arnya looked to Santino who had begun to pace.

Robert explained further. 'They were triplets, two now dead and one still living.'

The revelation brought the room to complete silence. Even Santino stopped moving back and forth. All three of them stood completely still beside the body. The grim news was slowly unravelling in a web of confusion and questions.

Arnya's pulse quickened. The sound was audible inside her head like the ticking of a clock. The deaths were connected. This proved it. 'Robert, can you give me access to copies of every test that's been done on each of the deceased? Anything that has come through here and any samples that were taken?' she asked. Evidence of whatever had caused these siblings to die, had to be there somewhere.

Robert hesitated. 'Give me some time and I'll see what I can do. Most of it's not back yet. We're inundated and barely coping.'

'They were fraternal, obviously,' she said. 'Is the third a female or male?'

'Female,' Robert answered.

Santino was shaking his head. 'What the hell does this even mean, Robert? Two dead and one living? Jesus.'

'It means that the siblings both died of what appears to be natural causes within days of each other. It also tells us that this is potentially something they passed to each other or something they both had. The fact that the third sibling is still alive says that she wasn't exposed to whatever it is – genetically or passed on – or, that she is going to suffer the same fate fairly soon.'

Arnya agreed. 'It also means that we need to work out why the third sibling hasn't died and why others who have had no contact with these two are dead.'

Santino raked his hands through his hair and leaned back against the sink. 'I'm not sure if this is going to lead us to answers or create more questions. Either way, it's bizarre. You're sure it was the same cause of death?'

Arnya could see the news had rattled him.

Robert answered. 'Looks just the same so far, but I'll know more once I open him up. It was probably a bit early for me to call you, but I wanted to at least give you a heads-up straight away. Sorry to say, but we'll have to make a report to CDC. We've got no choice, I'm seeing connections here as well and it's my job on the line, Santino. I'm just not willing to risk that.'

'Is there any chance you can hold off, just for 24 hours?' Santino asked.

Robert sighed. 'Maybe it's time to just hand it over, Santino. CDC will want all the information you have anyway. You've come this far and you were right about this being more than anyone first thought, but it's turning into something much bigger and we need to find out what the hell is going on here. We have to call them in.'

'Robert, we understand your position.' Arnya deliberately moved a little closer to him. It had been a long time, but she still knew how to appeal to his good nature. 'We're grateful that you called us first because it's definitely something we needed to know early. If you can hold off, we would be so grateful, but we're both also aware that you need to do what you have to, and I would never ask you to do something you're not comfortable with.'

Robert softened. 'I'll see what I can do. I might be able to hold off for a little while.'

Santino added. 'Let me know what you find, Robert. I'll make contact with the family and check on the surviving sibling. We'll go from there. And thanks for doing this. We really do appreciate the risk you're taking.'

'Sure,' Robert said. He shook Santino's hand. 'It's been nuts around here and,' he lowered his voice to a whisper, 'whatever this is, Santino, I'm worried. I've got a line of people breathing down my neck and to be honest, I don't know what to tell them. One of the families has gone to the Mayor and I've got a meeting with him tomorrow to review that case. Shit's gonna hit the fan soon, I'm telling you. If I were you, I'd get as far from this as possible, now. You do not need to end up back on the front page of every newspaper.'

'Thanks Robert, we really appreciate all your help,' Arnya said. She reached out a hand to shake as Santino had, but Robert leaned in slightly, as if he were going to kiss her cheek. When he realised, he quickly pulled back and took her hand.

'No problem, it was great to see you again,' he smiled. 'We should catch up for a drink sometime, for old times' sake. Might be nice to reminisce about the good old days.'

Arnya nodded. 'Of course, that would be lovely.'

As they left Robert to his work, Santino couldn't shake the feeling of dread that was enveloping him. 'Tell me you feel as worried about this as I do,' he said.

There was something in his voice that Arnya hadn't heard before. 'I'm trying not to jump to conclusions,' she said. 'I was trained to always rely on the science to do the talking, but I'll be honest, I'm getting a really bad feeling.'

'I've got more than a bad feeling, Professor,' Santino said.

Arnya knew exactly what he meant. They had come this far, but what next? 'I just wish we could put the pieces together to find out what all this means?' She felt frustrated and in over her head. 'The siblings, the similarities with the others, all of it. I just hope the last sibling doesn't suffer the same fate.'

'I'll drop you back at your office and chase up the family,' Santino said. 'The third sibling may well be the next one to roll in there and we need to find her before that happens.'

Arnya agreed. 'I'll spend time going through the files and see if anything jumps out at me. Hopefully Robert can get the additional information to me quickly.'

She watched him for a moment, seeing the sadness in his eyes. She couldn't imagine having to face a family who had already lost two of their children and, without even knowing it, were possibly facing the prospect of losing another.

CHAPTER

6

At her office, Arnya made a few calls and adjusted her diary to free up the week ahead. She wanted to concentrate on the cases and the meetings she already had scheduled could wait.

She stood up and stretched her body. The long spell of dry heat had been making her restless and keeping her from decent sleep, and the deaths were consuming her thoughts. It was easier to get up and work than it was to drive herself crazy trying to rest, but fatigue was setting in.

The files from Robert arrived at her office by courier, along with some additional police files from Santino. The note, in an envelope taped to the outside of the box, read:

> *Arnya, please find enclosed the case notes and test results that we have so far, as requested. The samples will need to be viewed here at the lab and I am happy to assist you at your*

convenience. Please give me a call to arrange. It was great seeing you.

Robert.

Arnya wasn't sure she agreed with the last part. Their relationship had not ended terribly well and neither had sought out the other for closure or resolution. They'd been great friends through medical school, but their relationship had slowly developed into more, mostly due to late night study sessions and high stress levels. Seeing him again was difficult, but she did miss their friendship and, in truth, Robert had been one of only a handful of people in her life that she had really opened up to.

She took the pile of notes from the box and organised them on her office desk with the case files Santino had provided. When there was no room left, she began placing them on the floor.

'What are you telling me? What connects you all?' she asked the faces of the dead who were looking back at her with their secrets hidden behind lifeless eyes. She wanted to solve this for them. She wanted to tell their families what it was that had ripped the victims from life and shattered their loved ones. She wanted the chance to bring them some closure and understanding of what had caused it.

Each case was different, other than the way they died. There was nothing about their lifestyle that was even remotely similar other than the basic things that most people have in common. Some were health conscious and fit, while others were heavy and, according to the notes, liked a drink and fast food. Nothing seemed to tie them together. Not even the preliminary toxicology results gave anything away. If they were going to dig further to look for other possible genetic links, a more intensive study of each of them and their family histories would have to be done. Notes and standard tests were just not enough to unlock this mystery.

Arnya opened her laptop and began to search articles and case studies for any possibilities. The next time she looked up, the sky outside had darkened to a steely grey and her empty stomach was crying out with loud groans. She rubbed her sore, tired eyes and packed the notes into the box they had arrived in. There was no point going on, her body was protesting the long periods of sitting. Her hunched shoulders burned, her legs were numb and her vision was beginning to blur.

Packing the box into the car, she headed home, stopping at her favourite Chinese takeaway to pick up dinner, but the faces of the dead, their stories and their possible connections, consumed her thoughts as the shop owner called her name again and again. He finally tapped her on the shoulder, pulling her from the vacant stare she had been casting at the wall.

She drove home with a nagging feeling that tugged at exhausted parts of her brain, telling her that there had to be some crucial clue, in the notes, in their lives, somewhere. She just had to find it. The thought of Santino facing the mourning family, who had lost not one, but two, of their children in the space of two weeks made her heart wrench with sadness for their loss and for his unenviable task. She wished there was something more she could do, but the only help she could provide would be to find the answers they so desperately needed.

She again unpacked and laid the files out on the floor of her apartment. Determined, she started at the beginning once again. Her eyes heavy and her body aching, she lasted little more than an hour before she was fast asleep on top of the notes. In her dreams her subconscious mind wandered through light and dark, places and dead faces and a feeling of having lost something.

She dreamt of her parents, feeling the sensation of her hand holding her mother's on one side and her father's on the other. They walked along the street like that, lifting her after every few steps, her feet launching into the air and kicking out in front of her. It was a feeling of utter joy and exhilaration.

Other faces appeared and then dissipated. Her father's best friend, Arthur, as well as a tiny Fox Terrier named Bubbles that she had loved as a small child. Through all of the images that filled her subconscious, simmering deep in her dreams but slowly rising to an unknown and unexplored surface, was a feeling of pulsating, raw panic. Her mind raced, searching for the reason for the troubled feeling, the kind that people get in the split second they realise they've lost their wallet or left the iron on at home, but the cause of her unease wouldn't surface, at least not in her subconscious.

Coming slowly back to wakefulness, her mind searched slowly at first and continued to increase in pace the closer she felt she was getting to the root of the feeling.

She sat upright, her eyes making desperate attempts to adjust to the dimly lit room as her chest heaved in great gasps. Her thoughts were foggy, still groggy from sleep, but as it cleared, a calm slowly made its way through her body, replacing the panic she had been feeling. It eased in the knowledge that her mind had finally made it to the root of the problem, far down in a dark abyss where no one could see it. It was clear, obvious even. She moved the papers around, checking the statements and file information. She had found the link they were searching for.

Santino boarded the flight to Phoenix and took his seat. The sound of the jet engines firing up sent a shot of nervous energy through him. He buckled his seatbelt and looked out the window at the ground staff moving away from the plane as it prepared to move out. He was heading to the home of Janine Graham, the third of the triplets.

While her two siblings had moved to LA to follow their dreams, Janine had been the dutiful daughter and stayed behind to be close to her ageing parents.

On the plane, the minutes passed like hours as he rehearsed the words he would use to ask a grieving family about their two lost children. Where to start. How to ask. Ways to get them to open up without destroying them in the process. He thought about the last part. Weren't they already destroyed? There was not much he or anyone else could say that would hurt them more than they were already hurting.

The closer the plane came to its destination, the more his anxiety grew. 'You've done this before. It's part of the job,' he reminded himself.

He ordered a scotch and settled back against the head rest. Two rows in front, on the other side of the aisle, he could see a little girl sitting on her mother's lap, colouring in a picture. When she held up the paper her mother praised the work and kissed the top of the child's head.

The innocence and love in the exchange was heartening to watch. To bring a person into the world, and then spend every moment tenderly loving and caring for them, created a bond that no separation could take away. He wondered if loved ones, who often said they could sense or feel their lost one near them, were still feeling that invisible connection. It was just too difficult to believe that everything about a person – their love, their smell, their laughter and their thoughts – were just gone. Blown away like the fluffy parachutes from a Dandelion.

He finished his drink and willed himself to pull back from the dark thoughts that were slowly creeping through him. He had a job to do and for the sake of the grieving parents, he needed to do it. This was their time to grieve.

When the plane landed, his anxiety rose. He collected the hire car, still thinking about the conversation he would have with them and how to start it. It wasn't long before he was parked out front of the Graham residence.

Inside, the grief was palpable. The air felt heavy in Santino's chest as he entered the narrow hall, behind the couple's only remaining daughter. He followed Janine to the sitting room where Bob and Carla Graham sat side by side in their armchairs, red-eyed and frail.

'Mum, Dad, this is Detective Santino, the one I told you about. He's looking into…' her voice faltered, unable to say the words, the unspeakable reality that both her siblings, their children, were dead.

Santino lowered himself onto the floral sofa opposite the couple who hadn't yet turned their attention to him. Carla's movements were slow and strained, she appeared to be medicated, likely with some sort of tranquilizer. Bob stared off at something unseen and spoke without averting his gaze.

'What's this about, Detective? We were… led to believe that there was not going to be any ongoing investigation.'

Santino spoke in a low tone. 'That's correct, sir, there is no formal investigation. I'm just gathering information and preparing some reports on these cases. I appreciate you taking the time to see me at such a difficult time.'

Bob turned his attention to Santino.

Santino took the queue and began the conversation gently. 'I was hoping to talk to you to see if there was anything you might have noticed with either Sydney or Taryn? Anything out of the ordinary, recently, or even prior to that, in their childhood perhaps?'

Carla flinched as the names left Santino's lips and tears fell from her red-rimmed eyes. She didn't brush them away as they rolled down to her small, receding chin and onto her lap.

Janine answered first. 'I've been in contact with them both by phone and email at least weekly, Detective, and they both seemed perfectly fine. Taryn was working long hours and training for some kind of soccer tournament, and Sydney, he had just completed a second degree in finance. They both seem… seemed great.'

Santino could see that she was desperately trying to hold it together for her parents, but the heartbreak and rawness broke through the cracks in her composure.

Bob was ready to talk. 'When the children were born we couldn't believe our luck. Three healthy babies, it was unheard of in those days. They were tiny, but all strong, with ten fingers and ten toes as we used to say.' His mouth moved from being pulled tight, almost like he was wincing, to forming a smile. 'When Sydney was a baby, he would constantly suck his fingers and toes or even his sisters' if they happened to be rolling around nearby. We were blessed, Detective, blessed to have conceived at all and blessed to be given two girls and a boy, a whole family that we had come to believe we would never have.'

'It was my fault.' Carla's eyes fixed forward as tears continued to fall. She nodded as she spoke as if somehow agreeing with her words before they had even passed her lips. 'There was something wrong with me. The doctors couldn't work out exactly what, but there was something wrong, I knew there was. I could feel it. When the doctor suggested we try some treatments that might help, I was petrified. But I wanted a child so badly, poor Bob had no choice but to go along with it. It was awful of course, but we conceived. You think that I'd have been over the moon, and I was, but I was also sure that the babies would die.' Bob reached over and took Carla's hand as Janine knelt beside her mother's chair.

She continued in a slow and measured voice. 'When we found out there were three babies, I didn't think I could handle it. I didn't think I had enough worry in me to be able to spread to three children, there were so many things in my mind that I was convinced could go wrong. Would they be healthy? What if they got hurt or sick or worse? I kept them so close, no sleepovers, no school camps or excursions for fear of something happening to them. And now this. It's my fault, I know it is. I think I did this to them. All the potions I took trying to fall pregnant, it probably affected them and did something to them.' Her sobs turned to heaves as Janine rubbed her mother's bony back.

Santino felt nauseated by the grief. It was raw and penetrating and brought with it a physical pain. It burrowed its way deep inside him, causing invisible scarring that would likely stay with him. He couldn't begin to fathom how these parents, or Janine, would ever recover from such a tragedy.

Bob took over. 'How do people just die like this, Detective? No one can give us any answers. How are we supposed to grieve for our children when we don't know what happened?'

'It's my fault,' Carla went on. 'I know it is.'

Bob reached out and touched her gently.

An uneasiness came over Santino. Their pain was bad enough, but their words were slowly reaching places in his mind that felt familiar. He had heard this story before; in fact, it was exactly the same. His heart felt as if it might pound right through his rib cage, and sweat was beading on his forehead.

He remained outwardly calm. 'I understand,' he offered. It felt completely ridiculous to even say these words, but in that moment, there didn't seem to be anything else to say. 'I am collecting all the information I can and if there are any developments, I will inform you immediately. I give you my word on that.' His promise sat in the air as he rose from the sofa.

Santino gave the family his condolences and thanked them for their time, excusing himself from the confines of their dark hell. At the door he handed Janine his card. 'Please call me if there is anything else that you need or if you have any questions at all.'

Janine tried to smile. 'Should I be worried, Detective?' Her eyes were pleading and filled with fear. 'I don't know what to do right now and I'm petrified, for my parents more than anything, but also for myself. Am I… next?'

He wondered how the hell he could answer that question without causing her further alarm. His conscience wrestled with what was the right thing to do. 'Please just take care and stay in touch. Given the situation it would be wise for you to speak to your doctor to rule out any problems. Your parents are understandably a mess and you'll need each other through this. Stay close to them and take care of yourselves.' He knew that pity was written all over his face. 'I wish I could tell you more, Janine, but I just don't have the answers. I'm truly sorry.'

Janine nodded, her eyes filling. 'Thank you, I will.'

Outside, the cool evening breeze filled his lungs like needles piercing tiny punctures in the inflated air sacs. He fumbled in the zip pocket of his bag for the cigarette packet he kept there for emergencies - like this, when he needed to remember to breathe. He'd had to do that on many occasions during the Fitzgerald trial when things got out of control and he risked letting himself fall over the edge into the psychological darkness he knew was waiting for the right moment to take him. But on this occasion, it wasn't grief that risked pushing him over the edge. It was a dawning realisation.

Lighting it up, he sucked in a long drag of nicotine that instantly made him light-headed. It calmed the dancing spikes that had erupted all over his skin. Taking out his phone, he dialled Harry's number.

'Hi Harry.' His voice was calm, but the phone shook in his hand. 'I need to ask you something.'

'Of course, are you alright? What's happened?' Harry said, clearly sensing his tone.

'When we first spoke, you mentioned to me that your sister was blaming all sorts of things like the treatments she had to conceive and the immunisation shots?'

'Yeah, that's right, along with everything else she ever gave Jason or fed him, or even bathed him in. They tried for five years to get pregnant and eventually tried one of those clinics, you know, where they take the egg and the sperm and...'

'IVF.'

'Yeah, IVF. Test tube babies they used to call them. What's this about? Have you found something?'

'Not yet, Harry,' he lied. He didn't know himself if what he was thinking was true. 'But we're working on it. I'll call you soon.'

'Hang on. I left you a message, did you get it? I've got Centre for Disease Control breathing down my neck, wanting any information we have on recent reported deaths that fit a particular criteria they provided. And I'm sure you can guess, it's the same as Jason's. You need to get down here. I haven't given them anything yet, but I think they're putting together a team. If they are, we'll have no choice but to back off.' Harry sounded exasperated and out of breath. 'I know I asked you to do this, Santino, but whatever's happening here, it's much bigger than anything we can manage.'

'Shit, Harry. I'm in Phoenix right now, but I'm heading back. We're on to something here, but I'll fill you in later. I'll call you when I get to the airport.' He ended the call before Harry could protest.

He took another long drag of the cigarette and dialled his voicemail. Arnya's voice echoed in his ears, almost sending him off balance on the pavement. He steadied himself against the car and took in her words.

'Santino, you need to get back here.' There was an obvious tremble in her voice. 'I think I may have found something. It might not be the cause of everything that's going on, but the link between some of the dead may be that they were conceived through In-Vitro Fertilisation. We'll know for sure once we look at the histories of some of the other deceased, but if this is in fact what's causing them to die, then this could be much bigger than we first thought. I don't want to alarm you, but if I'm right, then there are over 5-million people who could potentially be affected worldwide. Santino, we could have a global health crisis on our hands. Please call me when you get this.'

Santino felt the blood rush to his head. He was right. He was fucking right.

He got straight in the car, hitting the gas hard. Her words, 5-million people, replayed in his head as he weaved his way through traffic and into the airport terminal.

The flight felt like it would never end and by the time he reached the arrivals terminal, his phone was vibrating continually inside the pocket of his jacket. He ignored its constant and demanding presence. He couldn't deal with anything else right now. No more victims, no more cases. His head was swarming.

He passed the other passengers and the busy collection carousels, glad to have only a small piece of hand luggage. He headed for the exit where Arnya was waiting with her car engine running.

CHAPTER

7

Santino opened the rear door of the car and threw his hand luggage in before hopping into the passenger seat.

'How are you?' Arnya asked, careful not to launch into things too quickly as they drove from the airport.

Santino's bloodshot eyes, and the stubble that had all but taken over his usually well-kept face, answered the question for her, but she asked anyway out of courtesy. It had been a long few days for both of them.

'I just need to get cleaned up and have a decent coffee. I realise there's a lot to go over, but would you mind taking me home? We can talk there.'

'Of course.' Arnya wasn't sure if she should ask about his visit to the Graham family. Even though she hadn't known Santino for long, she cared about his welfare and wanted to know that he was okay.

'That wouldn't have been easy, seeing the family. How were they?' she asked.

Santino shrugged and reached over the back into his bag. He pushed two pain killers from their foil wrapping and swallowed them. 'Not good. I can't even imagine what they must be feeling.'

Arnya caught the slight hint of a choke in his voice and instinctively reached over to place her hand on his arm. She wanted to offer reassurance, but she feared that there was little that would bring comfort right now. What reassurance could you give someone in this situation, other than to let them know that you were there for them? She hoped he understood.

'I'm used to this kind of thing, dealing with grieving families and death, but this one really got to me,' Santino admitted. 'Where do we even begin with all of this?' he asked. 'If IVF is the cause, or even playing a part, then the implications are beyond anything I can even get my head around. Every time I thought about it on the plane, I felt as if the cabin was closing in on me.'

Arnya nodded slowly. He was right. The possibility that every child born using IVF technology since the late seventies could be at risk was something even she was struggling to comprehend. She was forcing herself to keep the panic at bay until there was concrete proof, but it was there in the back of her mind, pulling at her.

'We should begin by taking a step back,' she offered. 'At this stage we're making huge assumptions and getting ahead of ourselves. What we need to do is lay out everything we know so far and take another look at all the data. What we *don't* want to do is start panicking ourselves, and possibly everyone else if this gets out before we've even had a chance to properly consider the evidence collected so far. So, take a hot shower, grab some coffee and then we can get to work.'

Arnya pulled into a space outside the address Santino had given her. With an imposing curved and rendered frontage, the four-storey apartment building seemed to jut out from either side of the centre. It was very different from her plain, ultra-modern Lego-style block.

'I spoke to Harry and filled him in on the basics,' Santino said. 'He says that CDC are already knocking. They're rounding up evidence and they want any information we've collected, but I'd say they'll be keeping tight lips in order to avoid the media and any public questioning until they know more.'

'All the more reason for us to get to the bottom of this as fast as we can. Did he say whether or not they've come across the same information that we have?'

'It didn't sound like it,' Santino replied. 'I assume that the deaths have been flagged and the sibling connection will have raised alarms. They'll likely be starting where we were a few days ago, so I think we're still ahead of them at this point.'

Santino looked out the passenger window, scanning the apartment block.

'Everything ok?' she asked. His unsettled energy was making her feel uneasy.

'It's fine. Fitzgerald likes to put a guy on me every now and then, just as a reminder of his presence, and sometimes I can sense someone around. It's habit and paranoia more than anything. I'm used to checking, that's all.'

Arnya accepted the explanation, but she suspected it wasn't quite as trivial as he was making it sound. 'Even after all this time?'

'Definitely. You don't get to tangle with a guy like that without long-term consequences. And I humiliated him publicly. In his mind, this will never be over. He's made that very clear.'

When they got out of the car and crossed the street, there was a loud bang. It was so loud Arnya let out a scream. Santino pulled her to the entrance and left her there, running to the corner of the block to see what was happening. Across the street, something caught Arnya's attention. There was a man, standing in the shadows and watching them. She was too far to meet his eyes, but she knew they were fixed on her. She could feel it.

Santino returned, puffing and out of breath. 'Whatever it was, it's gone now,' he said.

'I saw someone, Santino, over there.' She pointed to the spot where the man had been standing, but there was no one there now. 'He was looking at me.'

Santino's eyes narrowed. 'Come on, let's get inside.' He ushered her up the stairs without saying anything more.

Arnya wondered if she was in real danger being there. Did Fitzgerald really want to harm Santino, and would he harm her?

'Are you okay?' Santino asked. He put the key into the lock, but didn't turn it, waiting for her answer.

Arnya forced a smile and tried to settle the fear that had ignited inside her. 'I'm fine, just a little rattled by everything.'

Inside the apartment, Santino gestured toward the kitchen and disappeared down the hall, calling back to her. 'Make yourself at home, I won't be long.'

Arnya wandered around the spacious apartment. Santino wasn't the stereo-typical LA cop, the kind Hollywood depicted in movies. She smiled to herself at the cinematic image of a middle-aged, dishevelled man with a filthy apartment, cluttered with pizza boxes and left-over take-out. Santino was well-groomed, meticulous and liked order. His apartment was immaculate. In the living area, black leather sofas and a matching armchair were placed in a rectangle around a gas fireplace. A large flat screen television was mounted on the adjacent wall. In spite of the neat, minimalist style, Arnya thought it lacked a woman's touch, and some books.

She made her way to the kitchen as the sound of the shower hissed through the partially open bathroom door and steam floated into the hall. Shards of the remaining daylight penetrated the top of the window, casting rays of gold that landed on the black stone bench top. She thought of her own apartment, which was currently a mess. She had been spending so much time at the office, she'd hardly been home.

'Make yourself a coffee.' Santino's voice found its way through the crack in the bathroom door. 'I might need several to get me into gear for this!'

She examined the shiny coffee machine that looked like it could make its way to outer space rather than serve up a short black. *'Make a coffee, he says.'* She quietly mimicked Santino's tone as if what he was saying was easy. She pressed one of the seven buttons that were lit up on the front panel and the machine responded with a whirring vibration. 'Shit.' She cursed and stepped back from it.

Santino had quietly emerged from the bathroom and was smiling smugly at her reaction. She laughed too, reminded how nice it felt to smile and hear the sound. He had definitely loosened up and looked much more relaxed. She pretended not to notice that he was only wearing a robe.

Santino pressed another button and the machine went quiet. 'Here, let me show you.' He took two cups from the overhead cupboard and placed them side by side on the bench. 'The machine is great, it's quick and easy, but when I have some time, I always use the percolator.' He turned the silver knob on the stovetop and filled the base of the percolator with water and coffee. 'This is from my mother's hometown in Italy,' he explained. 'The coffee's really good.'

Arnya was pleased to see his spirits had lifted, although she wasn't sure for how long.

'Now we let it simmer.' He placed it on the glowing hotplate.

'I'll grab the files,' Arnya said. It was no use putting it off any longer. They needed to get started. She fetched her bag and laid them across the coffee table and floor.

Santino returned in a shirt and trousers and brought in two coffees. He sat in the armchair across from her, looking at the papers that were now strewn across his hand-woven rug.

Arnya picked through the pages, highlighting lines and sections with a marker. The heavy feeling, a feeling of dread, washed over her again and was mirrored on

Santino's face when she looked up at him. The spark of joy she had seen only minutes earlier was gone.

'I'm convinced the IVF connection is the link, or at least *a* link,' she explained. 'I've already begun looking into the birth details of the case files we have and so far, every single one of them was conceived through IVF. The Graham case just made it easier to spot.'

Santino was silent. It was a lot to take in and process for both of them. Arnya squeezed her hands into fists and then unclenched, rubbing her fingers. They felt clammy.

'But what could it be about IVF that would be causing people to die all these years later?' he asked. 'We're talking a range of something like 30 to 40 years, based on the ages of the deceased, aren't we? That's crazy. Surely!'

Arnya flipped through her large pile of research papers until she found the one she wanted. 'Okay, a bit of background. The oldest living test tube baby, that we know of, to be conceived and brought to live birth through Assisted Reproductive Technology, what most people know as In Vitro Fertilisation, was born in 1978 and is now in her early forties. Her name is Louise Brown and since her there have actually been more than 5-million live births from IVF worldwide.'

Santino's chest tightened, the gravity of the number causing his body to tense as he tried to process what she was saying. 'Are we really thinking that 5-million people could potentially die? Jesus, Arnya, is this actually a possibility?'

She paused. Could she answer that confidently? Could she say it out loud? 'I don't know. We would have heard if Louise Brown had died. The media would have been all over something like that. Most of the cases we have here weren't born in the first years of IVF, so maybe it's something that came later, in the mid-eighties perhaps? A change to the IVF process?' Arnya rubbed her temples, feeling her head already beginning to throb. 'There are just so many unknowns here, Santino, it's nothing but guesswork right now, which is better than nothing, but still not fantastic when you're dealing with something of this magnitude. People's lives are at stake.'

Again, silence. She wondered how they had managed to find themselves at the centre of something so big it could change the world and have dire consequences for so many. How would they even tell the authorities or warn people if their suspicions were right?

She could see Santino was thinking through what she had told him.

'Where was Louise Brown conceived?' he asked.

'In the UK. The first clinics offering IVF treatment for patients in the US weren't popping up until later in the early-to-mid-eighties. There was a lot of backlash at that time, particularly from religious groups, and plenty of opposition to the research, so it was a slow burn to get it all up and running here. My dad's best friend, who was also my professor and my mentor, was very involved in the early pioneering days of IVF here in the US. I remember hearing him talk about it. It was university research-based initially, before the clinics began to emerge.'

'That's good to know. He might be useful as a contact if we need some specifics.'

Arnya agreed. 'Arthur would be glad to help if we needed him.'

'Okay, so given that all of the deceased, so far, are roughly somewhere between 31 and 38, then they're likely to have come from those early US clinics rather than from the university research programs?'

Arnya nodded. 'We'll need to look at that and get some more info for a timeline, but it seems that way. The problem is, there could be older or younger deceased that we don't even know about, so we have to be careful about restricting the timeline too much at this stage.'

'Good point,' Santino said. 'Could it be something about early IVF treatment as you said? Something they did wrong in the process that maybe got fixed as time went on?'

Arnya considered that suggestion. 'It's possible. But there's also the possibility that our deceased in this age group are just the first ones exposed to whatever it is, and the others will follow in time.' She thought about how to say the next part. 'It could be that this is just the first wave of deaths.'

Santino rested his elbows on his knees and buried his face in his hands. He rubbed his forehead with tense fingertips. 'How can that be? Are you telling me that these people, all 5-million or so, could literally be walking around like ticking time-bombs?'

Arnya looked back at the papers in front of her. 'As much as I hate to say it, yeah, it is possible, but we don't know for sure.'

'So, basically, they could have some sort of expiry? Reach a certain age or the right set of environmental factors and *boom*, that's it?' His voice sounded flustered and intense, hovering on certain words and accentuating the boom. He thrust his hands into the air and spread out his fingers. It looked dramatic, but Arnya could see how much it was upsetting him.

She softened. 'As I said, that's one possibility, but there are others too, Santino.' They were both desperate for a less horrific outcome for these people and their loved ones.

'Like what? Anything, please,' he pleaded.

'From what I've found so far, a study on 12-year-old IVF children that was conducted in Switzerland some years ago found there were significant abnormalities in their blood vessels in the body and lungs. According to the paper, 65 IVF and 50 non-IVF children were studied, and there were significant adverse changes in the developing blood vessels of those who were conceived using IVF.'

Santino's brow furrowed. 'Does that mean that IVF children are born with inbuilt abnormalities? Things that are already present in their DNA from birth due to the way they were conceived? If that's the case, why the hell would they keep allowing more and more babies to come into the world using IVF knowing that this would happen?'

Arnya could see he was agitated. She shuffled through the pile of paperwork to find another report while Santino went to the kitchen for more coffee. They both needed a distraction from the grim news she was delivering.

'Okay, listen to this.' She stood up and read from the paper she was holding. 'This study included the careful examination of relevant control groups. By doing this, the authors found that the problems observed were likely caused by events that influenced the embryo when in the test tube. Other research has recently also found elevated blood pressure and blood sugar levels in IVF offspring. And in 1992, research was conducted that found that abnormalities could be seen in the blood vessels of some children.'

Santino listened while he scooped coffee grounds from the percolator. Arnya continued to read. 'In 2005, they found increased blood vessel thickening in IVF newborns with low birth weight, showing that even foetal events could potentially influence cardiovascular health in later life. It now seems that even the environment of the embryo, be it in the womb, test tube, or lab, might also influence heart-disease risks in adulthood.'

'What does all that mean because you lost me on a few of those things?' Santino asked as he came back to the living room.

Arnya looked up. She took the coffee, knowing that the explanation would likely throw him further off balance. It was hard to believe, even for her. 'What this essentially means is that there have possibly been problems with this process and these children all along, we just didn't know it. These IVF-born people aren't yet old enough for us to see what breaks down, what goes wrong. It could be that this was going to happen all along. There is literally no test case other than watching what happens to them over time – or right now.'

Santino was shaking his head. 'Jesus Christ, Arnya. What they've actually done here is allow all of these people to be born without even knowing what the long-term outcomes might be. I've never even thought about it before, but that's just a huge lab experiment using people as the guinea pigs. Anything could happen to them in the long-term and no one even knows what.' He put his cup on the coffee table and crossed his arms. 'It's fucking unbelievable. It is essentially an on-going human experiment.'

Arnya's heart had begun to race. The adrenaline, the coffee and Santino's mounting anger were all having an affect on her. She tried to offer some scientific context. 'Having a child is one of the most powerful driving forces in human nature, Santino. The introduction of IVF was seen as something of a miracle of modern science. At that stage there was no reason to think that these children would be any different from the rest of us.'

'Isn't that what they thought when they had pregnant women take thalidomide? Or when they convinced people that smoking was fabulous? It's not that different, it's just that in this case it's taking a lot longer to see the outcomes. How have we brought more than 5-million people into the world without even knowing if something could go collectively wrong with them or if they might be prone to diseases or God knows what else?' His agitation was growing and so was his frustration. 'That might sound stupid or far-fetched, I know, but indulge me for a minute while I try to come to terms with this.'

Arnya could feel her own fear and anxiety intensifying. Her analytical brain told her to step back and not make any assumptions, but her emotional side was fighting against it. The more they discussed the possibilities, the more plausible they sounded.

Santino went on. 'We have 5-million people that have basically been created as an experiment. If they all had heart failure or got diabetes when they turned, let's say 40, what then? To do something like this with no idea about how the treatment might affect them or the mothers in years to come is insane. The drain on the health system alone would be crippling. Not to mention the trauma for the families. It seems so fucking irresponsible to have allowed it to get to 5-million with no idea of long-term outcomes.'

Arnya tried to calm the conversation. 'I understand, and I agree, believe me I do, but I suppose it's a topic that is completely subjective based on your standpoint. For those trying to have a family, they would argue that the risks are minimal and worth it. There has never been any reason to doubt the science or the process, or to think that something might go wrong. Obviously there are those opposed to it and they would argue from their own position on the subject, whether that be science, God, or whatever else. But regardless of any of those arguments, we need to focus on what is actually happening and not what the unknowns are right now. It's too easy to let our imaginations run away with us. We can't afford to do that.'

Santino continued to voice his fears anyway. 'And speaking of God, it makes you wonder about all of the opposition to scientific advancements like this.'

Arnya gave him a look, unsure if she liked where this was going.

Santino held his hands up for her to stop. 'No wait, hear me out. It's easy to look at all the religious protesters and say they're just radicals or nutters, but when you're faced with a possibility like this it makes you wonder if they had a point.'

Arnya stretched out her hands. She hadn't been able to get rid of the aching or the damp clamminess. She rubbed them along her pants to dry them. 'I wouldn't go that far,' she said. 'But that does actually bring us to an important aspect of this we need to consider.'

Santino stopped where he was. 'What aspect?'

'You were talking about radicals and nutters and people who opposed the science and you're right, there were a lot of them. They need to be considered in all of this.'

Santino stared at her. 'Of course we would always keep our options open for the possibility of something like that in any investigation, but I thought we were focussing on the medical aspects and the science. Are you saying we're not on the right track?'

Arnya huffed. She wasn't sure what she was saying, but it was obviously confusing them both. 'I'm not saying that we're on the wrong track. What I'm saying is we need to consider the possibility it could be something orchestrated by a radical group.' Arnya produced another stapled stack of papers from her pile. 'The position of the Catholic Church was clear from the very beginning, and they made sure their collective voice was heard. IVF research, and especially any IVF procedure actually being done, was initially kept fairly quiet. Religious groups put out lots of written information about the church's teachings and feelings on the topic and there was major resistance to the science, so it was kept virtually underground for a while. According to some of these articles, early IVF patients reported that the media fascination with IVF was intense, and the literature given to those first patients included advice about how to handle publicity. They actually told women not to talk to the media and to be careful about any enquiries.'

Santino gave that some thought. 'Maybe the church knew something that we didn't?' he asked. The comment sounded more emotional than intelligent.

Arnya explained. 'To be fair, it wasn't really the church that caused a lot of the resistance. It was more the fanatics, the radicals who were already spouting that the human race was doomed. They were the ones that picketed and made threats to the early clinics and patients, and they're the ones we should be at least considering.'

Santino's expression clearly showed his disbelief. 'What, like they've killed all these people to prove a point?' his voice had elevated.

Arnya shrugged. 'Anything is possible, you know that.'

Santino did know, all too well. 'Whatever the case, I still don't understand how you can continue to bring more and more people into the world without knowing what might happen to them. Why would any woman even want to participate in something that is literally experimenting on them?'

Arnya softened her tone. 'Santino, I know it's hard to understand, but from a scientific perspective, anything that doesn't have long-term testing to measure outcomes has its dangers. Anything. As far as I'm aware, there were no early indications that children born through IVF would be different in any way. Lots of these articles and studies talk about the *possible* long-term implications of the procedures, but they don't really offer any real concrete evidence of anything that would be considered a major concern. The science was solid. Or at least we thought it was solid, until now.'

Santino drained his coffee cup and refilled it again from the percolator. He refilled Arnya's as well and held it out to her. She hesitated, then took it, worried that she might never sleep again. It didn't matter anyway because at this rate, sleep was going to be a luxury neither of them could afford.

'I'm not convinced,' he said. 'I'm no scientist, but the more I think about it and look at all of this,' he pointed at the mass of paper strewn all over the place, 'the sicker I feel. Some of these studies were already pointing out years ago that there was evidence this process could bring about disease in the kids later in life. People are going to keep dying and it looks like there might not be a damn thing we can do about it.'

The thought that there were people out there - going about their evening with an invisible timer counting down their days, hours and minutes – made her feel sick to her stomach too.

CHAPTER

8

Several hours had passed since they had gotten back from the airport. Hours spent sitting on the floor going through piles of paperwork. Arnya could feel her limbs stiffening and her eyes were tired and dry. She was about to suggest they get something to eat when there was a knock at the door.

Santino shot her a questioning look and got up to answer. He leaned forward, peeping through the hole. 'It's just my neighbour Mrs Dawson.'

He opened the door allowing the scent of a pot roast to waft past him and fill the room.

'I hope I'm not interrupting, Detective, but I thought you could use a nice home-cooked meal. You've been in and out a lot lately and I haven't seen you with any groceries.'

Arnya grinned as Santino stepped back and allowed the tiny woman to pass him. She went straight to the kitchen and placed the dish on the bench top. As she set it down, steam escaped from the glass lid and the smell intensified.

'There's plenty of potatoes and veg in there. You really need to look after yourself better.' She smiled and placed her hand on his arm. The exchange was so warm and genuine, Arnya felt her sore eyes moisten just a little.

'Thank you, Mrs Dawson. You didn't have to, but it is so appreciated. We are actually starving and were just about to order in, so this is perfect.'

The small woman smiled at Arnya and took a plastic shopping bag from her arm. She handed it to Santino. There's a fresh baguette in there for you too. Make sure you eat it with the pot roast. You're getting thin.'

Santino thanked her again as she made her way to the door.

'He doesn't often have friends over,' she said to Arnya. 'You must be special.' She smiled and then disappeared into the hall outside his door.

Arnya laughed and raised her eyebrows at Santino when he returned from seeing her out. 'I think you have a fan there,' she said.

'She's very good to me. I think that she likes to mother me a bit, and I don't mind at all.'

'Well, whatever it is, she seems very sweet and that food smells amazing. I didn't realise how hungry I was.'

Santino got out plates and cut up the baguette while Arnya put the sections of paperwork they had gone through into ordered piles. As she did so, she found some text she had highlighted earlier about a study that suggested there was not enough evidence to support the idea that IVF could cause long-term negative outcomes.

'I wanted to show you this.' She held up the paper to Santino so he could see it from the kitchen. 'On one hand, we've gone over all of the evidence and established that the process does expose the embryos to things they wouldn't necessarily experience in a normal pregnancy, but on the other hand, there are also studies like this one that show there's actually not enough real data to prove this out-of-body exposure is harmful.'

'Fabulous,' Santino complained. 'It's like one study just discounts another if you look hard enough.'

He wasn't entirely wrong about that, Arnya thought. She had seen so many studies and papers put forward a new theory or idea, new research or investigation, only to be followed by a series of papers that would counter the idea or disprove the theory. It usually came down to the size of the study and the trustworthiness of the source, although lately she wasn't sure that she could trust anything.

'Maybe there's something else going on here entirely,' she said 'We can't discount the fact there are plenty of people who would like to prove that IVF is an abomination and a sin against God, and these days any idiot can get their hands on scientific equipment and tutorials online. Hell, there are people cloning animals and messing with IVF in their backyard sheds.'

Santino's head shot up and stared at her. His eyes were wide and he made a face, but went back to spooning the steaming pot roast onto the plates. He set them on the table with the bread and two glasses of wine. 'Come and eat before my head explodes.'

Arnya joined him at the table, the sight of the pot roast and bread immediately causing her mouth to water. 'Thank you for this,' she said.

'I think you mean, thank you Mrs Dawson.'

'You know what I mean,' Arnya said. The first portion of the pot roast made her tastebuds come to life. She wasn't sure if it was the fact that she hadn't eaten in so long - especially not a home-cooked meal - or that Mrs Dawson was probably the best cook on the block, but either way, the flavours of the food made her sigh with appreciation.

Santino finished in minutes, while Arnya savoured every mouthful. She almost couldn't listen when he went back to talking about the cases. She just wanted to sit at the table and enjoy the food and the wine for one more minute.

Santino shook his head before he even started talking. 'How can anyone be doing IVF or cloning or whatever from home? On live animals? That's disgusting. I can't stop thinking about it now. What if they create something awful, but living? It sounds like something from an old horror movie or a Stephen King novel.'

Arnya swirled her wine and nodded. 'The thing is, the equipment is easily accessible and you can find the science online – if you know where to look. There are individuals who believe they have the right to conduct their own research if they want to. They buy the equipment and do their own experiments.' Her jaw clenched. 'It's dangerous and irresponsible to say the least.'

Santino topped up both of their glasses, unable to come to terms with the idea. 'Why would anyone want to mess around with this stuff though? I just don't get it.'

Arnya wanted to bring the conversation back to the current situation. 'Okay,' she said. 'Before we get in too deep, why don't we get back to basics?' Arnya knew they needed to re-focus and pull them both from falling too far into the land of *what if?*

Santino relaxed back into the chair. 'Well, the basics would be explaining to me how this all works so that I can try to get my head around it. I mean, what actually happens during the IVF process?'

Arnya pushed the plate away and dabbed her lips with a napkin. She wondered how to easily explain one of the greatest medical advancements. It had turned man into a God and given him the ability to create life. They were going to have to start right at the beginning.

'A typical IVF cycle starts with the mother tracking her menstrual cycle and having a series of blood tests to check where she's at. At the right time she starts having hormone stimulation injections and then an ultrasound to check the size and number of the eggs. When the eggs are at the right size and the hormones reach the desired levels, she then goes into a surgical procedure to extract the eggs from the ovaries.'

Santino looked surprised. 'I had no idea it was so invasive. It sounds like torture, not to mention all the hormones and stuff being pumped in and messed with. Women really do get the rough end of it.'

'It's definitely invasive,' Arnya said, 'but as I said, the desire to have a baby can outweigh any concern or risk a woman might have. Many of the women in the very early days of IVF went through much worse than they do today. The science has come a really long way. They used to spend three weeks as in-patients, often staying in cabins in the grounds of the clinic that was treating them. The doctors would need to monitor their hormone levels, so they would have to collect their urine regularly. They would have to give samples every three hours, day and night. These days, in a standard fertilisation, after the hormones and harvest, the eggs and the sperm are placed together in the test tube where fertilisation occurs.'

'And humans are created. Actual human beings are the result. What do you mean by standard fertilisation?' Santino asked.

'Well, there's also another procedure called ICSI which stands for Intra Cytoplasmic Sperm Injection. This is where the sperm is actually injected into the egg.'

Santino was again shaking his head. Arnya felt like a school teacher trying her best to help a student grasp a complicated topic.

Arnya explained. 'But ICSI wasn't used until much later, so I'd say that if we're looking for clues related to IVF treatments in the timeframe we've estimated, we can rule it out, given that all of the deceased so far were born prior to its use in clinics.'

'So, that leads us back to the earlier clinics and their procedures,' Santino said.

Arnya agreed with him. It had to be earlier. 'Definitely. After the egg fertilises, the embryo is then grown in a culture medium for a few days before implantation into the mother. Any embryos left over are then frozen for later use if the first doesn't implant, or even if it does, they might use the embryos for later siblings.' Arnya got up from the table and went back to the piles of paper on the floor. 'I read something in one of these that was important. Hang on.' She picked up her bag.

Santino took the opportunity to clear the table. 'Refill?' he asked, holding up the wine glass.

'Thanks,' she said. If there wasn't so much at stake with all of this, she thought she might lock herself in her apartment and drown herself in wine and Netflix. It was a nice thought in comparison to the horror that was unfolding over wine and pot roast.

Santino refilled both glasses and placed hers on the bench. 'Thank God for wine,' he smiled.

'Here it is,' Arnya said. She climbed onto a stool at the kitchen bench across from him. 'This report says: The test tube parts of these events occur during a critical developmental period for the new embryo. This may be one reason why only 15 percent to 30 percent of IVF treatment cycles result in a successful pregnancy and delivery, because of a degree of *cellular stress* during the IVF process.'

'I hate to sound ignorant with this stuff, but I don't exactly get what that means, Professor.'

Arnya knew that no matter which way she tried to put it, it came out sounding like a science lecture. 'Basically, the cells are under stress and conception occurs in one in three attempts at best.'

Santino seemed to grasp that much better. 'So, do you think that maybe this is where we need to be looking – this cellular stress issue?'

'Hang on, there's more. It says, one potentially worrisome aspect of the recent French research is the implication that cellular and/or gene changes are occurring in the embryo - a cluster of stem cells that will go on to form all the organs of the body. If there are test tube environment-related changes that alter the development of healthy blood vessels in IVF children, this might mean other organ systems could also be affected in later life. This is an important topic for future research.'

They were both silent. Santino was staring out the window. He had an odd look on his face that seemed like a mixture of introspection and tortured thought. Arnya followed the line of his vision. It was dark outside and for a moment that calmed her. She was reassured by the knowledge that no matter what happened, or what they uncovered, there would still be constants like sunsets and darkness falling. Even if everything else changed, the sun would rise, rain would fall and life, for most, would go on, albeit, forever changed.

Santino turned to her. 'So, in trying to get my head around this and, stay with me here,' he tilted his head back, 'we're saying, what if fertilisation outside of the human body produced a live and seemingly healthy child, but one with a human 'use by' date? Basically, one with flaws not present in those conceived naturally.'

Arnya considered his summary. 'Based on this new study and what we're seeing now, that's… a very good possibility and not a bad summary at all for someone who hates the jargon.'

Santino looked back to the darkness of the outside world. 'Just like the poor Graham family, time just passes by, children grow up and families go about their lives, with no idea what's waiting for them. They forget to say I love you. They hurt each other and be selfish, never realising that time is ticking away towards their expiry date. And then one day, for no apparent reason, they just die with no explanation.' He shook his head. 'It is honestly just so tragic and sad. I don't even want to imagine what it would be like for all the others if this is true. All those people and all those families. It's the most terrifying thing I could ever imagine.'

Arnya's heart grew heavy. If it were possible for her soul to carry a weight, then it too felt weighed down. She fell silent.

'I think the Graham case is the one we need to focus on at this point,' she said after a long pause. It was an effort to bring herself back from the torrent of dark thoughts that were invading her mind. 'Surely the answer to all of this lies in why two of the three siblings are dead and one is still living. What is it about the last one that's different to the other two? They weren't identical, they were three separate embryos that all implanted, so external factors with the embryos is the most plausible explanation. Something that two were subjected to, but not the third?'

Santino picked up his phone as she spoke. 'Shit! Fifteen missed calls. How did I not hear it?' He gave Arnya a look that told her it wasn't good. 'We need to get everything we know to Harry Bryant.' He flicked through the call list and messages. 'If these are what I think they are, then we're about to be inundated with a whole lot more case files and an investigation much bigger than we can manage.'

Arnya sighed. 'Won't Centre for Disease Control just take it all?'

'Not if I can help it,' Santino warned. His eyes were reflecting a steely determination and his lips were pulled tight. 'I think if we can convince Harry to hand over all the initial notes we have, but not any of this more in-depth stuff, that might buy us a little more time so we can see if we're actually onto something. If we hand over the IVF connection too soon and it turns out to be wrong, we could end up the scapegoats for the whole lot, you know that. I've seen CDC in action and they'll do whatever it takes to avoid public panic or fallout.' His voice was low and his tone gave away his cynicism before his words did. 'If there is any opportunity to cover asses, especially their own and those that puppet them, they won't hesitate to use whatever means necessary.'

'Really?' Arnya couldn't believe that a government body charged with protecting the people could be so underhanded, but she had also been called naive more times than she could count. 'Even with something as serious as this?'

Santino turned up the corner of his mouth and gave her a knowing look. She wondered if he felt irritated by her naivety.

'I know exactly how these guys play the game – and it's all a game, no matter what the stakes,' he said. 'They'll play it down until it's contained and then pretend like it was nothing at all, while we end up the villains who scared the shit out of everyone before they, the *heroes*, fixed it.'

Arnya believed him, but she also knew that he'd had long-running feuds with many other cops and agencies, so it was hard to know if there was an element of exaggeration to his version of events. Regardless of whether or not he was speaking from first-hand experience or just bitterness, she trusted him and that was all that mattered.

'I know we need to be careful about how we proceed with this,' she said. 'It could get away from us really fast, but it's not like we have a whole lot of options here, Santino.' Her eyes were pleading and her tone soft. 'The problem is that we also can't sit on it too long otherwise, when it does come out, and it will, we'll be hung out to dry for not alerting the public immediately and potentially risking lives.' She didn't want it to sound like she was trying to protect herself over and above others, but she was worried, about both of them.

Santino met her eyes 'Damned if we do and damned if we don't.' His tone was matter of fact. 'Regardless of what the overall outcome is, and who ends up heroes or villains, we need a little time, just 48 hours or so to try to make some headway now that we have a better handle on where to focus.'

Arnya held the exchange between them, keeping her eyes fixed on his. 'I agree. But remember, we could be completely off base with our assumptions.' Her words were blunt. This wasn't the time for not speaking up. 'Nothing is certain and we still don't know for sure that we're on the right track. I guess it would be better to be accused of keeping it quiet for a short time while we did our research, rather than causing world-wide hysteria about something that turns out to be false. I don't want that on my conscience.'

Santino considered that for a moment. 'We'll need to go to Harry, though. I can't keep him out of this. We need as many hands as we can get for the short time we might have, and Harry can hopefully set us up with a small team. There's already a buzz out there. People will be sensing that something's happening and Robert is obviously swamped. The media are starting to report these strange and random deaths and Harry says CDC are sniffing, so it's closing in on us fast.' He looked at his phone again. 'Panic will follow. Even if they don't know what all this is about, people will make assumptions regardless. Flu, or a virus outbreak, or some kind of biological terror attack, whatever they can come up with that they can make fit the narrative.

If we don't find something concrete soon, it'll be out of our hands anyway.'

Arnya nodded. 'Agreed. Let's talk to Harry before this completely explodes.'

Santino went back to the coffee table. The strewn notes looked like a gust of wind had blown through and scattered them. 'If we spend the night putting all of the research in order, we can have an outline and a plan to present to Harry in the morning. We need to get him on side so that he'll give us the resources. We'll also need to get the names of some more of the deceased and find out what clinics the parents attended for their IVF treatments.' He pointed to the files. 'We can get some of those details from the families we've already got on file here. I'd say we've got 48 hours, max, before this completely blows up. We need to find that concrete link soon.'

Arnya ran her fingers across the back of her stiff neck, digging her fingertips in hard behind her left shoulder blade. She could tell that Santino was feeling the pressure too. The fact that within days they could be at the centre of a global health crisis was not lost on either of them.

'I'll go through the phone messages and see what updates have come through,' Santino said. He grabbed a notepad and pen from a kitchen drawer. 'Could you make a map of the first clinic locations from the year IVF began in the US? Maybe then we can start plotting the deaths based on those early locations.'

Arnya opened her laptop and started to search. She found two clinics in Virginia, but the third paralysed her fingers on the keyboard. Blood rushed to her cheeks and she was aware of a low thud in her chest. The name of the clinic was one she recognised. It was the clinic of her father's best friend, Arthur.

She knew Arthur had an early role in IVF, but seeing his clinic's name on the list of possible problem locations stirred an uneasiness in her. She wondered if any of the dead could have come through Arthur's clinic and if so, what did that mean?

Before she could finish the thought, Santino appeared in the doorway from the hall. He looked as if the wind had been knocked right out of him. He put his hands on the doorframe to steady himself.

'Jesus, Santino, what is it?' Arnya got up and went over to him. 'What the hell happened?' Fear and panic were washing over her, making her feel like she too might have to steady herself.

'I just got a call. Janine Graham and her parents are dead.'

Arnya felt herself step back as if that might somehow lessen the impact of the news. 'Fuck. How? What does this mean?'

Santino went to the cupboard and got out the whiskey. He put two glasses on the bench and poured, downing the large shot in one mouthful and handing Arnya the other. 'It was a murder-suicide, Arnya. Janine killed them and then killed herself.'

Arnya swallowed the shot and sat down on the kitchen chair. Her legs were buckling. This was exactly what she had feared. That the weight of knowing this news would drive people to do crazy things like this. 'Did they say anything else?'

Santino sat down across from her. 'Only that she left a note saying she couldn't sit around and wait to die and couldn't leave her parents to grieve another child.'

Tears had filled his eyes and he brushed them away.

Arnya sobbed.

CHAPTER

9

Feeling the first rays of the warm morning sun on her back as it streamed through the partially open blind, Arnya stretched out her cramped legs and pulled herself up to sit.

The shocking news about Janine Graham had taken some time to process, but it had also reinforced their determination and the fruits of their all-night labour had been plentiful. They now had a list of names of more recently deceased people who matched the criteria, and a map showing the location of every IVF clinic set up between 1981 and 1988 across the USA. She watched from the sofa as Santino brewed a pot of coffee and made an omelette. The mixture of smells was making her hungry in spite of how anxious and nauseous she felt.

'I know you probably don't feel much like eating, but once we head out that door, neither of us know what's going to happen, so I thought we could take a few minutes and have something decent to eat before we go. One last moment of normality,' he smiled.

Arnya appreciated the sentiment more than he knew. She wondered how she had ended up here, in the middle of all of this. Only a couple of weeks ago she had been getting up each day and doing little more than putting one foot in front of the other. This situation might be more than she could handle, something she probably shouldn't have involved herself in, but she felt alive and useful, and that was worth almost any risk she might face. The cases, Santino, the unknown, it all reignited a fire in her that she thought no longer existed, and for that she was grateful. Grateful to have made new and much needed connections like the man who now stood in the kitchen cooking her an omelette, and for old ones renewed, like Robert. Whatever the future held, it was better than the mere existence she had been previously living.

Santino placed the loaded plate on the coffee table in front of her. 'Thanks.' She smiled, taking a bite. 'This is delicious.'

'I like to cook.' He flashed her an almost shy look.

'Can I ask you a question?' Arnya said. She was unsure, even as the words left her mouth, if she should.

Santino looked up from his plate. 'Of course.'

'What happened back then, with the Parker Fitzgerald case and the media circus? Why did it blow up like that? What was the... real story?'

Santino reclined into the armchair with his plate on his lap. His shoulders fell and his lips pursed before he began. 'I'd been a cop for a few years, but I hadn't been with Homicide very long when I attended the scene of a murder victim, a guy called Maurice Stephens. Things seemed strange from the time that I got there. I could see the usual protocols weren't being followed. There were random people that seemed to be hanging around, and no one at the scene seemed concerned about it. In fact,' he straightened in his chair as if the next part of the story was crucial, 'when I raised it with another detective, he told me to just stand back and let him handle this one. At first, I thought that this was something different, sensitive maybe, like a celebrity or someone well-known that needed to be kept quiet, but later I realised it was something else completely.'

Arnya could see that telling the story was bringing back his frustration and disbelief about the whole thing. But there was something else. She could hear a sadness in his tone, a disappointment. 'So, you knew straight away there was something wrong?'

Santino had pulled in his bottom lip. He scraped his teeth across it, letting the skin fall slowly back to its usual position. He was taking his time to answer. 'I looked over the scene, checked the other rooms of the apartment - he was found in the living room - and asked a few questions. But I got the distinct feeling that no one wanted me doing any of that. I took some photos around the place, which isn't something I would usually do, the crime scene guys do that, but being fairly new at the time, I wanted to look it over later and cover all my bases. One of the other detectives told me to get rid of the pictures and put the camera away. That seemed really bizarre. What I thought at the time was that it looked more like they were cleaning up the scene rather than investigating it.'

'So, what was the connection to Parker Fitzgerald? How exactly did he know the guy, Maurice?' she asked.

'Maurice and Fitzgerald were lifelong friends. They met at university and were roommates. Fitzgerald was from a wealthy family, as you know - heir to a pharmaceutical fortune – which he's now just inherited. He was self-absorbed, privileged and pretty much the family's screw-up, always acting like the typical life-of-the-party with access to plenty of drugs and money to throw around. Maurice, on the other hand, was from a middle-class, hard-working background. His mother left them early on and the father did his best, you know, the usual story,' he shrugged. 'God only knows why he got tied up with that lunatic, but Fitzgerald befriended him, most likely because Maurice was brilliant and could be manipulated into doing all of Fitzgerald's school work. It was enough to lure Maurice in though. They stayed friends and ended up working together in Fitzgerald's family business.'

Arnya was confused. 'So why did he kill the guy, if he was his best friend?'

'Well, that's the 50-million-dollar question, and one that was never fully answered – for me at least. There was a lot more to this case than ever revealed publicly and as it was, Fitzgerald had so many people on the payroll that he almost got away with it all. He claimed Maurice was a hopeless alcoholic and was out of control. He was having violent outbursts and Fitzgerald claimed he was trying to help him.' Santino shook his head.

'But you don't believe that?' she asked.

'Not a chance. Fitzgerald was, and still is, a scheming, lying son of a bitch. There was something more, I have no doubt about it.'

Arnya could see the tension in Santino's face. Clearly, it was a very sore subject for him.

'Maurice was an alcoholic,' Santino continued. 'In the years leading up to his death he'd had some kind of breakdown and hit the bottle pretty hard. He'd gone downhill quickly, but there hadn't been any reports of violent behaviour or anything along those lines.'

'Do you have a theory then, why he killed him?'

'I've had many, but nothing that ever stuck. Nothing about that case was right. Everyone I thought I could trust was on his payroll and every time I voiced my opinion or raised something, I was shut down. But I knew in my gut there was more to it.'

'So, how did it finally unravel and end up in the media like that?' Arnya had seen the news reports, but they hadn't canvassed any motives for the killing.

'It was the pictures. When I saw the official crime scene photos that were submitted into evidence, they were completely different to what I had seen with my own eyes that day. The body had been adjusted. Things had been moved and removed. I had followed a few of my own leads and I knew by that stage that Fitzgerald was involved in some way. The LAPD was littered with people in Fitzgerald's pocket, so I did the only thing I could, I met with a reporter and leaked the story. Once it was out, Internal Affairs was in like a shot and it all fell apart. People started to talk to save their own asses and Fitzgerald was in the firing line, as well as a few other notable figures.'

'That must have been a crazy time. And tough for you personally,' she said. She wasn't sure that she would have had the guts to take on the whole city like that.

'The toughest thing wasn't being frozen out by the whole police department. The toughest thing was knowing in my bones that there was something more to it that I just couldn't work out. Fitzgerald had several people pay me a visit – numerous visits.' He pointed to a scar on the side of his forehead. 'For more than a year I was repeatedly threatened, tormented and even physically attacked by his thugs. Once the trial was over and Fitzgerald didn't get jail time, it didn't stop. Even now, Fitzgerald still makes a point of sending me birthday cards and the occasional, shall we say, gift.'

'Gift? What kind of gift?' She couldn't even imagine.

Santino rolled his eyes. 'Everything from snakes and spiders to cakes and donuts. It's his way of reminding me that he's always nearby, keeping an eye on me if you like. He likes to stay in control and make sure that I know it's not over. Maurice had something on Fitzgerald. I know it and he knows that I know it. That's why he continues to play these games.'

'Jesus, Santino. That's next level. Any idea what Maurice might have had on him?'

'Fitzgerald is a greedy son of a bitch, so it would have been about money. Something to do with some seedy underworld drug dealing probably, knowing that scumbag. There was no opportunity to push to look for something bigger back then. In the eyes of the cops, they had them all and it was done, but I wanted to take him down so badly. I got close a few times, I think.' He raked his fingers through his hair and folded his arms across his chest. 'But it became a bit of an obsession and I had to pull back, for my own sake. Harry helped me to see that.'

'Well, at least you got Fitzgerald, even if the whole truth didn't come out.'

'Maybe, but now he's just inherited billions. That's not justice in anyone's book,' he said. 'He sent me a thousand-dollar bottle of champagne when his father died recently. A reminder that he has even more money and power. But he's stupid because all it does is tell me that he's still afraid of me and he knows that I'll never completely let it go.'

Arnya couldn't believe the deep, dark underbelly of things that seemed to go on just beneath the surface, hidden and somehow protected. 'You see all this stuff on TV and in the news and you think you know, but there's so much more to it. I'm so sorry that you had to go through that.'

'I'm not,' Santino smiled. There was a trace of menace in his tone. 'And I'd do it all again. Although this time I'd be smarter. I'd dig deeper and make sure that I got everything I could get before leaking it. If I had done that the first time, I could have brought him down for good.'

Arnya took her plate to the sink while Santino packed up all of the paperwork. When he excused himself to the bedroom to change, she picked up her phone and put her notes in her bag. After the heavy conversation she had just had with Santino, she decided not to bring up the situation of Arthur and the clinic right now. She wanted to talk to Arthur herself first and see if he could shed any light on the situation that might help them. If anyone could provide some insight into those early years of IVF, it was Arthur.

CHAPTER
10

Captain Harry Bryant opened his office door and greeted the pair with pained, bloodshot eyes. Distraught families, confused officers and worried medical practitioners were all taking their toll on him. Before Santino even opened his mouth, Harry seemed to know that whatever he was about to say was going to be bad news.

Santino closed the door behind them and sat down in a chair beside Arnya. He watched as Harry opened the top drawer of his desk and pulled a small flask out.

'I have a feeling I'm going to need to brace myself for this,' he said. As he spoke, deep lines formed around his lips that were bitten to bleeding.

'Captain, this is Professor Sloane.'

'It's nice to meet you, Professor. Detective Santino has been singing your praises.'

'Thank you, Captain Bryant, although I'm not sure I deserve it. I don't think I've helped much at all.'

Santino shook his head in disagreement and then turned to Harry. 'We've been going over all the cases and talking to the families. You know I went to see the parents of the Graham triplets and spoke with Jayda Crane's parents. And Arnya has been following up with the others. The calls are coming in thick and fast, Harry, faster than I can even answer them, from every jurisdiction. It feels like the start of a tsunami.'

Harry cut in. 'It hasn't been much better here, believe me.'

'Well, we think we may have found the answer, or at least a link that could lead us to the answer.' Santino paused and Harry seemed to physically steady himself against the desk. He brought the flask to his mouth and threw it back, swallowing loudly. The liquid made him grimace.

Arnya took the opportunity. 'It appears, at this stage, that IVF is the connection in each of these cases. There's still so much to consider, and we can't rule anything out, but everything seems to point to IVF, or something in that process, as the common link.'

Harry wiped at his sweating forehead with the back of his hand. 'Are you fucking serious with this? IVF as in babies?' Harry sighed painfully, the sound almost bouncing off the walls of the small office.

He took another drink and then another as Arnya explained the IVF connection and how they had come to the conclusion. She read him the results of the studies she had quoted to Santino earlier. 'IVF does seem to be the strongest link. How or why, we don't know, but I'm convinced this is the connection,' she said.

Harry interlocked his fingers across his body, his large stomach pushing them so high they looked as if they were just below his double chin. 'So, you're telling me there have already been suspicions about medical issues relating to IVF treatment? Years of suspicions and studies that showed problems and no one bothered to fucking follow that up or warn people?'

Arnya tried to answer as best she could. 'There have been numerous studies done that have indicated children born through IVF could have any number of unknown issues in the future, particularly as they age, but no one has yet reached an age where we can see or study that in a significant way. Anything from the process involved with IVF, right through to human interference, could have led to the embryos becoming compromised and developing problems. We have to remember that this is all an unknown. IVF is barely 40 years old. No one can see the future and right now, it's looking like there could be millions of lives at stake.'

The room fell silent. Harry was a smart man who didn't need the ramifications spelled out for him. He stood up and paced behind his desk. 'Jesus Christ. My sister, Jason and all those other poor bastards.' He stood still, facing the window and wiped again at his damp face. 'I think we should hand the whole lot over to the Feds, Santino, before it gets out of control. This is way over our heads and we should distance ourselves before it really takes hold. We can't even begin to deal with something like this. It's insane.' He was shaking his head vigorously. 'How the hell could this happen in fucking America? Doesn't someone keep an eye on this shit, for Christ's sake? I can't even…'

Santino jumped in. 'Harry, I know that this has the potential to be catastrophic, but we need a little time. We need to get clear on what's happening here before the media get hold of this and people start going crazy. Give me a team, let us find out what's actually going on and then, when we have something concrete, we call in the Feds and give them everything we've got. If we tell them this now, what if we're wrong? And you know, Harry, you know that they'll bury it if anyone important is at fault, you know they will. Then what? Give us a chance to find out. For Jason. He's what started all of this.'

'This makes me nervous, Santino. We're not talking about a few deaths or even something treatable, are we? Are these people all going to die? Shit, I don't want that on my shoulders.' He slumped back into his chair. 'How many people are at risk here? Are you sure?'

'Captain Bryant.' Arnya stood up. She pulled the map from her briefcase and spread it out on his desk. 'This is what we know so far. All of the deaths have occurred in people under the age of 38. We have no idea why, but from the limited research we've managed to do, it seems that it might be something to do with conceptions that occurred roughly between about 1983 and 1988, but we can't be precise yet. Unless we start seeing younger or older people on the list, we should assume this timeframe for now.' She pointed to the black circles on the map. 'These are all the clinics in the US that were providing IVF treatment between '83 and '88. Initially, we mainly only received reports of deaths that occurred here in California, but since then, Santino has received reports of deaths right across the nation which indicate that they were possibly conceived in some of these clinics in other states as well.'

Harry looked lost as Arnya tried to explain. Santino leaned over her shoulder.

She continued. 'The big issue for us right now is determining if it is in fact IVF itself that is causing the deaths, or something related to the process at particular clinics. What we don't yet understand is why only some people conceived through the clinics have died, while others did not. For example,' she pointed to the clinic where Jayda Crane was conceived. 'Jayda Crane was conceived here and so was your nephew, approximately ten months after, but there were many more who were conceived before and after them that have not died, at least not yet.'

'Not yet? Jesus Christ.' Harry pushed his fingers through what was left of his hair.

'We have to be realistic here,' Arnya pushed. 'It's possible there are many more to come, Captain.'

'How many more?' Bryant asked.

'Up to 5-million people have been born through IVF worldwide, but if it's specific clinics and only here in the US, then that's much less,' Arnya said.

Arnya was doing a great job of explaining the situation, but Harry Bryant still seemed to be struggling to comprehend. 'But how is that possible? If it's the treatment itself, then why aren't they all dying? Why would it be sporadic like that?'

Santino answered. 'That's the question we want to try to answer before this thing gets any bigger, Harry.' This was his chance to push. 'Give me a team. 48 hours, that's all I'm asking for and if we're still in the dark by then I will gladly hand everything we have over to whoever you think should have it.'

He saw the concerned look that Arnya was casting his way. He knew that 48 hours was not enough time to look into the cases they had, let alone all of the others that were piling up with alarming speed, but it was likely the best they would get. Santino responded to her look of concern with a nod of recognition. He knew it was ambitious, but it wouldn't take the media long to start drumming up hysteria, and by that time the Feds would be pushing hard anyway and running with their own investigations that would likely lead them in the same direction. It was possible the Feds were already aware of the IVF link.

Harry slowly nodded his agreement, but Santino could see his Captain was nearing defeat. They were damned either way. Harry picked up the phone and spoke to someone, organising a team of six officers to assemble in the briefing room.

Harry got up. '48 hours, that's it, Santino. And that's if the Feds don't get wind sooner and swan in here in the next five minutes anyway. If they do, you hand it all over and you're out. 48 hours. God knows where this thing could end up. I don't want deaths falling back on me because I sat on it. Get in there, get it done and get as much as you can to prove your theory. Back everything up - you know the drill - and then hand it over.'

Harry led the pair into the meeting room at the end of the hall. The new team members shuffled nervously on their feet, unsure why they'd been summoned with such urgency.

'Thanks for coming in.' Harry's voice was raspy and strained. 'Detective Santino and Professor Sloane here are working on a special project and I have assigned you to their team, temporarily. I'm assuming you've heard the rumours buzzing around about the fact that there have been a number of somewhat unexplained deaths, so get them everything they need and do it quickly. This project is to remain classified, and I *mean* classified. Not your usual classified, where you still tell people you know because you think it doesn't really matter and no one will find out. This is CLASSIFIED. You do not talk to your families, your friends or even your goddamn dog about this. Am I understood?'

Each officer nodded their agreement, despite obvious hesitation. No one dared question Harry.

Santino stepped forward and briefed the officers on the cases so far. He left the technical aspects to Arnya. He enjoyed watching her come to life as she took charge of the room, addressing each of the officers and explaining the details. She was good at it and seemed to be at home in an environment like this. He felt a depth of gratitude to her. For her knowledge, unwavering support and her commitment, in spite of the fact that she owed him nothing. She could have easily refused to assist and simply gone back to her life instead of being dragged into this mess.

The people in the room were silent, their attention fixed on Arnya. They occasionally looked at each other and exchanged worried glances.

Santino could also see the fatigue on Arnya's face as she spoke, or perhaps it was a wearing down of her spirit. It reminded him of his own sense of impending doom and stirred feelings he was trying to suppress. No matter how tired or overwhelmed he felt, there was no stopping what was unravelling now. It was gaining fearsome speed and deadly momentum and how it would eventually come to an end was anyone's guess.

Arnya continued, moving the officers through the map and the details of the cases. He wondered why she'd chosen such a solitary career when her passion radiated as soon as she was inspired. It was hard to believe that she was a complete stranger only a short time ago. Since the Fitzgerald case he had vowed to never again rely on anyone, to trust or believe that someone was looking out for him, but now, watching her, he knew he had already broken that vow. He was depending on her completely, to be his eyes and ears in everything that he didn't understand with these cases. Science, genetics and the human reproductive system were a complete mystery to him. Without her he had nothing, but it was more than that, he was drawn to her, trusting her without reservation, something that felt completely foreign to him.

As Arnya finished her explanation, Santino could see the alarm on many of the officers' faces. The shock and the fear couldn't be contained, even by those who were used to hiding their emotions. He wanted to tell them that it was under control and they'd get to the bottom of this no matter what it took, but he couldn't. He couldn't give any assurances. Not this time. More were going to die.

$$-\!\!\!\wedge\!\!\!\wedge\!\!\!\wedge\!\!\!-$$

Santino scanned the meeting room. It was already stuffy and warm. It was now the team's central hub, buzzing with activity as voices jumped back and forth across phone lines, and keyboards tapped with frenzied fingers, searching for details of clinics, names, patient lists and anything else they could get in connection with the cases. The lists of names taped to the white board were growing rapidly as the officers worked at a ferocious pace. They eventually spilled onto the wall itself. Trays loaded with coffees came and went as night fell. By morning two things were abundantly clear. Firstly, the deaths were definitely localised to specific clinics across the US, but were apparently random within those clinics. And secondly, the six cases they began with were not the first deaths. The earliest they could locate, according to officers Moffat and Stevens, likely occurred several weeks earlier. However, there was no way of knowing for sure how many were in fact already dead and buried without having triggered any sort of concern.

'Listen up.' Santino clapped his hands to grab the attention of the team. 'I know you're exhausted, but we have a little over 30 hours before the Feds take over and I for one don't want to work my ass off just to have them come in and take it out from under us.'

No one liked the Feds taking over. The officers on the ground consistently worked day and night for little reward, only to have Federal authorities take over just as the case was all but solved, stealing every ounce of credit. Time and time again, officers were cheated out of recognition they deserved for work they put their lives on the line for. That injustice stirred the fire inside them all. Each knew what a case like this meant, what it had the potential to become, and no one was going home.

Santino gave the instructions. 'Collins and Green, you head to Judge Carlin's chambers and get the warrants we need for each clinic's patient files. Be creative with your reasons, we don't want too many questions. Moffat and Stevens, you stay on the phones and keep pin-pointing every new death that might be related. Rodriguez and Kelton, you need to follow-up every single name on these lists.' He tapped his pen on the sheet affixed to the wall. 'Find any that haven't yet been identified as an IVF birth. I want to give Harry an update and then see Robert James at the Medical Examiner's office so I can fill him in too, and I need to do that in person.' He turned to Arnya who was collecting her bag and some notes. 'Are you coming with me?'

Arnya took her phone from her bag. She looked up, but didn't meet his eyes. 'No, I need to see a friend, my old Professor. I'm hoping he may be able to help with a few things I can't get my head around.'

Santino moved in front of her so that she couldn't avoid his questioning eyes. 'Are you sure you're okay?' He asked in a lowered tone.

Breaking their exchange, she fumbled in her purse for her keys. 'I'm fine, truly. It'll be good to get out of here for a while anyway.'

Santino grabbed his keys and headed to the elevator alongside her. 'Meet you back here when you're done?' he asked.

The elevator reached the ground floor and Arnya stepped out. She looked as if she was a million miles away and Santino wondered if she had heard anything he said to her.

'See you back here,' she said.

Outside, Santino headed to his car, but not before noticing a hefty guy across the road who was staring him down. Santino kept his eyes on the man, feeling his senses sharpen. Fitzgerald seemed to be ramping up his game, being more obvious than usual. He had been fairly consistent with his approach in the last few years, but it was more distanced, not like this. Was it the inheritance of his father's empire making him feel more brazen? Maybe now he had more to lose than ever and wanted to make sure that nothing was going to undermine it. No matter the reason, Santino suspected the day was coming for them to face off once and for all. Fitzgerald had made it very clear that all was not over – and maybe that day was coming sooner than he thought.

CHAPTER

11

'Arnya, darling, I've missed you.' Arthur Hoffman looked up from his clipboard and took the pen he was chewing from his mouth. He said goodbye to the younger doctor he had been chatting to and placed his notes on the bench of the nurses station. 'To what do I owe this delightful pleasure?' Arthur wrapped his long, slender arms around the woman he had always considered a daughter.

Arthur was a brilliant man in Arnya's eyes and an exceptional doctor with a huge heart. Although retired, he refused to spend his days on the golf course with most of his friends and former colleagues, preferring instead to volunteer and give his time and knowledge to his community. His latest endeavour was helping out at a local aged care facility.

'Well, I missed you of course, Arthur!' Arnya smiled and pulled back so that she could see him. He had aged so much in the last few years, but his smile never changed in spite of the lines that had formed around his mouth and chin.

'You never were a good liar, Arnya, and flattery is also not one of your strong points, so that must mean that you need me for something.' He smiled back. 'Not that I'm complaining. Walk with me, I'm making my rounds.' He pointed down the corridor of the brightly lit ward.

Mrs Jacobs was their first stop. 'Good morning, Mrs Jacobs, how are you today?' he asked. He took her pale, wrinkled hand in his. Mrs Jacobs didn't respond verbally, but the sparkle in her eyes and quivering smile was evidence of her pleasure at his arrival. 'She loves me most days,' he said to Arnya, while winking at Mrs Jacobs like a naughty schoolboy. 'This is my friend Arnya, she's here to visit me,' he added.

While the frail patient turned her eyes to Arnya, Dr Hoffman checked her medication chart and clinic notes.

Arnya admired Arthur's ability to connect with his patients, despite their physical or mental barriers, more than anything else about him. He reminded her so much of her father, but also of everything she was not.

While Arthur moved from bed to bed, joking and making small talk with those that could no longer respond or interact, Arnya's heart grew heavy in her chest. The forced pleasantness of the ward, with its bright curtains and indoor plants, could not hide the truth of what went on there. The desire to brighten the cold, clinical space was done so admirably by staff with good intentions, but nothing could mask the smell that always lingered in these places. It was the smell of death in a place where patients came to die.

Room after identical room of similar afflictions on different faces; Alzheimer's patients, frail people with no control of their extremities or emotions as a result of Parkinson's, and the wandering demented. Arnya looked to a nurse who was helping a patient out of bed nearby, marvelling at what special and strong souls it took to care for these most vulnerable people. No matter how many years of study she completed or how good her qualifications looked on paper, she felt she could never measure up to the strength of character of carers in roles like this.

'I do actually have something I need to talk to you about, Arthur. And it's important.'

Arthur turned to face her, picking up on the seriousness in her tone. 'Of course, come with me.' He linked his arm through hers and led her to the cafeteria down the hall, a welcome relief from the confronting human side of medicine, the stark reality of what people so often become and what they have little or no control over. As she had walked through the ward, she was glad she made the decision to leave medicine and pursue a career that didn't force her to look into the eyes of sick, sad and dying patients. Any amount of regret for not living up to the expectations - created by herself or her father - was far outweighed by the feeling of dread and sadness that she felt when dealing with patients and their desperate families.

Arthur fetched the coffee and then pulled up a chair beside her. He placed his hand over hers. 'You seem worried, what's the matter?'

'You know me. I've never been good at dealing with sick people.' She forced a smile. 'I'm much better with numbers and formulas.'

'Of course,' Arthur said, 'it was silly of me to take you along. Seeing the deterioration of human beings can be very confronting. Drink your coffee and tell me why you're here.'

'I'm involved with something, Arthur, something that I think has the potential to be disastrous. And I need your help.'

'Disastrous? I sincerely hope that's an exaggeration.' He smiled, not yet grasping the seriousness of the situation.

'I'm not sure if you've seen the news,' Arnya said. 'There have been some cases lately, people that have been dying suddenly with no reasonable explanation. There was one at a grocery store and another at a gas station. And there are many more.'

Arthur listened taking small bites of his donut between sips of steaming coffee. 'Yes, I did see something in passing, but I didn't take in any of the details. What's this all about, Arnya?'

'I think there's a lot more to it that hasn't been reported yet, but it will soon.' She could feel her voice wavering, just saying the words. She looked around to make sure there weren't others close enough to listen. 'There's something going on here, Arthur, and it's big.'

Arthur's smile disappeared. 'Okay. This all sounds a little dramatic, Arnya. I'm assuming you have this information first-hand and not from some tabloid media beat-up?'

'I wouldn't come to you without something solid, you know I wouldn't,' she said. She felt slightly annoyed by the suggestion that she might. 'I've been working with a detective on a series of deaths that seem to be odd in nature. Natural, but unnatural if you know what I mean.

There were only a few at first, but now the numbers are climbing and we think we're on the brink of something catastrophic, Arthur. We think... that it may be related to IVF treatment or at least early IVF clinics.'

Arthur continued to listen attentively as she explained their findings. If he was concerned by anything she was saying, he wasn't showing it.

'I'm not sure I agree with your assumptions,' he declared when she had finished. 'This is a very big guess to make without clear scientific evidence, Arnya. You of all people should know that. This is something that could affect the lives of countless people and have political and global ramifications. I think you should leave this to the authorities to handle. This is not your area of expertise at all.'

His words stung her. Had he not heard all that she had said? 'Arthur, the evidence, the links, the families of the deceased. It all points to this. I'm working with the authorities.' He was dismissing her like she was a child wanting to play on the big kids' swing. It wasn't like Arthur at all. He'd always encouraged her relentless fervour to question everything and never stop at the easy or the obvious.

Arthur folded his arms. He seemed cross with her and she could see the slightest clenching of his jaw. 'That may be, but it's not enough, Arnya,' he said. His tone bordering on harsh. 'It's not even close to enough to be making such a broad statement like that. You're talking about things you know very little about. You're in no position to be making such outrageous claims without something more solid.' He shook his head as if he was disappointed. 'You're playing with fire, you must know that, and why would the authorities involve you in such a thing? You're doing research work, not crime fighting.'

Arnya could feel a hot anger rising inside her, flushing her neck and burning her cheeks. 'Arthur, the evidence points to IVF as the cause of these deaths and they're piling up fast. All I'm asking is that you look at some of these cases and tell me if you see anything else and if you draw the same conclusions. That's why I've come to you.' She hesitated before adding, 'your clinic came up on one of the lists of clinics we're looking at.'

Arthur paused as if measuring his response before saying anything. 'When your father passed away, I promised him that I would look out for you, dear girl, that I would help to guide you and always be there for you. I can tell you right now that if he were alive, he would not want you getting involved in something like this. Making claims like this could ruin you and all you've worked for. Do you really want to risk losing everything on a whim? Concentrate on your research and getting the grants you need. Let the authorities deal with this.'

Arnya was shaking her head. Arthur had said nothing about his clinic or the possible IVF link. 'No, there's more to this, Arthur, please! Don't dismiss my concerns like I'm still a little girl or a student with a theory. What if it's not a coincidence? Even the Medical Examiner believes there is something happening here and the Police Captain. It's not fair to dismiss me like this. What if my assumptions are actually right? What then?'

Arthur looked around the cafeteria. He leaned in closer to her and lowered his tone. 'Then it's best that you are as far from the fallout as possible. You are swimming with sharks and you'll get eaten. Take my advice and step away now. Politics and government and medical cases are like a black hole that will suck you in and spit you out. I'm telling you, Arnya, have nothing more to do with it.'

Arnya's stomach sank. Arthur Hoffman, a man she had known and loved her whole life, stared back at her with eyes she didn't recognise.

Kissing her forehead, he got up from the table and collected his rubbish. 'I have to get back to my rounds.' He stopped and flashed her the smile she recognised and the very one that had brought her comfort so many times when she'd had no one else to turn to and needed counsel. 'Please make some time to come and see me and we'll do something nice, have dinner or catch a movie.' He disappeared through the doorway leaving Arnya rooted to her chair feeling more confused and hurt than she had when she arrived.

For some reason Arthur had stone-walled her. He hadn't even questioned what she had uncovered or the fact that reputable people were on the same page as her. If it was to protect her from harm or embarrassment, or maybe even to protect his own reputation and his work in the early clinic, she could understand. But he was stern with her and that left her feeling uneasy. He owed her an explanation.

As she left the building, the dread had become like a mould, working its spores into every place it could find. She had never felt more determined in her life.

'Jesus, Santino, tell me you're onto something,' Robert said when Santino entered the autopsy suite. 'This place is packed to the rafters. We're drowning.'

Santino walked over to where Robert was working on the body a young man in his early twenties. One side of his face had been completely blown away. 'You might not be in the mood to hear what I have to say once you hear it,' Santino warned.

Robert lifted his glasses and stepped back from the body, peeling his latex gloves from his hands. 'Okay, you've got my attention.'

Santino looked around him before continuing. 'We think we've worked out what might be going on with these cases and it's... beyond fucking belief.'

Robert raised his eyebrows. 'Let's hear it then, by all means. I'm open to anything at this point.'

'We think the link is that all of the dead were conceived through IVF. We're not 100 percent sure, but possibly something to do with that or the process involved in handling the embryos, given the sporadic nature of the locations, is now causing them to die.'

Robert retreated to his chair. 'Shit. Are you sure?'

'We're not completely sure yet, but we're pretty confident. Bryant has given us some time and a team to follow up on what leads we can, but with what's going on out there, I'd say we don't have long before the Feds take over.'

Robert leaned back, tilting his chair and looking up at the ceiling. He lowered his gaze and rubbed his forehead. 'Are you really sure? CDC have already been breathing down our necks for info and stats. They're onto the deaths, so this shit will blow up, Santino, it'll send people bat-shit crazy if it is IVF. The entire world will lose their minds.'

'I know, that's why we begged Bryant for some time to get enough evidence together so that we could be sure, but also to see if we can work out what part of all this is the problem,' Santino explained. 'The team is working on it as we speak and Arnya's gone to see an old Professor for some expert advice. But we're working against the clock and time is running out, fast. Christ, it's just too big to get your head around.'

'Yeah, I'm not sure I agree with you on the working it out part. I'd be handing this over to them right now and running for the hills.' Robert's eyes widened. 'And Arnya, what if she gets caught up in it all? Her career could be ruined.'

Santino pulled up a chair beside Robert. 'You're right, but that's even more reason for you to understand why I'm here. I have a small team that Bryant has allocated, but I need more. I need you and your expertise, Robert.'

Robert snorted and scanned the room. 'Look around, Santino. Does it look like I have a line-up of help here? I'm barely keeping my head above water. I can't take a lunch break, let alone time out.'

'Robert, within days, even hours, this could literally turn into a massive health crisis with millions of lives at stake. When that happens, I hate to sound callous, but,' he pointed at the gurney, 'your gunshot and stabbing victims will be taking a back seat regardless. One of the juniors can step in, surely.'

Robert rubbed his chin and squinted. He looked more ruffled than usual and seemed to be wrestling with his thoughts. 'The thing is, I'm not sure I want to get involved,

Santino. I know that sounds selfish, but shit like this has a tendency to get out of control very quickly and you know how much I love the media. They're a bunch of parasites only out for blood. You know that better than anyone. I don't want to end up some bloody scapegoat down the track because, let's face it, there always ends up being some poor bastard that somehow bears the brunt. As I said before, people *need* someone to blame and I'd like to be as far from that someone as possible.'

Santino wasn't the only one who had been crucified by the media in this city. Robert had taken his fair share of media criticism in stories about mishandling of autopsy information, overspending, and accusations of items missing from bodies. And those work issues were nothing compared to his personal life. He had been scrutinised several times for being at a horse track during his lunch break and for getting a little *loose* at a local night spot.

'There's something else.' Santino fixed his eyes on Robert's. He wanted to be sure that Robert took this seriously.

'What is it, Santino? You're freaking me out.'

'Fitzgerald's been ramping up the pressure on me for some reason. I don't know why or if he's planning something, but I need someone to have my back. If anything happens to me…'

'Santino, come on. Shit's hitting the fan everywhere and you have plenty of people who would like to see the back of you. Don't you think you might be a little paranoid?'

Santino kept his eyes fixed. 'It's him, Robert. I know it's him. He's all but taken out a billboard. You know he's determined to get me out of the picture permanently and I think he's decided it's time. I just need to make sure that someone else knows. If anything happens, I need to know that someone will make sure that son of a bitch doesn't get away with anything.'

Robert tilted back in his chair and squeezed his eyes shut. 'Fucking hell. This is too much.'

'Just tell me you'll do it, Robert. I'm not leaving until you swear.'

'Yes, okay. Of course. I swear that if anything happens, I'll make sure.'

Santino stood up and pulled his vibrating phone from his pocket. 'What is it?' he said into the receiver.

Robert took an energy drink from the chemical fridge and popped the top. He offered one to Santino who waved it away.

'What do you mean she's on the list?' he said through clenched teeth.

Robert stopped and listened.

'She can't be, have you double checked your source info?' Santino spun on the spot where he was standing, as if he wasn't sure which way to walk. 'Her surname is Sloane with an e, are you absolutely sure it's her?'

He listened intently and then pushed at the buttons on the phone with ferocious fingers. 'Christ, Robert, Arnya's on the list. I don't think she even knows.'

'What list?' Robert's eyes had widened and his face flushed with rushing blood.

'The list of people born through the clinics we're looking at. Arnya is on one of the lists. She's at risk like all the others. And I don't think she has any idea.'

'What does that mean?' Robert said. He moved closer and forced Santino to look at him. 'Stop for a second and tell me what's going on?'

Santino looked up from the phone. 'I don't know, but it's possible that at this point, Arnya could die like the others. I need to find her.'

'I'm in, Santino, whatever you need. I'm in. Tell me what to do.'

'Professor Sloane, Detective Santino needs to speak with you urgently. Can you wait here while I get him?'

Arnya had barely set foot in the police station door before the officer had approached her. 'Of course. Is something wrong?' Arnya answered. The officer disappeared without a response.

'Arnya.' Santino appeared in the doorway and gestured for them to move to another office to talk privately. 'I've been trying to contact you.'

'I went to see a colleague, I told you. My phone was off. Should I be alarmed? because I'll admit, you're worrying me.'

'Sit down and I'll explain.'

'Sit down?' She let out a laugh that was stifled by a nervousness she couldn't hide. She watched Santino, reading his body language and his tone. He opened a cream folder and laid the contents out in front of her.

'After getting the warrants, Collins and Green rounded up the original patient lists from some of the IVF clinics. Some clinics had been closed or sold to larger ones as the treatments gained ground, but they were able to track down a fair few. These sheets have the names of all of the patients that were treated between 1983 and 1988 at each of the clinics. Green started organising the deaths we know about so far into groups based on the clinic they were conceived in, but he's still working on it.'

'Okay, that's great. Once they've organised them, we can begin to look for any patterns with the dates, times, embryologists etc.'

'Arnya... there's something else.' He hesitated as Arnya searched his face for answers. 'They found something that I thought you needed to be aware of. Maybe you're already aware.'

Her brow furrowed. 'Santino, what's this about? Already aware of what?'

Santino shook his head and exhaled slowly. He didn't know how to say the words. 'One of the clinics, one in Boston, listed a patient by the name of Sloane, Heather. Your father's name was William and your mother's was Heather, wasn't it?' The urgency that was evident in his tone moments ago had given way to a slower and gentler pace. 'Arnya, did you know that you were conceived with IVF?'

Arnya opened her mouth to answer, but no sound came out. Her lips, heavy and full of rushing blood, refused to come together and form coherent speech. Her mind raced, filling with memories and worrying possibilities and conversations. 'It's not possible.'

Santino reached out and took her hands in his. 'I'm so sorry you had to find out this way, I didn't know how to tell you.'

'There has to be a mistake.' Inside her head, her voice didn't sound at all like her own. This voice sounded distant and pained. It sounded like a wounded girl who had been hurt by a mean world or a bully in the school yard. 'They would have told me, Dominic. They would have told me if I was an IVF baby. The information has to be wrong.'

The words came out more like a plea than a statement as tears filled her eyes. Her hands gripped his fingers tightly and held them as if they might pull her out of this nightmare.

Santino squeezed her hand for reassurance and then gently let go. He fetched her a cup of coffee from the pot and put in extra sugar as his mother would do whenever there was bad news to be handled.

While she watched him pour the liquid into the cardboard cup and lump a teaspoon of sugar into it, a thousand thoughts flooded her with the ferocity of an unanticipated wave crashing hard against rocks. Her childhood. Her mother's assurances - when she would beg for a brother or sister - that they only ever wanted one child and could not improve upon perfection. That sweet, comforting voice rang in her ears and brought with it an anger that began to surge. Memories of her father's particular interest in infertility and reproductive technologies, and Arthur's clinic, brought the anger surging to the surface. She got to her feet and walked the length of the room in one direction and then the other.

Arthur knew about this, she was sure of it. Maybe this explained his behaviour earlier and his insistence that she stay far away from it. He didn't want her to find out. Her father must have asked him to keep their secret, even in death.

'Why would they keep this from me?' she said. 'Why would they make that decision for me, to assume that it was something I didn't need to know or deserve to know?

They died without ever telling me, Santino. What kind of parent would do that?'

Santino moved closer and turned her shoulders toward him as the composure she was desperate to maintain deserted her. Taking both of her hands in his he studied her face and gently wiped away the tears that were sliding down her cheeks. His grip tightened on her hands, but he could not form any words that would comfort her. She understood the implications of the situation better than he did. Nothing he could say would bring her any comfort due to the knowledge that she already possessed.

Overwhelmed by conflicting emotions that engulfed her mind, Arnya buried her head in his chest. To hell with the professional boundaries she set for herself.

Santino put his arms around her. 'I know this must be impossible to process,' he finally managed, 'but I'm sure they only did what they thought was right. Concentrate on now and what we can do about it.'

Arnya's legs felt like someone had drilled into them and filled the space with a heavy lead, buckling her beneath the weight of an unknown future.

Officer Moffat appeared with a bottle of cold water. 'Thanks, can you give us a minute?' he gestured for Moffat to leave and then knelt on the floor in front of Arnya. 'We will get through this, I promise you. I won't let anything happen to you, but you have to trust me. We can still do this. We can help these people. The deaths at these clinics are sporadic, there's a good chance you're not going to be one of them.'

Them, she thought. It had already become *Them*, as in those who were destined to die with no warning and no possibility of saving themselves, and *Us*, those who were safe and could continue going about their lives and planning for the future. She wondered now if she was in the *Them* or *Us* category.

Santino pleaded. 'Please, trust me. We can get to the bottom of this if we stick together, we have to, especially now.'

Arnya's nod of agreement was unconvincing, even to her. She wanted to be as sure as he was that they would find some answers and, more importantly, that they would be able to stop anyone else from dying. But she wasn't sure. 'There's just so much at stake and so many people who could be affected,' she said. 'How do we even navigate any of this, let alone stop anyone else from dying? It feels like a losing battle.' Her eyes were stinging and her head throbbed.

'We just keep trying,' Santino's tone was low and firm.

For the first time Arnya had a sense, a real sense, not just a guess made by someone who wasn't in the exact same shoes, of how each and every one of *Them* would feel if they knew; helpless and hoping with every ounce they had in them, that they would be one of the ones that didn't die, while at the same time, racked with guilt for knowing if not them, then someone else.

Santino was watching her intently, looking for a sign that she believed what he was saying.

'What choice do we have?' She posed the question without following it with an answer. There was no choice. She would have to trust Santino, a man she barely knew and who had, in a short space of time, turned her life completely upside down. She wondered if she would have been better off sitting in her office, worrying about grants and funding and been none the wiser about the fact that she might be about to die. She straightened her back and squared her shoulders. More importantly than trusting Santino, she needed to trust herself. If anyone was going to get her out of this alive, it was herself.

'I need to wash up,' she said, regaining her composure.

In the bathroom the mirror revealed a tear-stained face, smudged with black eyeliner and puffy eyes. Arnya splashed her red skin and closed her eyes as she tried to re-order her thoughts and force them in a more positive direction. There was work to be done. The time for tears was over.

The buzzing of her jacket pocket penetrated her haze. The text read:

Can I see you? I want to talk. Hope you're ok. Robert.

CHAPTER

12

As Arnya entered the team hub at the station, the busy room that had minutes ago been filled with noise and ringing phones was now at a standstill. The officers were all standing, gathered in a loose huddle around Santino. All eyes turned to her. She smiled and summoned a voice filled with strength and determination. 'I want you all to know that I'm fine. We're all here to get to the bottom of this and the sooner we do that the better, so let's get back to it.'

The faces stared back at her with unsure eyes. They looked for reassurance and Santino gave it with a nod. Slowly, the room leapt back to life. Santino stepped closer to Arnya. 'Are you sure you're alright to keep going? I'm not going to pretend that I don't need you, because I do. We'd be lost if we didn't have you right now, but I also realise that this is your life we're talking about, so if you want to walk away and take time for yourself, I won't try to stop you.'

Arnya thought about what he said. *Her life*. Was this going to be it? Would she die having barely taken the time to really live? 'The best thing I can do right now, for myself and for all of the others who don't even know that they are in the same boat, is to focus on finding out exactly what this is and if there is any way to stop it.'

Santino half smiled. 'Thank you,' he said, but his eyes said more. His eyes told her how grateful he was to have her there and that he knew how hard it was to keep going.

Arnya changed the subject. She didn't want to talk about it anymore. She'd made her decision and it was time to push on. 'I went to see Arthur earlier, my old Professor. I'm worried, Santino.'

'Worried? What did he say?' Santino asked.

'I didn't mention anything before because I wanted to talk to Arthur first, but after speaking to him I'm even more concerned.'

Santino gently took her arm and moved over to the corner of the room away from the others. 'I'm confused. Does he have some kind of connection to all this?'

She struggled to articulate her scrambled thoughts. This was Arthur. Friend and mentor. How the hell could he be connected to this at all? How the hell had *she* become connected to this?

'I think it's possible, but I'm not sure. When we were making the lists back at the apartment, I saw that one of the clinics on the list was Arthur's, the one in Boston that you mentioned. Remember that I told you he had some involvement in the early years and that my father always spoke about how pioneering Arthur was and how much he admired him? The fact that his clinic was in question prompted me to go and see him and find out if he could help us. Obviously, that was before this new information about my own conception.' The thought that Arthur still hadn't bothered to tell her, in spite of what she had explained to him, made her blood pump harder.

'I thought if I could just ask him about it, that might give us some insight into what was going on at that time and how these deaths could have been triggered. But he wouldn't budge and that's not like Arthur at all. It shocked me actually.'

'Wouldn't budge how?' Santino questioned.

'I asked him, more generally, about this situation and told him about our suspicions, but he literally shut me down. He was cagey and pushed me away almost abruptly. He pretty much told me to stay out of it and that I was out of my depth.'

'Do you think he might just want to distance himself from it? Not get involved?' Santino asked.

'Possibly. But I know Arthur. I've known him my whole life and he has always been very direct and honest. He's hiding something, I know he is.' She was sure of that now.

'Any idea what that might be, or why? Did he give anything away at all?'

'Now that I know my parents used IVF, it could be that he didn't want to talk about it, I suppose, but it felt like more than that. I could sense it. He was very loyal to my father, but he warned me away from the whole thing as if the entire subject and everything I put forward was off limits. I got the feeling that he knew something more and that terrifies me. He told me I was playing with fire and I should walk away from this investigation.'

Santino thought for a second. 'Do you think we can go back and push him a bit harder? See what he has to say if we make the conversation official?'

'I think we keep going with...'

The door to the hub opened and Harry Bryant appeared, a look of exasperation contorting his red face. He made a beeline for Santino and Arnya. 'Feds are on their way,' he announced. 'Can you bloody believe it? I'm not sure if they've come through their own leads or if someone tipped them off about your investigations here, but either way the ball is in motion. They're sending a team to take over all investigations – ours and others. Apparently, we're not the only ones looking at this and they want it all contained.'

Santino bit down on the inside of his cheek in response. 'Fucking hell, how long have we got?'

'Not long,' Harry said. 'It's already turning into a frenzy. The media are catching on and spreading a torrent of bullshit as usual, although I think the IVF link may well have come from one of ours. From what I can gather, no one else seemed to have made that connection before which is why I think they've been tipped off by someone inside our ranks. It's why they're coming here first. However, we might want to rethink admitting that we were the first to come up with the theory if this goes to shit and turns out to be something else.'

Harry clapped his hands hard causing a series of loud thuds to echo through the room. 'Listen up. Feds will be here in an hour, two at the max. Any leads to follow, get it done fast and tie up any loose ends you're working on. I want to hand this over to them clean and with nothing that can blow back on us down the track. The media won't be far behind, so when that happens, all hell will likely break loose, so do what you can and after that, it's out of our hands. Go home and get some rest and whatever you do, do not talk about this to anyone!'

Harry nodded at Santino and left a room full of stunned and disappointed faces.

'Right,' Santino commanded. 'We're not finished here. We've got limited time, but we can still make some progress. Listen up, I want you to continue to log everything, but also duplicate it. There's a folder on the shared drive with my name, save all duplicates in there and make copies of any hard copy materials and notes. You'll need to do it fast. We'll convene in the break room to debrief once the Feds are here and have what they need.'

The room roared back to life with a renewed urgency.

'So, we're out?' Arnya asked. 'That's it?'

'Not exactly. Feds will take over, but we can continue running with what we have. We'll be sidelined and without the resources, but that doesn't mean we're completely out of the game.'

'But Harry said…'

Santino held up his hand for her to stop. 'Don't worry about what Harry said. He needs to make sure that all loose ends are tied up and everything is handed over, but he won't stand in my way of following up leads. He started all of this, remember?'

'What can I do to help?' Arnya asked.

'Make sure everything we have is being put into the drive for us to take,' Santino instructed. 'I'm going to copy all the file information and grab my notes from my desk so I can get them out to the car. We'll need to hurry.'

When the Federal agents arrived, they were swift in taking control. Within minutes, a swarm of agents had taken up the spaces where Santino's team had been. Leading them was Agent Troy Boffa.

'Long time no see, Detective Santino. Is there anything else, any extra tidbits you may have left out that you'd like to share with us before you head out?' Boffa asked. He surveyed the room.

'Nope, I think you've got everything,' Santino answered. He'd come up against Boffa on several occasions throughout his career and the best course of action was not to poke the bear.

'You should have handed this over hours ago, Santino,' Boffa said. He was flicking through a file of one of the deceased. 'I could have you for this.'

Santino was about to respond, intending to give him a serve about how hard his team had worked and what they had put in to get this far, but Arnya stepped in.

'With all due respect, Agent Boffa, no one even knew what *this* was until we made the connections that you'll now be working from. We still don't have all the information we need.' She pointed to the plotted map on the wall, strewn with red dots and ruled lines connecting points to each other. 'But without the work of *this team* – and I mean all of this team - you'd still be looking at a series of unexplained deaths with no connection whatsoever.'

Boffa smirked. 'We'll make sure that your contribution is duly noted,' he replied. Disdain oozed from every word.

'But, if it turns out that keeping this from us for as long as you have has led to people dying unnecessarily, you'll be credited for that too, I can assure you.'

Arnya appeared to be on the verge of launching a full-scale retort. Santino placed a hand on her arm to calm her and mouthed, 'leave it'.

Heeding his warning, she stepped back and picked up her bag.

'Do I need to check that?' Boffa asked.

Arnya's face burned and her eyes flared. 'I dare you.' She straightened her back and held his stare.

Boffa smiled and opened the door for her. She stormed past and out into the corridor with Santino following behind her.

'I'd advise you all,' Boffa called after them, 'to keep your mouths tightly shut about your work here. We'll take it from here and that includes talking to media and informing the public of any new information. We will decide what this is, not any of you. Am I understood?'

Arnya turned her back on him and continued down the hall.

'You okay?' Santino asked when they were out of sight.

'I'm fine. That man is an insufferable pig. Who the hell does he think he is?'

Santino laughed and took her bag from her shaking hands.

'I'm not shaking because I'm upset,' she explained. 'I'm shaking because I'm angry, no - furious.'

'I know that. Boffa's a bastard, always has been. I've been unfortunate enough to deal with him before. Don't let him get to you, he gets a kick out of it.'

Arnya's shoulders fell back to their usual position. She was about to say something when her eyes fixed on a TV screen at the far side of the room. Without dropping her gaze, she headed toward it.

'Shit,' Santino said, pulling alongside her.

A news reporter was standing outside the entrance to an emergency room filled with people. Without even hearing the report, Santino knew exactly what she was saying.

'Well, looks like it's well and truly out now,' Arnya said. She was shaking her head. 'The whole thing is about to go completely crazy. If only we'd had a little bit more…' She seemed to lose her train of thought as footage on the screen showed dozens of people of all ages in lines at emergency rooms and doctors' offices. She went closer and increased the volume.

> *'As dozens of people continue to arrive at hospitals, medical centres and local doctor offices, the American Medical Association is calling for calm.'*

Another face appeared on the screen. The greying man from the AMA spoke with a forced calm that was easy to spot.

> *'Right now, people are worried, but what we need people to understand is that they are not in any immediate danger. We are taking this seriously and looking into the reports that there have been a series of deaths that may or may not be linked to In-Vitro Fertilisation, but these are rumours and have not been substantiated. I repeat, they have not been substantiated. Wide-spread panic and overloading much-needed hospital emergency resources is hindering our ability to assist those in*

immediate need. The Federal Bureau of Investigation and the Centre for Disease Control are looking into every aspect of this situation and will provide updates as they come to hand. In the meantime, please, stay calm, and alert the authorities if, and only if, you have an emergency.'

Santino pointed to the news ticker captions at the bottom of the television screen.

Great Britain, Australia and Canada now working with US authorities.

'Maybe they're seeing similar things,' Arnya said. 'Australia was actually the first country to achieve an IVF pregnancy, but it didn't result in a live birth. After that, England was successful with the birth of Louise Brown in 1978 and then Australia in 1980, followed by the US. We need to find out if the UK and Australia are seeing similar deaths. If they are, then we can narrow the possible causes to something involved in the actual fundamental workings of IVF. If they're not, then we'll know that the problem lies with something local to our clinics here in the US.'

'Detective Santino?'

Santino and Arnya turned in the direction of the voice. A small blonde woman, one of the team that Harry Bryant had assembled, was approaching.

'Officer Kelton?' Santino said. She was fairly new to the department and he'd only spoken to her a couple of times.

The woman smiled and looked at Arnya. 'I'm Kathryn, I was helping out in there before the big boys arrived.' She grimaced.

Arnya smiled and Santino stepped forward. 'Of course, Kathryn,' he said. 'We really appreciate the time and effort that you put in with this. I only wish we could have done more.'

Kathryn pursed her lips. 'That's why I'm here, Detective. I think we still can.' The small woman lowered her voice and stepped into a side area that led to the stairwell. 'I'm actually a data analyst and somewhat of a tech expert. The FBI have asked me to stay on with their team to assist.'

Santino smiled. 'I would say congratulations - career wise - but I'm guessing that's not why you're telling us this.'

'I've seen your work, Detective, and I know your reputation,' she said. 'This isn't just about what's going on here or about me trying to further my career. I have a son. He's ten...' Her voice trailed off as she struggled to finish the sentence.

Arnya stepped closer and put a hand on Kathryn's shoulder.

Kathryn put her hand up and inhaled to steady herself. 'He's an IVF baby.'

Santino could see that her hands were shaking and she was fighting to hold back tears as she explained.

Kathryn smiled and pulled herself straighter. 'This isn't about me. It's about all those people out there who are dying and their loved ones who are scared out of their minds. I know that I can help and I don't trust them at all.' She pointed at the hub where the agents were assembled. 'I trust both of you.'

Santino swapped a glance with Arnya. It was nice to hear, but he wasn't sure that there was much more they could do, at least not for Officer Kelton. 'Okay, tell us what it is that you think we can do,' he said.

'I overheard Boffa saying that if they find solid evidence of the IVF connection then they'll bury it. They're planning to come up with something else, another story. Something more... *palatable* was the term he used. He didn't say this to us of course, but I heard him saying it quietly to the other agent, the big one.'

'Palatable? How?' Arnya said. 'What does that even mean?'

Kathryn was shaking her head. 'Boffa said that he was waiting for word from higher up about how to proceed, but it was likely they'd be shutting down this research and turning the focus towards a virus or something else. They're looking for something easier to blame that will make it more manageable. Something they can claim to fix so that the public will be reassured.'

Santino hadn't said a word.

'Tell me this isn't happening, Santino?' Arnya implored. 'Surely they wouldn't deliberately deceive people like this just to cover their own asses. And for what? To look like the heroes or protect someone higher up the food chain? Who are they even protecting?'

Santino's tone was flat and matter of fact. 'Scandals like this lose elections. They make people who are supposed to be in charge look like they made mistakes and were careless. I know you find it hard to believe but people in powerful positions will go to any lengths to cover themselves and stay in those powerful positions. Kathryn's right. By turning this into a virus, something they can then try to control and *fix*, they become the heroes of the story instead of the villains. It becomes an opportunity to get the public to trust and put their faith in them, rather than throw their anger at them. They'll bury it for sure.'

Arnya shook her head. 'No. I won't let them. They won't get away with it. If I have to go public, be the fall guy, I will. I'm not afraid. People deserve to know the truth, not to be lied to just so politicians and rich fat-cats can save face and get re-elected.'

'You don't have to sell it to me, Professor,' Santino said. 'I'm with you all the way. But it's not as easy as that. We need to tread carefully and build a case. If we just burst in with guns blazing, they would shut us down, make us out to be crazed lunatics caught up in the hysteria and God only knows what else. They'll fabricate substance abuse or blame a breakdown or illness and anything else you can dream up.' He rubbed his forehead and closed his eyes. 'No, we have to be smart and play the game. The only way forward is to collect enough irrefutable evidence and build the case so tight that they can't get away from it.'

'I'll be your eyes and ears here,' Kathryn said. 'If the two of you can set yourself up with a base to work from, I'll feed through anything important as it comes in. I have a couple of personal contacts from the IVF clinic that I used for my treatment and I'm just waiting for a call back from one of the nurses there. I think I might already have something to go on.'

Santino's senses prickled with the conviction in her voice. 'What is it?'

'I got to know a few of the nurses at the clinic quite well while I was going there for treatment. You spend so much time there, it's difficult not to make friends. The clinic was one of those on the list, so I gave them a call just to see if there was anything they might be able to offer, some insight, that sort of thing. I knew that one of the nurses in particular had been at the clinic almost since the beginning when it opened. When I asked her if there had ever been anything out of the ordinary happen, or anything that she saw or heard that had struck her as odd, what she said took me a bit by surprise.'

Arnya stepped back out into the main hall and scanned the area for movement before moving back in to listen.

'She mentioned something about a man, some years ago, who had repeatedly called the clinic ranting about *ticking time bombs* and other stuff. He'd become quite persistent, a bit of a serial pest I believe, but she couldn't tell me any more because she had patients to see. She said she'd give me a call back when her shift was over later tonight.'

'Did she say anything else?' Arnya asked.

Kathryn shook her head. 'Not really. Only that he had been connected to the clinic somehow in the early years but had gone off the rails or something. I'm hoping she'll be able to tell me more when she calls back.'

'That definitely sounds like it could be something,' Santino said. 'We'll head to my place and set ourselves up there. Anything you can provide will be appreciated, Kathryn, but please, don't get yourself into any trouble with them in there. Trust me, their bad side is not a good place to be.'

Kathryn smiled. 'I appreciate your concern, but my son is more important to me than anything else, including this job.'

Santino nodded. 'Then let's see what we can do.'

CHAPTER

13

Santino pulled the car into a space outside his apartment building. It was a warm evening and the day's heat was slowly being released from the pavement.

'Do you think there's anything in what Kathryn said about the nurse?' Arnya asked.

'There could be.' He paused and seemed to be deep in thought. 'But the guy she mentioned could also be just another nut job, like she said. We know there are plenty of people who still believe even now that scientific procedures like this are a crime against God. Right now, I'm not sure that I completely disagree with them.'

Arnya tilted her head so that she could look at him over her sunglasses. The last thing they needed right now was for him to start swaying towards a radical standpoint, but they needed to consider every possible angle. 'When I was doing the research, I did read a few excerpts online about some religious views on IVF,' she said. Arnya pulled out her phone and began tapping. 'Most of the information is about opposition based on the Church's teachings and that's fair given their belief system, but there are some views that are pretty blistering. Listen to this from one of the more radical religious sites I came across.' She read from the article on her phone. 'IVF can be described as an experiment on a large scale, using children as subjects. It is an abomination in the eyes of God and while parents may think that it will bring an end to their heartbreak of infertility, the wrath that God will bring down upon them will be far worse than anything they ever imagined. When the time comes, God will make sure that anyone who had a hand in acting against him and his way is dealt with swiftly. Their time for judgement by him will come.'

Santino was watching her intently. 'Shit, that's a pretty strong statement to make publicly. Clearly, they don't have a PR person watering things down for public consumption.'

Arnya continued to scroll. 'That's just one of hundreds of sites spouting stuff like this and some of it is much worse than that. It seems, especially in the early years, that everyone had an opinion on IVF.'

'Stay here,' Santino said suddenly. He got out quietly and took a look around.

Through her window, Arnya looked too, but there was no one that seemed to be looking back at her.

Santino led the way up to the apartment. Inside, Arnya laid everything they had brought across the table and floor of the living room.

Santino disappeared into his office. 'I'll print off what we need from the hard drive,' he called back.

Arnya could hear the whirring of the printer churning out page after page. The sound was so soothing she almost didn't hear the buzzing of her phone in her handbag.

'Arnya Sloane speaking.'

'Hi Arnya, this is Kathryn Kelton from the station.' Her voice was hushed on the end of the line. 'I just spoke to the nurse I was telling you about.'

'That's great, Kathryn. What did she say?'

'She confirmed that some years ago there was a guy, an older man she said, who had started calling the clinic repeatedly and then began showing up there on and off.'

Santino returned to the living room and Arnya hit the speaker button so they could both listen to Kathryn. 'She said that it wasn't just that clinic either. He had been harassing other clinics as well, ranting about deaths and nature and human timebombs. It was enough to unnerve a few people at the time, including this nurse. She said that one of the doctors at her clinic had called all of the staff into a meeting to address the situation. He had explained to them that the man had actually been somewhat of a pioneer in the early IVF years and had worked across several clinics, but he'd had mental health issues and fallen on some hard times.'

'Did the guy continue to show up?' Santino asked.

'She said that he'd been pestering them for some time. Just standing out the front and in the foyer rambling and shouting warnings, then one day he just stopped coming and that was that. No one ever mentioned it again.'

'Did she say or give any indication as to how long ago this was?' Arnya asked.

'Yes, sort of. She said that it started around 2008 or so, and maybe occurred over a couple of years on and off. It was only every now and again in the beginning, but it got worse as time went on and at one point, they had to call the police. Not long after that she said she had taken some leave and gone overseas and when she returned, everything was back to normal and she never saw him again.'

Santino interrupted. 'Was she able to give you a name or any other detail that might help us identify him?'

'No, I did ask, but she couldn't recall any other specific details. She said that she only remembered the situation because to her it seemed quite strange at the time, but no one else was too fazed by it. They used to get death threats and abusive phone calls all the time in the early years, as well as picketing from religious groups, so people just ignored it and things continued on as normal after that.'

'Thanks Kathryn. Can you let us know if you uncover anything else?' Arnya asked. 'We'll get to work and see if we can find out who this guy might be.'

'I'll keep you posted,' Kathryn whispered. 'They haven't made any progress here as yet. Idiots are still getting set up and drinking coffee.'

When she hung up, Santino laid the printed pages on the floor beside the other documents. 'So, for some reason in roughly 2008 a guy who had presumably been involved in some way with the early IVF clinics was going around spouting about people dying and being ticking timebombs. That's definitely not just a coincidence.'

'The question is,' Arnya said, pacing the line where the carpet of the living room met the dark grey tiles of the kitchen, 'what did he know all those years ago that we can't even work out now? And how did he predict this? If that is what he was doing.'

Santino went to the kitchen to put on a pot of coffee. 'Given what's now happening, it's just possible that this guy could hold the key to what this is. We need to find out who he is, and more importantly, where he is.'

Arnya came back to the sofa and opened her laptop. 'If we search up the people who were involved in the early clinics, perhaps someone will stand out.' She punched in a Google search and clicked on Images. 'Any of these guys familiar?'

Santino came to look. 'They all look a bit odd,' Santino teased. 'I'm not sure there's any point doing this. We have no idea what this person looks like or who we're even looking for.'

'Perhaps Arthur will be in these pictures somewhere,' Arnya said. 'Maybe he'll know something about this guy. Not that he's likely to talk to me about it given his attitude towards the whole thing, but I could ask.'

She scrolled through a few more of the search images. Mainly male faces, all looking important and intelligent. Santino move closer to look over her shoulder. She snapped the laptop shut in frustration.

Santino reached across to stop her. 'Wait. Let me look at that last one you had on the screen.' He picked up the laptop and studied the picture. In the photograph, three men, scientists, according to the caption, were standing at the foot of a staircase. The title of the accompanying article was 'The faces behind the science that is changing the world'.

'What is it?' Arnya asked. 'Do you recognise someone?'

It wasn't the faces Santino was interested in. It was what was behind them. On the wall to the left of the staircase was the logo for Alpha Pharmaceuticals.

'Shit, what the hell do they have to do with it?' Santino said. His puzzled expression reflected the questions racing through his mind.

'Who?' Arnya asked. She was desperate to decipher whatever it was that Santino was seeing in the picture.

'There.' He pointed to the logo and name. 'That's the Fitzgerald family company. As in Parker Fitzgerald.'

'So, these guys,' Arnya took the laptop and opened the website the picture was from, 'according to this, were all scientists doing IVF work.'

'Why would they be at Alpha?' Santino asked. His unease was evident on his face.

'They must have been supplying funding or maybe pharmaceutical products used in the labs. Could this guy have been a part of that? Maybe a clinician?' Arnya said.

'I have no idea. There would have been dozens of people involved, but seeing Alpha Pharmaceuticals there, that makes me really worried. If Fitzgerald has had a hand in any of this, in any way, I swear to God it will be the end of him. I can't believe this.' Santino grimaced as he tried to comprehend the possibilities.

Arnya could sense the heightened emotion in his response. 'Let's just take a step back before we come to conclusions without any supporting evidence. Just because they are at Alpha doesn't necessarily mean anything. They are research scientists, so it's not exactly out of the scope of normal. What we do know is that Kathryn said this guy was working across multiple clinics, so that could mean a doctor, nurse or a clinician.'

Arnya got up and went to attend to the bubbling coffee percolator Santino had forgotten about. She was keen to settle his increasing suspicions.

'But why?' he pushed. 'Why would clinics have someone who is working across multiple sites? Wouldn't the clinics have been in competition? Why would they be sharing someone around?'

Arnya agreed. He had a point. 'You're right,' she said. 'Clinics would have been secretive about the work they were doing, especially early on. It's not likely they would have allowed someone to go from place to place.' She shrugged and handed Santino a cup. 'The only thing I can think of would be someone who assisted with the clinic set-ups. Staff would have needed initial training on how to care for the embryos. These were emerging processes that could make a huge difference to the developing embryos. That's the only reason I can think of for someone to be working across multiple clinics.'

Santino took the coffee and smelled it. Arnya noticed that he seemed to relax his shoulders slightly as he took a sip. 'Was there anything specifically new?' he asked. 'Anything that changed around the early eighties when these kids were being conceived?'

Arnya thought for a minute. She was trying to remember a particular paper she had read. 'From what I recall, there were lots of advancements over the years. There was one in particular though that occurred around 1984. Basically, a couple of IVF doctors published a paper with a formula called Human Tubal Fluid, or HTF which was able to mimic the real environment an embryo would normally be exposed to. They could use this new formula in the process for better outcomes,' she explained.

Santino put both hands around his cup and paced the living room from one side to the other. 'So, is it possible that something in the composition of any fluid used, or the environment of an embryo, could have been wrong or tainted, and that's what is causing the problems?'

Arnya huffed. She felt frustrated with their inability to find a logical explanation. It was like having a jigsaw puzzle with a few missing, but crucial, pieces. 'Possibly. Sort of,' she said. 'The environment definitely plays a factor, but the deaths are random, even in the clinics, so they wouldn't be switching the culture medium all the time. There has to be something more, something we're missing.'

Santino flipped the laptop back open. 'What if we print off some of the photos and ask the nurse to take a look. She might recognise someone. It's a long shot, but it's about all we've got to go on right now.'

'Couldn't hurt,' Arnya said. She almost tipped the mug of steaming coffee into her lap when her phone again lit up with Kathryn's number. She answered and put it on speaker.

'Sorry Arnya, but can you and Santino get down here right now?' Kathryn's voice sounded muffled, as if she was half covering the mouthpiece with her hand.

'Of course, Kathryn, what's happened? Are you alright?' Arnya asked.

'I'm fine, but I have a priest who has come in here after seeing the news and he says he might have some information that could help. He told me it's about a guy who used to come into confession a few years back and he thinks it might be related to the stuff on TV. I've got him in a side room away from the Feds, so come in the back entrance. He's in interview room three.'

'We're on our way.' Santino grabbed his jacket and keys.

Outside, the streets were littered with people who were visibly distressed. 'Santino, this is bad,' Arnya said, heading toward the car. 'These poor people are panic-stricken, look.' She pointed to a group a short distance up the street who were waving protest signs above their heads.

'It's only going to get worse. The more people that die, the more the public are going to go into a frenzy,' Santino warned.

'How can people be so cruel though? To make signs saying that God is punishing those who have sinned. How does someone who is facing the possibility of death, or losing their child or loved one through absolutely no fault of their own, deserve that kind of treatment? It's just awful.'

'People can be cruel, Santino said. 'Times of chaos and fear bring out the best and worst in human nature. Some spring into action. They join in anywhere they can to help and bring comfort. And others, well they find their own way to blame and shame and say I told you so. I know it hurts.' He reached out and touched her shoulder. 'But don't focus on that now. We know which side we're on and we have to keep moving forward.'

Arnya stared at the protesters as they passed. She jumped when a woman holding a sign saying, *Test-Tube Babies Will Burn In Hell*, slammed her fist against the car window. 'Jesus, get us out of here.'

'It's nice to meet you, Father,' Santino said. He took the man's hand and shook it gently, placing his over the top, the way he had seen his father greet their priest at church. 'We really appreciate you taking the time to come down here.' He gestured toward Arnya who was standing by the door. 'This is my colleague, Professor Arnya Sloane, and you've already met Officer Kathryn Kelton.'

'Good to meet you, Father,' Arnya said. She too reached over to shake his hand.

Santino pulled out a chair from behind the desk and offered it to Arnya before sitting opposite the priest.

'It's really no trouble,' the elderly man replied. 'I just hope that what I have to say is helpful in some way and I haven't wasted your valuable time. Things are certainly getting crazy out there. People are in quite a panic.'

The priest pointed a long, bony finger toward the window and adjusted his position in the chair. Santino watched as he intertwined his fingers and rubbed his thumbs together.

'Officer Kelton mentioned on the phone that you had been seeing a man for confession some years ago and you thought there could be a link with these deaths?' Santino asked.

Arnya reached into her purse and pushed record on her phone as the priest began his story.

'Thank you for relaying that, Officer Kelton,' the priest said. He turned his attention to Santino. 'It wasn't exactly in confession as such, not in the formal sense. It was more like a conversation between friends, albeit a very troubled friend. I think he just needed someone to talk to, you know, to get things off his chest and ease his sorrows. I can't be sure, but I think it was around 2007 when I first began seeing him. I noticed him in my church one evening. He was sitting in a pew towards the back, staring at the altar and muttering quietly to himself. I thought I might have seen him earlier, perhaps at the Sunday afternoon service a few times, but he looked somewhat dishevelled that night, so I wasn't sure. I let him be at first, but he came in a few times when the church was empty, and one evening I was finishing up when I saw him sitting in that same spot. I don't usually like to interrupt a parishioner in quiet reflection or prayer, but I felt compelled to check on him.'

The priest looked about the room. Santino followed his gaze. 'Would you like some water, Father?'

The priest nodded and reached into his pocket. He held up a small tablet. 'Blood pressure,' he smiled. 'The Lord has decided that I need to lessen my intake of salt.'

Santino laughed as Kathryn fetched the water. When she returned, Santino noticed that her eyes were bloodshot and her cheeks flushed. It was a reminder of what was at stake for Kathryn's son and Arnya, as well as countless others.

'What was it about the man that made you go over to him that night, Father?' Arnya asked.

He swallowed the pill and seemed to contemplate the question. 'I think that perhaps it was the sense of desperation I felt from him. Even from the back of the church I could tell that he was in crisis, in pain.'

'Uh-huh, what happened next, Father?' Santino asked.

'I went to him and asked if he needed anything and when he turned and looked up at me, his eyes were red and swollen. He stopped muttering and for a moment he was quiet. I sat down beside him, giving him the time I thought he needed to gather himself. After a few minutes he said, I'm a terrible sinner. I've committed terrible sins against God and Man and there's nothing I can do about it. He said he had created some kind of ticking bomb and that one day, only God knew when, it would explode and people would die. I assumed he was speaking metaphorically of course.'

Santino could feel Arnya's eyes on him, but he held his on the priest. 'Did you press him further? Did he say anything else?' he asked.

'Yes, much more over those first months.' He shook his head and wiped his forehead with a handkerchief from his pocket. 'I tried to push him about the bomb, I was very concerned, but the more I talked to him, the more I thought it was just the ramblings of a very ill man. There was no actual bomb as such. He just thought that he had done something that would hurt people one day.'

'Was he physically unwell?' Arnya asked.

'You could call it that. His mind and spirit were tortured and that had led him to the drink, as is the case with many a troubled soul. That first evening we talked for more than an hour, and over the next few months and years I saw him at least a dozen times, although he was deteriorating rapidly by then.'

Santino asked, 'During those conversations, Father, I hope you don't mind me asking, but what did he say that led you to believe it might be connected specifically to these deaths we're seeing now?'

The priest leant forward and took another sip of water. 'There were many things that he said during those conversations that troubled me, Detective. You have to understand, he spoke about things out of logical order, all over the place, as if he couldn't order his thoughts, so it was hard to decipher or make sense a lot of the time. He spoke of his time at university, studying science and the awards he had won. Then he would jump to where he had been that day and begin to ramble incoherently. One time he spoke about working in some sort of medical field, but I'm not sure what. He said something about another man, maybe a brother or someone he cared for like a brother. He kept saying that they weren't supposed to hurt anyone. They had a plan that was going to make them a lot of money, but he said that the science had a flaw and that it gone wrong and people would die. You have to understand, he was very much rambling by this stage and he believed that people were watching and following him all the time. The last conversation I had with him, he said that what they had done was the beginning of the end of everything and could unravel for generations.'

'Any idea what he meant by that?' Santino pushed.

The priest shrugged. 'Not really, definitely not at the time, but he had also mentioned that he wanted to make it right. He wanted to warn people and give them a chance, but he was trapped. Even though he was in a bad way, he did seem genuinely fearful. He would spend the entire time, while he spoke, looking over his shoulder.'

Santino could see that the priest's account was upsetting Kathryn. She stood still and quiet, but her legs were shaking. He could tell her worry for her son was increasing.

Arnya asked, 'Do you think he might have had genuine reason to fear someone?'

'Not then, not really. Many people who have substance abuse or mental illness can have paranoia and sometimes delusions. It wasn't terribly out of the ordinary for the many lost souls I've seen over the years, although the way that he spoke when he was lucid, in an educated way and with such conviction, it did make me wonder if it was true, even if it was at times disjointed and confusing to follow.

Some time later I did wonder if I had made a terrible mistake in not taking him more seriously.' The priest wrung his hands in his lap. 'But there was no way to know, Detective.'

'I'm sorry, Father, I don't follow. No way to know what?' Santino asked.

Father Kelly explained. 'The last time I saw him he was barely functioning. He was rambling more than ever, but in those ramblings, he told me he had decided to tell people the truth. That he couldn't live with it any longer and it was only a matter of time before they would begin to see it anyway. I dismissed it, given his state, and the fact that it was likely no one would listen to anything he had to say given his decline, but a week later I saw him on the news. He was dead.'

Santino felt a shockwave ripple through him and saw it mirrored in Arnya's eyes. 'What happened to him, Father, what was his name?' Santino pushed.

Father Kelly met Santino's fiery eyes. 'He was murdered. His name was Maurice Stephens.'

Santino braced against the chair when he heard the name. Years of pent-up anger, suspicion and regret hit him hard, ploughing through his chest and causing it to pound. He looked to each of the other people in the room and wondered if they could see his rapid breathing through the fabric of his shirt.

Through tingling, numbing lips Santino asked, 'You're sure, Father, you're 100 percent sure it was Maurice Stephens? The man who was murdered by Parker Fitzgerald?'

The priest reached for the cross around his neck and held it between his fingers. He bowed his head. 'I'm absolutely sure, Detective.'

Pangs of nausea and a rush of adrenaline hit Santino like pellets from a shotgun. 'I mean no disrespect, Father, but why didn't you come forward? Why didn't you tell someone what you knew?'

The priest let out a heavy sigh. 'I did. At least I tried. I came here, to this very station, twice and tried to tell them, but I was dismissed and told that it wasn't relevant to the case. One of the officers told me that they were far too busy to be concerned with the ramblings of a dead man and so I should let it go. I have to admit, I wondered myself if there was anything to what he had been saying, and as God is my witness, I pray that this isn't what we are seeing now. To know that I could have done something...'

Santino could feel a fire igniting inside him. The cops, Fitzgerald, all of them had covered it up, just as they had everything else. He had known it, but to hear it now was almost too much to comprehend. 'We appreciate you coming in, Father. Could I ask that you don't repeat what you've told us here? Just for now, until we figure all of this out.'

'Of course, I understand. I live in the apartment at the side of St Cuthbert's parish, if you need anything further. I hope you find the answers you're searching for. I'll be praying for all of you.'

While Kathryn walked the priest to the back exit, Santino paced back and forth across the interview room. 'This was the piece of the puzzle that I could never figure out. Whatever they did, this was the reason Parker murdered Maurice. Seeing Alpha in that picture, plus

Maurice's ramblings and warnings, and now this? Maurice is the man visiting the clinics.' He stopped and faced Arnya. His heart was still pounding and his forehead was damp with sweat. 'Maurice must have been stirring up too much trouble for Alpha and that's why Fitzgerald killed him.'

Arnya stepped closer to Santino and placed her hand on his arm. Her heart was thudding too, but she knew the hell Fitzgerald had, and continued to, put Santino through. 'That may be, but how do we prove it? We need to find something to link Alpha to these deaths,' Arnya said. 'We need to go over every detail of what happened when Maurice was killed. There has to be some evidence somewhere that links Maurice and Alpha to the clinics. If we've managed to uncover this much, then there's more.'

Kathryn poked her head back through the door. 'I have to get back to the hub, but I'll call if anything else comes up.'

As she closed the door, Arnya called out to her. 'Kathryn, wait.'

Kathryn stepped back in. 'Thank you so much. You're taking a big risk in helping us and I want you to know how much it is appreciated.'

Santino added, 'We also know that you must be worried out of your mind about your boy.'

Kathryn's eyes filled and she covered her face with her hands. When she looked up there was so much pain in her expression. 'I am, but I have to get back.' She wiped at her tears and straightened. 'I'll keep you posted.'

When she disappeared down the hall Arnya turned back to Santino. 'Tell me everything. From the beginning.'

'We need to get down to the evidence room,' Arnya insisted. 'If Maurice had been planning on telling the truth somehow and outing himself and Fitzgerald for whatever it is they had done, he must have left something, something we can use to prove all this.'

'There's no point,' Santino said, his tone resigned. 'We can look, but I guarantee you that anything he left would have been destroyed. I told you, there were lots of random people at the scene that day and it looked like they were all working to cover up rather than investigate. Whatever these two did, Fitzgerald didn't ever want it getting out and he was willing to murder his best friend to make sure.'

He paused and went over to the window. 'But if the deaths didn't even start until recently, I just can't get my head around how Maurice knew it was coming.'

Arnya was rubbing her temples as if the act might help her brain to unravel the details. 'They did *something* to the IVF process to cause this, they had to have, but for what reason? What reason would anyone have to want to orchestrate a mass killing that would occur decades later? Is Fitzgerald a religious man? Was he trying to teach the world some insane lesson?'

'Fitzgerald's only religion is money, I can assure you. If there's any reason behind all of this, and if he is the driving force, the outcome would have been to make money or gain power. He is a greedy, spoiled, low-life scum bag and whatever he's done is now causing hundreds and soon, possibly thousands, of people to die.'

Arnya nodded. 'The priest said Maurice claimed there was money to be made, but for him it was the science. What if he was doing an experiment, something that would allow him to watch it unfold and see what the outcome would be over time? Nothing would be out of the question at this point.'

She watched as Santino's expression turned to a scowl. 'The thing is, if they did do something that's causing all this, can it even be undone?' he asked. A tone of defeat had crept into his voice.

She didn't know the answer. 'Even if we find out the truth, we may not be able to stop it. We may very well have to watch thousands die without a damn thing we can do about it.' She said the words knowing that she might be one of them.

'Arnya, I'm sorry, I didn't mean to...'

The realisation brought a heavy silence down on both of them. There was a grim inevitability in the words that couldn't be ignored. They both knew what it would mean. Arnya would have to face the possibility that she was already dying. Even if they found their way to the truth and could hold those responsible to account, it didn't mean they could save lives. It didn't mean they could save *her* life.

Santino spoke first. 'C'mon, let's get back to the apartment,' he said. He silently kicked himself again for being so blunt. He knew that all this talk of death affecting her, even though she tried not to show it. 'We can grab a bite and then have a look at the original crime scene photos I took when Maurice was killed. Your fresh eyes might be better than mine at spotting something out of the ordinary. God knows I've looked at them enough times.'

Before they could leave, the door to the interview room swung open and Boffa appeared. His frame filled the doorway. 'You never know when to quit, do you, Detective? In some ways it kinda works in my favour because now I have the absolute pleasure of informing you that, from this moment, you are officially suspended.'

Santino moved closer and squared his shoulders. 'On what grounds, Boffa?' he demanded.

'On the grounds that you have deliberately impeded this investigation by holding back evidence vital to the case, as well as causing public panic and refusing to take direct orders. On top of that, if I find out that you've kept back anything else from this investigation, I'll have you up on charges, do you hear me? I may do it anyway, you and Harry Bryant. Now, get the fuck out of here!' He stepped back and pointed to the exit.

Santino held Boffa's stare defiantly. He took Arnya's arm, leading her to the door before she could get involved in another verbal stoush with Boffa, but he wasn't quick enough.

Arnya pulled herself from Santino's grip and turned to Boffa. 'Agent Boffa, if you haven't noticed, people's lives are at risk here. Does it really matter who comes up with the answer, as long as someone does?' She looked him up and down from head to toe and back to his eyes, contempt oozing from her. 'Surely even someone like… you can agree with that.'

'You listen to me, pro-fessor,' he separated and accentuated the title. 'Your bullshit ideas about this being some In-Vitro science master fuck-up is being shut down as we speak. Official statements from the very top will likely be made by morning, so unless you want to be right in the line of fire of every Federal agency, I suggest you step down little lady. You do not want to go into the pool and swim with the big boys because you will sink. The issue here is an antibiotic-resistant virus, likely brought in from overseas, we're not clear where yet. We already have our labs working on a new antibiotic to deal with it. Case closed. Now, go back to your life, your apartment, your cat and your little university office before you really see what we're capable of.'

CHAPTER

14

'I can't believe this,' Arnya stammered. Her eyes were wild and her veins pulsing. In the precinct carpark she got into Santino's car and slammed the door hard before yanking on her seatbelt. It jammed at the tug and refused to budge.

Santino hopped in beside her. He leaned over, gently pulling the belt and sliding it across her lap to fasten it. 'It's okay, just take a breath.'

'It's complete bullshit and he knows it,' she shouted. 'How can they get away with this? Every shred of evidence points to the IVF connection. It's a complete cover-up. This is the US of A for Christ sakes. I never would have believed that my own country...'

'Arnya, they know what something like this will do.' Santino's voice was calm and even. 'What it's already doing. Look outside, look at what's happening.' Santino had pulled out onto the road but slowed down to allow a group to pass. He rolled down the window to hear their chant, but could only make out a few words about truth and God.

He pointed to a larger group assembled on the lawn of a nearby park. 'Listen to them, look at their signs. They're demanding answers, calling on the government to explain. The government, and some others with heavy pull, will lie and cover up the truth because it's the easier road. This is the reality and, in truth, it happens all the time, much more than you could even imagine. If the IVF link was proven, the fallout for them financially, personally and politically, would be catastrophic. Financial claims, wrongful death suits, and chaos. It's not just the government, believe me. There will be a lot of influential people who could lose a lot and they will likely be weighing in on this.'

'Well, so be it!' she exclaimed. 'They can't just lie, Santino. People elect their officials and they expect to be told the truth. They can't just make things up to suit their agendas. It's wrong.'

'And that's what we're here for,' he assured her. 'We know the truth. We have the power to expose all of this, if we can just get what we need. But that also makes us targets, Arnya, you have to know that. Boffa knows that we're liabilities and he's banking on us just giving up. But I'll be honest, if he finds out we're still following leads, he won't hesitate to act and that won't be just a dismissal.' He turned to look at her, not wanting to alarm her further, but needing her to understand. 'People disappear and it'll come from way above Boffa. No loose ends. Ever.'

Arnya shook her head and slapped her hand on her thigh. 'This is bullshit! I can't believe I'm even hearing this. I was born in this country. I've paid taxes and voted for these so-called leaders, and none of it means anything. And now you're telling me they'd happily make me, and God knows how many others, disappear if it was deemed necessary.'

Santino could feel the anger and the hurt behind her words. He felt pangs of guilt for making her see the ugliness behind all of this, but he had decided it was better to tell her the truth, even if it enraged her. She needed to know. 'Arnya, the banking industry, pharmaceutical industry and plenty of others have a lot of political sway. It's not just a matter of politicians making decisions. Sometimes the only reason the politician is there is because they were put there for a purpose by powerful people.'

Arnya stared at him. Her eyes were wide and her mouth open, but no words came out.

Santino pulled into a parking space on the street outside his apartment. 'We need to be extra careful now. Boffa said some stuff in there to rattle you.'

She looked out the window, checking their surroundings. 'What stuff? I'm not sure anything he said could rattle me more than I already am. Everything is rattling me,' she said, a resigned expression on her face.

'He mentioned that you should go back to your apartment and your cat. He's watching us, and he wants us to know it.'

Arnya sat back in her seat and let the information sink in. She hadn't even taken in the words when Boffa had said them, let alone realised it was a deliberate and calculated warning. 'Shit, would they really be watching us?'

'They most definitely are watching us. I've suspected all along. Boffa thinks we're still snooping around so he's probably got someone checking on our whereabouts and reporting back. We need to keep our wits about us. Come on, let's get inside and see what we can find.'

Inside the apartment, Santino got the crime scene photos from a locked filing cabinet. He spread them out across the coffee table in front of Arnya. 'These are the originals that I took at the scene.' He grabbed his laptop from the kitchen bench and opened it, plugging in a USB memory stick he had in his hand. 'And these,' he said, swinging the screen around for her to see, 'are the photos that were submitted by the police as the *official* crime scene photos. There was a lot missing by then, as you can see.'

Arnya studied the pictures. 'How did they think they were going to get away with this? Were they all in on it?' she paused before answering her own question. 'They had to be.'

'To this day, I still honestly don't know. The senior guys on the scene were pushing their weight around and calling the shots. The rest of us there were just following whatever we were told. But you know, after I blew the lid off it all, not one person came forward and backed me up, so all I can assume is that they were either in on it, paid off, or just too afraid of the repercussions.'

'That's ballsy, Santino, I have to say. That must take some guts to do that in the face of all the backlash and the threats.'

Santino shrugged. 'It's a choice between right and wrong, plain and simple. There's no in-between or blurring of the lines.' He turned his attention to the photos. 'Now, tell me, did I miss anything in these photos?'

Arnya looked at them one by one, comparing them against the laptop photos submitted by police at the trial.

She shook her head slowly. 'I don't even know what I'm looking for. Maybe we're wasting our time with this.'

Santino sat beside her. 'I don't think so. We know that Alpha Pharmaceuticals was involved with the IVF clinics somehow from that photo we found on the internet. And we know that Fitzgerald killed Maurice to keep him quiet, that's for sure.'

Arnya began making a note of hardcopy photos that were missing from the police trial photos.

Santino continued his re-cap. 'Maurice was a drunk and losing his grip, but he was a smart man, he had to know he was playing with fire and that his life might be in danger. The priest confirmed that. Wouldn't you make sure that whatever you had on Fitzgerald was safely tucked away? Obviously, he knew he was being watched and possibly followed, so he would have been discreet.'

Arnya slowly flicked through some more pictures, searching every inch of the glossy paper. 'The priest said that on the last occasion he saw Maurice, he seemed determined to reveal the truth,' she said. 'But if you were going to reveal something that could potentially see you killed or imprisoned, how would you do it? What would you do?'

Santino stood back up. He walked over to the kitchen and then back to Arnya as if the movement might help his racing brain to concentrate. 'It totally blows my mind to think that this is all related.' He turned to face Arnya and answer her question. 'Okay, well I'd be pretty cautious to start with. Fitzgerald had likely warned Maurice, and even threatened him to keep quiet, so if I was Maurice, I'd take everything I had - any notes or photos or evidence to back up my claims - and hide it all somewhere safe, where they couldn't get to it.'

'Good. Now, where would you hide it? In your apartment? In a bank? At your parent's house?' Arnya asked.

'Good question. I don't know.' Santino went to the kitchen and poured them both a wine. He handed a glass to Arnya. 'There's no way I'd hide it at home. Not unless I had a hiding place that I was sure would never be uncovered. Just hiding it in an air-conditioning vent or under the floorboards, or something like that, wouldn't be enough. They'd easily find it in a place like that and we have to remember that Maurice knew Fitzgerald better than anyone. He would have been able to anticipate Fitzgerald's moves.'

'And the cops would have done a thorough look too, wouldn't they?' Arnya asked.

Santino scoffed. 'I'm sure Fitzgerald would have told them to tear his place apart. Fitzgerald would have been making sure that no stone was unturned, especially a stone that could lead back to him. And he would have had his own men comb the place as well.'

'So, somewhere else then?' she asked. 'Maybe a friend's place, a rented locker or a storage shed? Depending on how much there was to hide.'

'Possibly, but that just doesn't sit well with me,' Santino said. 'We have to remember that he was drinking heavily and not necessarily thinking straight most of the time. I really wonder if he would have had the presence of mind to be that organised. The priest said that he was rambling and often incoherent.'

Arnya nodded her agreement. 'But he might have done it well before it got to that point. If I was him, I'd have put it away for safe keeping from the beginning. Surely if he knew Fitzgerald well, he would have known what he was capable of.'

'I think you're probably right,' Santino conceded. 'Even before his decline or the decision to reveal the truth, he might have had concerns about the information being found. If I'd been doing something illegal, especially something that could be dangerous, I'd be making sure the evidence was well hidden and far away from me.'

Arnya held another photo up against the laptop screen to compare the scene. There were several pictures that were similar to Santino's version, but items had been moved or taken away. 'I still find it hard to imagine what they could possibly be trying to achieve. There doesn't seem to be anything to gain by killing so many innocent people. Not one theory makes sense to me.'

Santino shook his head and let out a long sigh. 'I think Fitzgerald is a narcissistic mad man who would do anything for money. Maurice was a genius, but easily manipulated. Mind you, after what the priest said about Maurice claiming he was interested in the science, maybe he was just as mad as Fitzgerald. You'd have to be mad to get involved in anything that could lead to what we're seeing now. There was money to be gained in all this somewhere and we just have to work out where.'

Arnya's analytical mind couldn't make sense of it. 'But what? What could the experiment have been for? If he messed with the process somehow then it had to have at least two possible outcomes to satisfy him and Fitzgerald too. One, it would need to have the potential to make them a lot of money, and two, test some kind of scientific theory of Maurice's.'

Santino shrugged. 'It sounds like something out of an old science fiction book – one of those horrible war stories about humans being experimented on. Do things like this actually go on right under our noses? I like to think that I'm switched on when it comes to knowing that there's some shady shit that happens in this world, but this is beyond me.'

Arnya thought for a minute. 'Well, there was the case of the triplets in the *Nature versus Nurture* experiment. Are you familiar with it?' Arnya asked. The case had always interested her.

'No, and I'm not sure that I want to be,' Santino replied with a weary smile.

Arnya decided to tell him anyway. 'I'll give you the brief version. Basically, identical triplets were taken at birth and placed in three different families of varying wealth and social structure. These boys were never told that they had siblings and the families they were placed with were also kept in the dark. They were studied over the years to compare their development and it was only by chance that the three boys eventually came into contact. One of the boys attended a university where his brother had been a student the previous year and it began to unfold. It's quite a heartbreaking case to read. One of the boys eventually took his own life.'

Santino dropped his head and closed his eyes. 'Fucking hell.' After a moment he looked up at Arnya. 'That has just disintegrated the tiny sliver of faith that I had left in humanity. How do these doctors or scientists, or whatever they are, think they should be in a position to play God like this?' he said. 'For those boys, their lives were little more than a social experiment. And for the others, the ones used as guinea pigs during war to test poisons and drugs, and for our IVF victims now, it's pure evil.'

Arnya could feel his revulsion. 'I'm sorry, I know it's upsetting. Let's get back on track. She turned her attention back to the photos. 'Were there any keys put into evidence? He must have had a set of house keys or car keys or something?' Arnya asked.

Santino returned to the table and picked up the photos he had taken. 'It was so long ago. It's hard to remember after everything that happened. There would have to be, I guess.'

They scoured the photos together.

'There!' Arnya pointed to one of the photos Santino was holding. 'Look, on that table at the back, near the door. There's a set there, I can see the tag.'

Santino brought the photo closer to his face and squinted. 'Yep, there is. But the question is, where are they now?'

Arnya grabbed the laptop and flicked through the official police photos. She tapped again and again until she spotted them. 'They're with the other evidence. They'll be in the evidence locker. Look.' She spun the computer around for him to see.

'We need to get those keys,' Santino said.

They both knew there was no way they could go back to the station. 'Boffa will be looking out for us,' Arnya said. 'He'll arrest us both if we try. It's too risky.'

'Call Kathryn. She'll have full access to the evidence room.'

Arnya shot him a worried look. She wasn't comfortable asking Kathryn to bear any more risk than she already had. 'I hate dragging another person into all this, Santino. It's not fair on her and if she loses her job over it, or worse, it'll be on our shoulders. Don't forget, she has a young child.'

'You heard her earlier, Arnya. Losing her job means a lot less to her than the possibility of losing her child. She wants in on this and we need her help, plain and simple. We have no choice.' He paused and turned to face her squarely. 'Are you scared?' he asked.

Arnya looked up, surprised by the suddenness of the question. She let her hands fall to her lap and breathed in and then out in a long, slow release before answering. 'A bit, I suppose. I don't think I've really let myself think about it yet, but I'm afraid that when I do, I won't be able to pull myself back from it. I guess I'm in the same boat as a lot of other people, not knowing.' She wasn't sure how honest she should be with him, given what they were already dealing with. 'Being faced with your own mortality is pretty confronting. I just thought I'd have done so much more with my life before contemplating the possible end of it, that's all. That's the only thing that really weighs on my mind. All I have to show for myself is a messy apartment and an inherited cat.' She smiled briefly before her eyes filled with tears.

Santino placed his hand on her arm. 'You've done so much, don't sell yourself short. Look at all you've achieved. I, for one, think you're an inspiration.'

The comment was sweet, but she didn't agree. 'Thank you for saying so, but I work in a boring job that I've slowly grown to hate, live in an apartment that feels empty and lonely, and my cat is the closest thing I've had to a relationship in a really long time. It's not exactly what I had hoped for my life.'

'Well, lucky for you, you're going to have plenty of time to do all the things you've always wanted to do. This isn't over, not by a long shot,' he assured her, his hand still resting lightly on her forearm.

Arnya smiled trying to blink away her tears. They made her eyes sting, but she resisted the urge to wipe them. The last thing they needed right now was for her to crumble. 'I hope you're right, but I fear that even with a second chance I'll stuff it up. I wouldn't even know where to begin. I haven't cultivated any friendships or relationships, and even if I started dating right this minute, by the time I got through the awkward stage, then the getting comfortable stage, and finally, onto the falling in love part, I'd probably be too old to even start a family or enjoy it!'

Santino laughed. 'I suppose us men are lucky like that; we don't have the loudly ticking biological clock, constantly banging in our ears. But I do understand, believe me I do.'

Arnya gave his hand an appreciative squeeze. 'You should make the call to Kathryn. She has a lot of respect for you and I think it will mean a lot to her for you to ask.'

While Santino called, Arnya took her phone from her purse. She looked at the message Robert had sent her earlier. Her fingers paused over the text. Was there any point in responding? What if all of this was fate, some last-ditch attempt by the universe to bring her and Robert back to each other? What if by not responding she was again pushing away a chance at having something with someone? Something that might actually lead her towards the kind of life she had just spoken to Santino about. But what if she did text him back and then she ended up like all of the other unlucky ones, dead without warning?

Her fingers hovered for another second before she put the phone back down.

Santino came to her side with a pillow in his hand, still giving instructions to Kathryn. When he finished, he handed it to her. 'Kathryn is going to see what she can do, but for now, we'll have to wait. Get some rest, we both need it.'

Arnya didn't argue. She took the pillow and curled up on the sofa. Within minutes of her eyes closing, she was fast asleep. She didn't move all night.

In the morning Arnya woke with an almost panicked start. She sat up abruptly and called out to Santino. He was asleep nearby on the rug. He raised his head and looked up at her.

'What time is it?' she asked.

Santino checked his phone. 'It's seven.' His voice was raspy and he cleared his throat.

Arnya got up to fetch her phone and turn on the television but instantly regretted the decision. 'Santino, look at this,' she said.

Santino sat up and rubbed his face. 'Jesus,' he muttered. 'Turn it up.'

The looming health crisis that could potentially affect thousands of Americans, and possibly more across the world, is developing. We're crossing live now to Agent Troy Boffa, lead investigator for the FBI, who is holding a press conference as we speak.'

Boffa began to speak.

The health system is already reaching crisis point as people react to incorrect information that has been repeated from various sources. We are asking people to stay calm and not overcrowd an already bursting hospital system. There is no need to panic. The information that has reached the media has been grossly exaggerated and at this point, we still do not know what we are dealing with. I can confirm that we have had multiple, possibly related deaths, but there is no clear or direct indication of a link as yet. The reports that these deaths have been directly related to people who were born using assisted reproductive technologies, such as IVF, have no basis and we are asking that people go about their usual business. The Centre for Disease Control is working to identify exactly what we are dealing with. If you were a person born through assisted reproductive technologies, there is absolutely no need for concern. I repeat, there is no need to present to hospitals or medical clinics unless you are in fact unwell or have a medical emergency. Please keep in mind that by clogging up the hospital system unnecessarily, you are keeping people who are in need of medical assistance from getting help.'

Arnya sat down on the arm of the chair, her eyes still on Boffa who was now taking questions from the large media gathering. He was giving little away, likely because they had nothing and were already planning their next move, a move that would spin the focus onto something else, something more *palatable* to the general public.

'I need to see Fitzgerald.' Santino grabbed his keys.

Arnya spun on the spot, turning to face Santino. 'What? Why? You can't do that.'

'I need to see him face to face. I can feel him out and get a better sense of his involvement, I know I can,' Santino said.

'What does that even mean? There was irritation in her tone. 'Is that some kind of man code or show of power? Because if it is, get over it. Going to see Fitzgerald is a stupid idea. And risky.'

Santino smiled. 'No, not like that. Kathryn is going to get into the evidence locker and get hold of those keys, but I want to rattle Fitzgerald. I want to put him on edge, make him believe we know a lot more than we do. I'll make him think that I'm giving him a chance to come clean. That's when he might do something stupid. That's when he'll make a mistake.'

Arnya wasn't convinced. 'But even if he does do something stupid, what are we supposed to do about it? We don't have a plan. We're not even part of this investigation anymore.'

'Maybe not, but as I said, it might be enough to get him worried. If he has any evidence stashed, he'll likely go straight for it to cover himself. I'll have someone keep an eye on him after my visit and see what he does. If we're lucky and he has any evidence stashed, he might just lead us straight to it, although I'm not quite that optimistic. What I do want is for him to know we're onto him. We have a pretty intense history, and this time I'm not going to let him get the upper hand. Fitzgerald will react, I know he will.'

Arnya let her guard down. 'Do what you feel is right, but I think our time would be better spent researching and following up solid leads. What is he likely to even tell you? If he's the kind of man you say he is, then he'll just tell you to stick it, and that would be best-case scenario. From what you've told me of your past with him, it could also be the worst thing to do, and dangerous.'

'It'll be enough to stir him up,' Santino said. 'And that's exactly what I want. We need to get under his skin and pressure him now. The clock is ticking.'

Arnya shook her head and closed her eyes. She wondered if he meant that *her* clock was ticking. She knew it was. 'I still don't understand why you'd want to poke that hornet's nest, but you presumably know what you're doing.'

Santino softened. 'I can guarantee you that I do not know what I'm doing, but at this point we have to do something and this is it, it's our one chance to really get this moving. He'll already be well aware of what's going on and if he's involved as deeply as we suspect he is, then me showing up will let him know we're already making the connections back to him. He is the missing link to all of this Arnya, and it's time to bring that to a head.'

'Just be careful, please,' Arnya pleaded. 'I don't want to be left to deal with all this on my own. I'll wait here for Kathryn to get back to me about the keys.'

He faced her, momentarily averting his eyes from the intensity of her gaze. 'Arnya, if I don't come back... call Harry immediately. He'll know what to do.'

CHAPTER

15

Parker Fitzgerald ran his short stubby fingers through what was left of his wiry hair. 'What the hell do you want?' he asked when Santino was led into the office. His tone was civil but warning. 'Did you come to thank me for the champagne? It was a nice one, wasn't it?'

'Just a few questions, that's all.' Santino responded in a flat tone.

Fitzgerald lifted his chin. 'Well, ask away, I've got nothing to hide, Detective, although I do question your motives for this little intrusion.' He pushed back, tilting his expensive chair behind the oak desk.

Santino made a point to scan the room. The large corner office was like a fishbowl with windows on two sides that looked down upon what Fitzgerald would consider the peasants below. The ceiling was high, overdone with far too many lights and the remaining walls were covered with grotesque art. The outer area of the top floor was carpeted with a dark grey, hard-wearing pile, but in true Fitzgerald style, his office had a marble floor. Santino showed his distaste, making a face before turning back to the obese man behind the desk.

'Looks like you're doing pretty well now with your father gone,' Santino said. It was time to cast the bait.

'Yes, well we all miss him terribly of course, but I can't complain.' Fitzgerald stood up and walked to the wall of windows. 'Are you going to get to the point here, Santino, or should I just have you removed now?'

'I know you, Parker, and I know how much you like to weave your stories, so I thought I'd come here personally and give you the chance to weave me a good story before I uncover the truth. We both know that I'll find my way to it eventually. Why waste both of our time?'

Fitzgerald rolled his eyes in a theatrical manner. He added to it a raucous and forced laugh. To anyone looking on, unaware of the man and his standing, he would have looked slightly unhinged.

'You don't know anything, Santino. You're just a washed-up, pathetic, whiney little pretend cop who thinks he's some sort of hero because you told some bullshit version of a story and dobbed on your mates.'

Parker put his hands out in front of him and began to clap. 'Well, good for you, how'd all that work out for you, Santino? Looks like you're pretty much exactly where you were when I last saw you. Grovelling for information because you don't know how to actually man-up and do anything yourself. Oh wait, now you don't have any back-up either, do you? Let me guess, no one will work with you, given that you're a no-good snitch?'

Santino smirked, letting Fitzgerald say his piece before folding his arms across his chest, mimicking Fitzgerald's earlier move. 'Is that what you think? Funny, because the way I remember it, you were the pathetic excuse who tried to pay off anyone you could with your daddy's money so that you could keep the fact that you murdered your own best friend a secret. Now, how did that turn out? Well, you were convicted of manslaughter and I went back to my life.'

Fitzgerald grimaced. 'You think you're so damn clever, don't you? Always did. Sitting there like the sanctimonious piece of shit you are. I went back to my life too, if you didn't notice.' He swung his arms about the room. 'This life, actually. This very lavish, expensive life, full of booze and women and parties and money. The kind of life you will only ever dream about.'

Santino kept his eyes on Fitzgerald. 'I guess you did. But unfortunately for you, this time you're not going to get off so lightly. This time you'll be held accountable for what you've done.'

Fitzgerald let out a deep, stifled groan. 'I paid my dues, Santino and you know it. You can't touch me now, so fuck off!' He pointed at the door and motioned to one of his men just outside. The man approached and came toward the office, hovering by the door.

Santino smiled. 'You may think you've paid your dues for what you did to Maurice, but I've got you now. I know the real reason you killed him and when I prove it, you'll say goodbye to all this.'

Fitzgerald again gestured to his man, this time to leave them. When the man had turned away, Fitzgerald came around to Santino, meeting him eye to eye. 'You don't know anything. Maurice is dead and buried and there's not a damn thing you or anyone else can do to change that. Whatever you think you're going to find, go your hardest because there's nothing there, I can assure you. You know me better than that. I didn't leave a trail. Now, toddle off, back to your little Professor and your insignificant little life before you really make me mad.'

Santino smiled, teeth showing, and stared right back. 'You're wrong, Parker. Maurice wasn't like you, was he? He was clever and came from humble beginnings, unlike you and your rich kid, party boy ways. You were a fuck-up who needed a clever friend to do all your work for you. Everyone knew it, even your father knew it. You were the son that he wished he never had.'

Parker was furious, spit gathering at the corners of his pursed lips. 'Don't talk about my father, you fucking bastard…'

Santino pushed on. He wasn't backing down now. 'Whatever happened between you, Maurice knew all along that you'd turn on him, didn't he? You forced him to do what you wanted and then you cast him aside like trash, just like you do with anyone you're finished with. But he was so much smarter than you ever gave him credit for. He had a contingency plan, something no one knew about, not even you or the goons you had following him. And now, with your handy work strewn all over the news and the body count piling up, you're finally going to pay for what you've done.'

Santino turned and swung his arm from left to right. 'Take a good look around and soak in all this wealth, because you're going to lose it all. As God is my witness, you will pay for this.'

For a split-second Santino saw a knowing look pass over Fitzgerald's face. What Santino said was enough to give him pause and Santino knew it. Fitzgerald had taken the bait.

'Get the fuck out of here, you son of a bitch. You're a dead man, you understand me? You're dead. I'll be behind you every minute of every day, every second. Watch your back, Detective.'

Santino held his hands up in defeat and turned to leave. 'Maurice knew you too well, Parker and he knew that you would eventually get rid of him. Did you know that for years he had been calling the IVF clinics and in his drunken haze had been ranting about the fact the two of you had done something terrible? This is what you did. This catastrophic loss of innocent life is your handy-work and you know it, we all know it. The thing is, I know how this story ends, now I just have to work out how and why it started. Don't say I didn't give you the chance to come clean and minimise the damage. I'm sure the judge and the public will find that piece of information very interesting.' As his threats hung in the air, Santino headed for the elevator.

When he reached the fresh air outside, Santino let out a long, heaving breath. He could still feel his heart pounding against his rib cage. From this point on he would have to assume that Fitzgerald's goons could strike at any moment. It was just a matter of time.

He crossed the street and signalled to the two officers he had stationed outside. The game was on.

Arnya was standing in Santino's kitchen, but she wasn't alone. Robert had arrived unexpectedly and Santino hadn't yet returned from seeing Fitzgerald, which was worrying her. The sound of keys jangling outside the apartment door brought a wave of relief.

Santino entered, his face red and his hair damp with perspiration. He was surprised when he saw Robert. 'Robert, what are you doing here? Did something happen?'

Arnya wondered if he had noticed the interaction between the two of them as they stood awkwardly on opposite sides of the bench. She knew that Santino had a sense for picking up on body language and she was sure that hers was screaming, *I'm uncomfortable.*

Robert spoke. 'Nothing happened, other than the fact that the entire city's gone to shit. I'm getting a walloping from the Feds and the politicians, and at this point it looks like a good chunk of the population is dropping dead. There are literally cases popping up everywhere. It's a shit storm.'

Arnya interrupted. 'How did it go with Fitzgerald?' She was concerned about how Fitzgerald might have reacted. 'You got out in one piece, so I suppose that's a good sign.'

'As expected,' Santino said. 'Fitzgerald was cocky at first, but he knows we're on his trail. From now on we can assume he'll have eyes on us at all times.'

Arnya scoffed. 'Exactly how many sets of eyes are on us at this point in time? And how are we supposed to get around without any of them following?'

'We don't,' Santino said. 'We let him see us. We let him think that we have more than we do and we back him into a corner. He'll go for anything he has hidden and we'll be watching him.'

Robert chimed in. 'What if he gets rid of something that could implicate him in all of this? Then what?'

'I've got someone watching him and his guys. He's only got a small crew that he trusts completely, so if any of them move, we'll know about it. It's a risk, I know that, but we have to take the chance.'

'Jesus, this sounds like some 007 shit.' Robert's body language was giving away more alarm than his words. 'I'm a doctor, not a hero. I don't want to end up in my own morgue. I think you should back off, I really do. This is getting too dangerous.'

'We have to see this through.' Santino's voice was slightly raised.

'I don't think we do,' Robert argued. 'It's time to get out and get as far away from this as possible. I'm out, Santino, I'm done.' Robert's phone rang in his pocket, interrupting his speech. 'Sorry, I need to take this.' He excused himself and walked a short way down the hall.

Deflated, Arnya sat down on the sofa in the living room. She picked up the photo of the keys from the table and held it up. 'Kathryn's on her way with these. What's our next move?'

Santino sat in the armchair across from her. 'Our next move is to see if these keys mean anything, and I pray to God they do.'

'Are you sure about all this, Santino?' Arnya asked. 'The whole thing seems really risky and if Fitzgerald is the monster you say he is, I can't say I'm not a little worried.' She leaned forward and put a hand to her eyes, her head dizzy.

'You okay?' Santino asked, reaching for her as she stood up, blinking and shaking her head.

'I think so. I'm not sure.'

'How do you feel? Is it just dizziness?'

Arnya knew he was worrying. 'Yeah, I might have moved too quickly, that's all. We've barely slept or eaten, I'm probably just a bit lightheaded.' She exchanged an unintentional look with Santino, aware that the fear in her eyes was already showing. It was too late to hide it. She rubbed her face and stepped away from him. 'I'm sure that's all it is.'

Robert came back from the hall. 'I have to get going, but keep me posted. I won't give you my leave-it-alone speech again, just please stay safe.' He grabbed his bag and headed to the door. 'Arnya told me about the keys in the photo. Let me know if you find what they lead to.'

'I might duck home too and get some things, I've barely seen the place,' Arnya said. 'I need a change of clothes and a few other things anyway. I'll be quick.' She grabbed her purse, realising she didn't have a car. 'Can I take your car?' she asked Santino.

He was about to answer when Robert spoke instead. 'Let me drive you, please. I'd be happy to.'

Arnya looked at Santino who was watching her intently. She could tell that he was ready to offer an excuse if she gave him a signal. She decided not to. 'Sure, that would be great. Thank you, Robert. I can get a cab back when I'm done.'

Robert jingled his keys and led the way. 'I wasn't sure you'd want to ride with me,' he said when they reached the car.

Arnya shivered. The early evening air was cool and she only had a thin shirt on. 'It's all ancient history as far as I'm concerned, Robert. Isn't it?'

'Um, I'm not sure about you, but I feel like we never actually resolved anything,' he said slowly. He seemed to be looking for her to say something, but she didn't, so he continued. 'We walked away in separate directions and that was that. It's been bothering me for a long time. I wish I'd contacted you sooner, or at least tried.' He unlocked the car doors and waited until she was in the passenger seat. 'I just think it would have benefitted both of us to talk things over and feel better about the way we ended it. I guess we were both unsure how to approach it. I didn't know how, or what to say.'

Arnya remained silent.

'Didn't you ever think about it? About contacting me?' he asked.

'Of course I did,' Arnya said. 'But every time I contemplated calling or coming to see you, I convinced myself that there was no point. You know I'm not good with the feeling stuff. I never have been. I told myself that we had a thing and it ended. That happens. That's life. We both had careers and dreams and the stars didn't align for us, that's all.'

He turned his eyes from the road to look at her. 'But I always wondered if they might align at another time. Maybe things weren't right back then, but...'

Arnya was staring straight ahead. She had wondered. She had wondered more times than she would ever admit to anyone, including herself. There were sleepless nights staring up at the ceiling and obsessing about whether she had made the right choices or walked the right path. There were even times when a body was curved in behind her and Robert had still entered her thoughts. When she was having sex with other men, she would think about the passion she and Robert had shared. Her body would ache to feel that passion again – with him.

'I've thought about you a lot over the last few years, Robert. I wondered what we might have been like if we'd made it work and tried a little harder.' She laughed. 'I even picked up the phone to call you a few years back. It was the only time I got so far as actually dialling the number.'

Robert sighed. 'Why didn't you? If you'd called, I would have answered and things might be a lot different now, different to all this.'

Arnya looked at him quizzically. 'None of this would be any different if we had gotten back together. Everything that's happening now would still be happening, we just would have been in a different position with all of it.'

Robert nodded. 'Of course, I didn't mean to say it that way or upset you. I was thinking about me personally, that's all. I wish that things had taken a different path. Sliding doors, I guess, you know, what could have been. We could still change it, you know? We could…'

'Just over there on the right,' Arnya pointed to her building, cutting off the conversation. Even though it wasn't completely dark out, she noticed straight away that there was a light on in her apartment. Robert was saying something, but she didn't hear it. 'My light is on,' she said out loud.

'What light?' he asked.

Arnya pointed up to the third floor. 'The light is on in my apartment.'

'Is that a problem?'

'I didn't leave any lights on. Everything was off when I left.' She could feel a sense of unease crawling over her skin.

'Do you think someone's been in there?' Robert asked.

Arnya unbuckled her seatbelt and got out of the car. 'I guess I'm about to find out.'

Robert killed the engine and got out too. 'You're not going up there alone. Fitzgerald is a nasty bastard, believe me. You don't know what he's capable of.'

'Fitzgerald? What makes you think this would have anything to do with him?'

Robert shrugged. 'Santino went to see him and now Fitzgerald feels threatened, perhaps? Makes sense, doesn't it? That he'd be watching and possibly send someone to check you out or scare you?'

'Maybe,' Arnya said. She took out her phone. 'Boffa made a few comments as well to let me know he knew all about me. I'll call Santino on the way up and tell him.'

Santino was on the line as they entered the apartment. 'It's trashed,' Arnya told him, taking in the scene, a look of desolation on her face. 'Every single thing I own is in piles on the floor. Everything's broken, everything.' Her voice was wavering. She didn't have anything of significant value, but it felt valuable to her, and it was all in mounds like piles of rubbish. It hurt to look at it.

'Just go to the car and come straight back here. It's not safe,' Santino insisted.

Arnya held back her tears. 'I'll see if I can find a few things I need and then I'll head back. I don't even know where my cat is.'

'Make sure Robert stays with you, and be quick. I don't want either of you hanging around there too long.'

Arnya hung up and tucked the phone into her pocket. She followed Robert, who had moved into the kitchen. 'They've certainly done a number on this place, haven't they?' he said.

She could feel her eyes welling. The idea that someone had been in her apartment, whoever it was, in her space, rifling around, felt so invasive. 'Let me just grab a few things, can you wait?'

'Of course, get what you need and then I'll drive you back.'

'Thanks Robert, I appreciate it.' She reached out and touched his arm.

Robert smiled and leaned in to hug her. She let him, even though it felt strange. 'It'll be okay, this will all sort itself out in time. I'll make sure that he doesn't hurt you.'

His words made her feel uncomfortable. They seemed odd and out of place, as if he had already closed the case on it, but she didn't have the energy or the will to dissect why or to get into a discussion about it.

Arnya went to the bedroom and pulled out an old sports bag she used to take to the gym in her college years. She sat on the edge of the bed, reminded of how simple life had seemed then. No threat of death looming, or people following and threatening her. No need to try to save lives that didn't even know they were about to be lost. No real complications other than her love life, Robert, and university exams.

She grabbed some clothes from the clean laundry she had done only a few days ago. It felt like a lifetime ago now. Back then she had been thinking things through while putting the load on and wondering what these cases were about, with no idea where it would soon lead.

'You okay?' Robert asked, appearing in the doorway. 'You look a little lost.'

She hadn't realised that she was clutching her clothing to her chest and staring at the wall.

'I feel lost, Robert. I really do. This is all happening so fast and my mind is swimming.' She looked up at him. 'What if this is the end? What if all these people die – and I'm one of them?'

Robert moved over to the bed and sat beside her. He took her hands in his. 'All of this is nuts, and scary, but that doesn't mean you're going to die too. It just means that we don't know what the outcome of all of it is and speculating won't do anyone any good. I know it must be terrifying. God knows, I would be out of my mind if I was in your shoes, but for now let's just get you to a safe place.' He picked up the bag at her feet. 'Come on. Let's get this packed and get out of here.'

Arnya got up and placed some things in the bag. When Robert's phone rang, he excused himself, leaving her to her thoughts once again as she collected toiletries. She wondered if she would even need any of it. Even if the IVF situation didn't kill her, there was a good chance that if she didn't back off and keep her mouth shut, she'd disappear. 'Stop being so damn dramatic,' she told herself.

When she went to the hall to collect her runners from the cupboard, she could hear Robert. His voice was low and the conversation sounded tense. She inched further toward him, just in time to hear him say a few curse words and see him smack his finger hard on the screen. He reached into his pocket and pulled out a small bag, tapping it on the side of his hand between his thumb and forefinger. He leaned in and sniffed hard, pinching his nose as whatever it was worked its magic. Arnya pulled back, worried that he might see her watching. She'd never known Robert to use drugs, but then again, she didn't exactly know him anymore. People can change a lot over time and, other than what she had seen in the newspapers or on TV, she knew little to nothing about Robert's personal life. In fact, she felt as if she knew little to nothing about anything anymore.

Arnya went back to the bathroom. 'Everything alright?' she called out.

The question caused Robert to jump. He stuffed his phone and the bag back into his pocket.

'Sort of. Work, breathing down my neck as usual, you know how it can be.' He appeared at the door.

His answer made her feel uneasy, just as she had earlier. She could tell he wasn't being truthful. It may have been a long time since they were together, but he had never been good at lying. 'If you're sure? Robert, I'm happy to talk if you need to.' She looked at him through the bathroom mirror.

'Nah, it's nothing, really' He stared at the floor as he spoke. 'Bureaucracy at its finest. How about you?' he asked, looking up at her reflection. 'Almost done?'

'Yes, I think I have everything. I need to leave some food for the cat though, I have no idea where he is.'

Robert followed her to the kitchen. 'Can I ask you something?'

'Sure,' she said.

'You said before that you thought of me over the years…'

Arnya turned to face him. 'Of course I did. Many times. But as I said, it just didn't feel like the right time for us.'

Robert dropped his eyes. 'And now? Do you ever think there could be a right time?'

Arnya smiled and moved closer, placing her hand on his shoulder. 'Just look at us now, Robert? How can we be sure of anything?' Right times almost sound ridiculous. Looking back, I realise that a right time is just something that we create in our minds to avoid making hard decisions.'

Robert leaned over and kissed her cheek. 'Maybe after all this is over, we can get together some time for a drink. Maybe we can finally have that conversation that's waited all these years. I want to make changes in my life, do better, you know?'

Arnya stiffened. Ten minutes earlier she would have said, sure, that would be nice. But right now, she just wanted to get out of there. 'Let's deal with one thing at a time. If we all get through this, then maybe we can revisit that.'

Robert looked at her intently, but said nothing as he picked up her bag and took it to his car.

CHAPTER

16

At Santino's apartment building, Robert walked Arnya to the door. He lingered when Santino answered, making small talk before saying his goodbyes.

'That seemed a little awkward,' Santino said. He let the words sit for a moment before adding the question he really wanted to ask. 'Was Robert trying to rekindle an old flame?' He picked up the photos from the coffee table and began studying them.

'Something like that, 'Arnya said. 'I guess all of this craziness has got us all contemplating our existence to some extent. It kind of makes you wonder about the road not travelled and the *what if's.*'

Santino agreed. He wasn't usually in the habit of spending too much time wondering what might have been, but occasionally his thoughts did wander to the idea of having a family and kids of his own. He'd let go of that a long time ago and his lifestyle didn't exactly fit in well with that scenario, but maybe, if the time was right, he would make a change, start a new version of his life, one that included all those things he'd pushed aside. There was that so-called *right time* again.

'I'm sure it does, but more importantly, are you okay?' he asked.

'I'm fine, really. It was just a bit upsetting to see my place like that, but I'm fine and Robert was really helpful.' She hesitated before continuing. 'Do you think he's okay? You know him fairly well and I haven't seen him for a long time.'

Santino looked at her, his brow slightly furrowed. 'What do you mean, okay? Did something happen?'

'Nothing happened, he just seemed like he was on tenterhooks and when he took a call…'

The ringing of Santino's mobile snapped them both from the conversation. 'Santino,' he answered. 'Kathryn?' He pulled the phone from his ear and put it on speaker. Arnya moved to his side.

'Santino, I'm on my way to your place with the keys from the evidence locker, but I think I'm being followed. There's a Ford, a black one, it's been on me since I left the station. I think you should get out of there, now!'

Santino looked up from the phone at Arnya, his eyes narrowing. He mouthed the word, fuck.

'Kathryn, you need to get off the road and out of sight. Arnya's place has already been ransacked. We can come to you,' he said.

'No, you don't understand. You need to get out of your apartment, now!' Kathryn's voice was insistent. 'I've just heard the call on the radio. Boffa has sent patrols to take you in. Turn on the TV and you'll see. Parker Fitzgerald, the big pharma guy, has accused you of attempting to murder him. You're going to be arrested.'

'Kathryn, just get off the road and stay safe,' Santino said. 'We can meet up in an hour at the Crypt Cafe. Corner of Rowe and Coventry. It has a lower level. Go down there and wait for us, and park out of sight. We'll be there as soon as we can.'

Santino turned on the TV while Arnya collected up the case files and photos. She stopped to look up, searching Santino's face for answers. 'What the hell happened with him today?'

Santino was shaking his head. 'Nothing happened.' He grabbed his things. 'Fitzgerald is making his move. I knew he would, I just didn't know what that move would be, but this is it. Come on, let's get out of here. We need to get those keys from Kathryn.'

'Is she in danger, Santino? They won't hurt her, will they?'

Santino stopped and met her worried eyes. 'I don't know. I don't even know which *they* we're talking about. It could be Fitzgerald or the Feds. I'm guessing it's Fitzgerald rather than Boffa. Boffa is too consumed with diverting the public to care about anything else right now.'

'So, the worst-case scenario is likely and it's the rich sociopath?' she said.

'Unfortunately, yes. Fitzgerald is capable of anything at this point. Let's get to Kathryn and make sure she stays safe. I'll call my guys who are watching Fitzgerald and see if there's an update.'

In the hall, police lights reflected around the walls, filtering in through windows on the lower floor. 'Go to the back stairs.' He ushered Arnya down the two flights and out into the darkness at the rear of his apartment block.

'How are we going to get the car? It's out front,' Arnya said.

'Wait till they go in and we'll run for it. We'll be away before they even realise. Go around to the side and keep watch. They're only looking for me, so you'll be safe. I'll wait. Bring the car around to the back block and I'll jump in there.'

Santino watched as Arnya moved to the side of the apartment block before making a run for the Lexus. Within seconds she turned the car into the side road, picking Santino up as instructed. 'I hate to admit it, but this feels weirdly empowering,' she grinned.

Santino watched as she put her foot down and took off. 'It suits you,' he joked.

'Right, where is this place?' she asked.

Santino pointed ahead. 'Make a right up there and then hit the freeway. I'll show you from there.'

'God, I hope Kathryn is safe. I'm really worried for her, Santino.'

'How did they find out? That's what I want to know,' he said.

'Find out what? About Kathryn helping us, or the key? Maybe Fitzgerald doesn't know.'

Santino's face tensed. 'He knows. And someone tipped him off. He's got someone, or more than one, on the inside.'

'I thought this was just retaliation for you going to see him today. You said you rattled him, maybe he just got spooked.'

'He did get spooked, but that explains the attempted murder bullshit. Following Kathryn, that's something else entirely. He knows she's helping us and someone's tipped him off. That's how he knew to have her followed,' he explained.

'Who though?' Arnya asked, pressing harder on the gas.

'Make a right and then pull in. It's just up there on the left.'

Inside the cafe, Kathryn was sitting at a table in the back of the lower section. She was biting her nails and tapping her leg. When she saw them coming, she waved them over.

Arnya went quickly to her side. 'Are you alright? You must be scared out of your mind.' She squeezed Kathryn's shoulder.

'A little,' she admitted. Her green eyes were wide and her hands were shaking. 'It just freaked me out when I realised what was going on.'

'What happened when you went to the evidence room?' Santino asked. He sat down at the table. 'Did anyone see you or talk to you?'

'I went down there and Jensen was on, you know the old guy who's been there forever.'

Santino nodded. He knew who she was talking about.

Kathryn continued. 'He's a sweetheart. I think he was asleep actually. He barely flinched when I went in. It took me a while to find them and when I came out, there was a younger officer there. He saw me as I left and I got the feeling that he was watching me, so I pretended to leave and waited behind the stairwell. As soon as he thought I was gone, he made a call to someone and told them I'd accessed the Maurice Stephens evidence. That's when I took off out of there to come to you, but I didn't realise I was being followed, not at first.'

Santino clenched his fist under the table. 'I knew Fitzgerald had someone on the inside. It doesn't surprise me. There's likely a few more too. Was this before or after the attempted murder accusation surfaced?'

'It was before. After I heard him on the phone, I went straight out to the car. That's when I heard the call go out to bring you in and I phoned you.'

Santino paused, considering the timeline of events. 'So, the accusation was made after he knew the evidence had been accessed,' Santino said. 'That would have been the final straw after what I said to Fitzgerald today. He knows I'm on to something. I'm surprised he didn't do it a little earlier though, right after I left. He must have stewed for a while about how to shut me down.' Santino shook his head.

'I'm surprised he didn't just have you killed,' Arnya said. She was suddenly furious that Santino had put himself in such danger.

'That would be too easy, and obvious,' Santino said. 'It's all a game to him and he wants to win, but not without a bit of cat and mouse. He thrives on it. He wants to see me suffer so that he can look me in the eye and say he won.' He turned his attention back to Kathryn. 'The young cop at the desk would have alerted him that you were accessing the evidence. He'll be really out for blood now. He knows we've got something, he just doesn't know exactly what. He wants to slow us down, but not take us out of the game which is why he's levelled that murder threat accusation.'

Arnya gasped. 'This is no game. People are dying!'

Santino felt bad for saying it like that, but it was the truth. 'And what about the Feds?' He asked Kathryn. 'Where are they up to with the investigation?'

Kathryn rolled her eyes and shook her head. 'They're treading water to be honest, and Boffa is spending every minute just dealing with the media fallout. He's spinning a web of lies and being puppeted from above. From what I could tell, they're already putting out the virus idea. It's nuts out there and people are in panic mode. If I wasn't on the inside, knowing that so far it's only people in the 30 to 40 age group, I'd be a mess too. This whole thing has a life of its own. I'm not sure anything will stop it now, at least not until there are some real answers, or at least some believable lies.' Kathryn put her hand in her pocket and handed Santino the set of keys in an evidence bag. 'I hope they're worth it,' she said.

'So do we,' Santino smiled. 'We can't tell you how grateful we are, Kathryn. You've put everything on the line and we know what a big risk this has been.'

'I'm glad I could help, I really am.' The love for her little boy and her worries for his safety were etched on her face.

Arnya's words gave away her fears. 'You can't go home tonight. Is there somewhere you can stay?'

Kathryn nodded. 'I'm leaving the car here and my brother is picking me up in ten minutes. I'll be safe, don't worry. He's got my son with him and I'll go to my parents' place in the country for a few days. I need the break anyway and I want to spend my time with my boy. I don't care about anything else.' She forced a smile. 'Look after yourselves.'

Santino got up as Kathryn did. He went around the table and gave her a hug. 'Keep that little boy of yours close. I promise we'll do everything we can to get to the bottom of this.'

Kathryn smiled and reached out for Arnya's hand, squeezing it. 'Take care,' Arnya said, before Kathryn disappeared up the stairs.

Santino sat back at the table and studied the keys. The first two were similar and looked like normal house keys, but the third was different. It was older and cut with a strange pattern at the head.

'What do you think?' Arnya asked.

'I think we're crazy and that this hunch better pay off.' In spite of his gentle humour, they both knew what was at stake.

'Are there any marks or writing on the keys? Indicators of where they might be from?' Arnya asked.

Santino held them up for her to see. 'These two are standard door keys, probably from his apartment, but this one's different.' He held up the third key on the ring. 'This one's not for a door. It's smaller and has this weird pattern.' He ran his finger along the top of the curved edge. 'Maybe a lock box or something like that? It's too small for anything else.'

'Well, that narrows it down. But how the hell do we track down a box? And who would even know it exists?'

'It wasn't in the evidence, I know that much. And I don't recall seeing anything like that at the apartment or in the photos.'

Arnya shook her head. 'From what we know, Maurice was drinking heavily and had ostracised himself from most people. I suspect the only person that he was actually confiding in at that time was Father Kelly when he would visit the church.' She shrugged. 'If he told anyone at all, it would most likely have been him. It's a long shot though, and the priest said there was nothing else that Maurice told him.'

'Yes, but people can often have their memory jogged when they see or recognise something. We need to show him the key – even if only to rule it out.'

Arnya agreed. 'The next question, then, is how do we get out of here and get to him without ending up in a cell or worse?'

'We be careful and if we do get stopped, I'll resist and cause a scene. No matter what happens, you go and just keep going.' He handed Arnya the keys. 'No matter what, okay?'

She took them, even though she wasn't sure that she could follow his instructions. 'The priest was from St Cuthbert's, wasn't he? That's not too far from here.'

Santino got up from the table and took her hand. 'I wouldn't have been able to do any of this without you, you know that. I truly am grateful.' He held her gaze and squeezed her hand.

'I know you are,' she said quietly. 'For a scientist with a desk job and a detective with a bad reputation, we make a pretty good team, don't we?'

Santino smiled. 'Yes, we do. I just hope we stay that way.'

Outside, they hailed a cab. 'St Cuthbert's please, on Martin Place,' Santino directed as the driver pulled away from the curb.

The driver sighed loudly. 'There's a whole heap of people picketing on Fairfax. I'll have to take you around.'

'That's fine,' Santino said.

The driver looked into his mirror, clearly eager to discuss the situation. 'The whole country's gone off its head. People are dying and the religious nuts are picketing about God's wrath and how he's teaching man a lesson. Not to mention all the families of the poor bastards dropping like flies are storming the hospitals and government buildings in a frenzy. People have lost it. Crazy shit this is, it's making everyone lose their minds.'

Arnya looked at Santino. Her heart was heavy and sad for the panicked people whose lives had been turned upside down. They didn't know where to turn or what to do. 'We're running out of time, Santino. Look at it out there.'

The cab driver turned back to them again, sharing more of his observations. 'Yeah, it's crazy. Let me break it down for ya, because it's pretty messed up. Basically, there are rumours it's somehow related to IVF, which is kinda mind-blowing if it's true. Or maybe you believe what the Feds are selling, about some kind of new virus thing. That's a load of dog crap of course, but I'm betting on the IVF connection. That's what's making people even more crazy. It's like some kind of lottery where you don't know if the next ball to drop is the one with your name on it. Anyway, they're droppin' like flies and even with all the supposed brilliant minds of our time, they still can't figure out why the hell it's happening. On the flip side, all the God-botherers have decided that it's God's wrath, you know? Like he's had enough and is finally punishing us for our sins, as if every day isn't punishment enough.' He moved his chewing gum from one side of his mouth to the other and gave it a few chews before continuing. 'They reckon it was a sin against God to create test tube babies in the first place. I remember when it first started. Today, this one guy on a street corner was hollering that if God decided that your union should bear no fruit, then that's God's will and God will have his reasons for it. The whole thing is just crazy town if you ask me. I've never seen anything like it in my whole life. And don't even get me started on the government and their cover-ups. Everyone is lying.'

Santino stared out the window, watching as people walked back and forth in lines across the pavement with hand-written signs. They weren't even about test tube babies, they were about sinners and Hell and a litany of other things. He felt the cross that was dangling at his chest. For everything good, there was an equal and opposite. He hated that kind of religion, the kind that used faith to divide and destroy instead of to unite and overcome. Divide and destroy was definitely the way it seemed to be going.

The cab pulled up outside St Cuthbert's. 'There you go. Got you here in one piece and neither of you exploded, so that's good.' The driver seemed pleased with his own humour.

Arnya got out quickly. She had seen and heard more than enough. Her phone buzzed in her pocket, the ringer on silent. It was Arthur. There were two earlier missed calls from him. She dialled her voicemail. Arthur's voice was hushed and hurried. He said he had been watching the news reports and worrying for her. He pleaded with her to step back from this situation and call him. He wanted to talk things over and make sure she was safe.

She hung up and dropped the phone back into her pocket. Not even Arthur was going to make her step back from this. Nothing would.

When the door opened, Father Kelly looked as if he had been asleep. He rubbed his eyes and pulled the robe around his pyjamas. 'Detective, this is a surprise. Um, please, come in.'

'We're very sorry to bother you, Father, but we really need your help. It's urgent.'

'Anything, son, anything I can do to help, of course. I've been watching the television and praying all evening. Times like this always bring out the very best and very worst of humankind.'

'They certainly do, Father,' Santino said.

'Please, follow me.' Father Kelly led them through a side door and into a sitting room. It was modern, but had only the most basic furnishings. A small table with two chairs and a kitchen area with a bar fridge and storage cupboards. It was enough for one person and a visitor, but not much more.

Arnya stepped forward and held out the keys. 'Father, Maurice Stephens, the man you were seeing here at the church, he had this set of keys and we were wondering if you knew anything about them, or saw him with them when he came here?'

The priest took the keys and studied them. 'I'm really not sure. Maurice came and went and most of the time he was dishevelled and rather inebriated. I don't recall seeing him with anything like that. There was one time he came - it was cold out, I remember that. I noticed him in the back of the church and I went to see if he was alright. He was shivering and looked unwell. I brought him back here and gave him some tea to warm him up. He had something with him that night because I remember him putting it on the table.' He pointed to the square table against the wall near the tiny kitchen.

'Do you remember what it was?' Santino asked. Without even thinking, he reached for the cross at his neck as if it might help in some way.

The priest shook his head. 'I wish I did. Maybe it was a bag or a case? It wasn't that big, but it was large enough for me to notice it and I remember that he carried it under his arm, not on his shoulder. I'm so very sorry, I can't remember more clearly.'

Arnya reached out and put her hand over his. 'It's okay, Father, but did anything else happen that night, did he say anything that might be relevant? Anything at all. Please, take a moment to think.'

The priest walked over to the armchair and sat down. 'I'm trying to recall. He came in here, and as I said, he had something under his arm. He put whatever it was that he had on that table.' He pointed again to the small dining table. 'He sat down over there on the sofa and I made a pot of tea. He looked very unwell that evening, as I said, and we talked for a while, but things seemed to be pretty jumbled in his mind.'

'How so?' Santino pressed.

'He talked about being a sinner, as he often did, but also about people watching him. I think he said that he had been waiting for something, but when it didn't come, he knew that something had gone wrong. He was worried and scared. He asked for forgiveness, oh wait...' Father Kelly looked to the ceiling as he tried to clear memories that were distant and foggy. 'He asked me for a set of rosary beads, so he could pray, yes that's right.'

'And did you give him the beads?' Arnya asked, her body tingling with the hope that they were on to something.

The priest thought for a moment. 'Yes, I went to get a set from the office.'

'And where was Maurice while you went to get them? Did he stay in here?' Santino asked.

'Yes, he stayed here and drank his tea. When I got back, he thanked me and I remember that he said something very odd, something about science and religion being in conflict and man, eternally driven by greed, being the master of his own demise. Those weren't his exact words, but it was along those lines. For someone who was quite erratic, it was a profound statement that caused me to pause and consider its meaning.' The priest shrugged. 'That's it I'm afraid, I wish I had something more for you, something more useful at least. If only I'd thought to make a note of our talks.'

'No, Father, you have helped, believe me. Thank you so much once again for taking the time,' Santino said.

As they left, Arnya turned to Santino. 'What now?' She felt let down by the discussion with Father Kelly.

Santino stopped at the bottom of the church steps. He stared at the night sky. Arnya wondered if he was asking for help from above or just trying to clear his thoughts. Without answering her question, he turned and headed back to the door. 'Wait, Father, there's one more thing.'

The priest swung the partially closed door back open. 'What is it?'

'You said that when you came back you gave him the beads and then he left.'

'Yes, that's right.'

'Think hard, Father, please. When he got up to leave, holding the beads, did he go to the table and fetch the item he had put there?'

Father Kelly thought for a moment before meeting Santino's eyes. 'No Detective, I don't believe he did.'

CHAPTER

17

Parker Fitzgerald inhaled his cigarette and let the putrid smoke escape in one long breath. He looked to his right-hand man, aptly named *Chimney* on account of his square brick-like frame and hot temper, to confirm that Santino was taken care of.

'Everything's in place, Mr Fitzgerald. When they come out of the priest's place, the boys will grab them.'

'Do not fuck this up, do you understand me? This cannot get away from us.'

The hefty Chimney checked his messages. 'Jackson's on watch at the church now. He says they came out, but went straight back in, like they'd forgotten something.'

Fitzgerald bellowed. 'This piece of shit cop has been on my tail for years and it ends today. Those useless fucking cops should have brought him in by now. Whatever he's got, or thinks he's got, goes away with him.' He stood up from the desk and walked to the window on the southern side of the office. 'Fucking Maurice. He was so damn weak. I liked him better when he was a poor, pot-smoking genius from the wrong side of the tracks.'

'What about the woman? The doctor that's with him?' Chimney asked.

Fitzgerald turned on his heels, his glare enough of an answer. Chimney took the cue and tapped away at his phone.

'Fucking Maurice,' Fitzgerald muttered. 'Not even being dead in the ground will shut him up.' His phone rang on the desk. He took in another drag of his cigarette before answering. 'So, now you're interested? Why the change of heart? I thought you wanted nothing more to do with it?'

He made a hand gesture for Chimney to leave.

'Let me guess,' he continued. 'You're worried about your precious reputation all of a sudden? Let me just make this really clear for you. We made a deal and I don't make deals lightly. You're into me for a very large sum and in order to pay that off, you'll get me every single thing I ask for. The alternative is that I hand your debts back to the crew I took them from and we all know where that leaves you.' He listened for a minute before hanging up.

Pacing back and forth, he dialled another number. 'It's me. Don't speak. Just listen,' he commanded. 'The only thing you've given me is your bullshit assurances. I've given you time and you've done nothing. The deal is off. I'm grabbing them now.'

He slammed down the phone and waited, knowing the pleas and promises would come. His phone lit up with a message:

If you go down, I go down too and I'm not willing to lose everything. I'll find out what they have. We need to know before you grab them in case they've buried it. Be smart.

Fitzgerald sat back in his chair, lighting another cigarette and drawing it in, long and deep. He pressed a button on his desk phone and Chimney re-appeared. 'Tell them to hold off grabbing them until I say the word. I need to get some information first.'

Chimney tapped furiously at his phone.

Fitzgerald rocked back in his chair. 'All these chicken-shit sad-sacks are going down. None of them have the guts, never did. Not one of them ever had the foresight that I had. Weak. Plain and simple.'

Chimney seemed unsure if Fitzgerald was talking to him, but he nodded and agreed anyway.

'They pretend to be smart men, but they're not. I'll fuckin' bury Santino, that maggot, and the others if I have to. They'll go down for all this before I will. I'll make sure of it.'

At the church, Santino had more questions for the priest.

'Father, whatever Maurice had with him, it might be here in the church somewhere. He may have left it here for safe keeping.'

Father Kelly was shaking his head. 'I can't even begin to imagine where.'

Arnya spoke up. 'When you left to go and fetch the beads from the office, how long were you gone?'

'Only a few minutes, five at the most. I wasn't sure where I put them initially, so it took me a little while.'

Santino walked to the door. 'In that time, he had to have been able to hide the item and get back here before you returned.'

'Yes, I really wasn't gone very long,' the priest said.

'Do you think it could be here in the residence somewhere?' Santino suggested.

Father Kelly shook his head. 'We renovated last year. Everything was moved out and then back in. If there was anything hidden, it would have been found then.'

Arnya moved toward Father Kelly. 'Father, would you mind re-tracing your steps that night? Could you go over to the office and get another set of beads? If we do everything that you can remember doing that night, we might be able to work out how far we can get in that time. It will give us an idea where to look.'

Father Kelly got up. He headed to the door and disappeared.

'Right,' Santino said. 'You have a look around here and I'll go out to the church and see how much time I have.'

Arnya began searching the room. In the church, Santino went straight to the altar. He had five minutes at the most.

He checked behind the altar, and then under the pews and along every aisle. There were cupboards at the back of the church, either side of the exit door, but they were filled with candles and other items. Santino walked back to the front entrance doors and checked the foyer area. There were no obvious places for someone to hide something. He looked up at the ceiling which was high and unreachable without scaffolding of some kind. Stained glass windows filled with images and scenes from biblical stories lined the long walls. They reminded Santino of sitting in church as a boy, holding his mother's hand, afraid of the stories of Hell and the devil. Santino wondered if Maurice had chosen a church specifically. A last attempt at seeking forgiveness for whatever he had done. A man of science, turning to religion to seek what all his intelligence and understanding could never give him.

Santino looked upward. 'Maurice, help me out here. You wanted me to find this, didn't you? You knew at some point someone like me would come looking. Help me find it now.'

Arnya appeared in the doorway. 'Time's up. Any ideas?'

Santino approached her and shook his head. 'It's here somewhere, I know it. I can almost feel it'

'He could have put it anywhere, Santino. We may not even be in the right place. Perhaps he did take it with him that night and Father Kelly just doesn't remember.'

Santino shook his head and looked back out over the church. 'Maurice wanted it this way, I'm sure of it. He wanted the evidence of what they had done to lie here, the only place where it could be forgiven. If he knew what was coming somehow, then it explains why the church became so significant to him. Science and religion have always been at odds, particularly in relation to creation. I think that maybe he felt as if they had intervened in what was meant to be God's work and in turn they would be punished. It's here, I know it is.'

Arnya sighed. 'Okay, but how do we get inside his head and work out what he would have done with it?'

Santino marched back to the side of the church where Father Kelly was standing. 'Father, when Maurice would come here, you mentioned that you would often find him sitting in quiet reflection.'

Father Kelly then followed Santino to the altar. 'Yes, that's right. He would come and just sit, sometimes for hours.'

'And did he always sit in the same spot?'

Father Kelly nodded. 'Yes, he did. Just over there on the right-hand side. In that pew towards the back.'

Santino walked to the pew Father Kelly had indicated and stepped along until he almost reached the middle. 'About here?'

'Yes, about there. Maybe a little further,' Father Kelly said.

Santino sat down as Arnya and the priest approached. They waited at the end of the pew and watched Santino slide into position. He leaned forward, lowering his shoulders, his head bowed, just as he had as a child when attending church. The seat in front of him was quite close to his forehead and the floor below was solid when he banged his foot hard against it. With his eyes closed, he reached down and felt beneath the seat to the left and then to the right. Opening his eyes, he looked along the pew toward Arnya and then to the wall on his right. The thin aisle that ran between the wall and the pews caught his eye. A strip of dark red carpet ran the entire length, but a little way along, it seemed to lift slightly.

'Father, can you come over here?' Santino said. The priest made his way along the pew until he was standing beside Santino. 'What's that?' Santino pointed to the carpet.

Father Kelly leaned over to see where he was pointing. 'The carpet runner?'

'The area where it seems slightly lifted,' he said. 'A few rows up.'

Arnya had gone two rows ahead and come along the pew. She leaned down to look at the floor just in front of the confessional.

'There's a cavity under the floorboards there', the priest said. 'It hasn't been opened for a decade though. It's just a very small empty space that contained an old gas line valve, I think. Maurice couldn't have known it was there.'

Santino leaned back down to look. 'Yes, but if you sit here, where you say that Maurice would sit, you can see that the carpet runner lifts slightly in that spot. If he sat here long enough, he probably would have noticed it and maybe checked it out.'

Arnya moved forward and lifted the section of carpet that covered the area. 'There's a trap door. Can we roll this carpet up from the end?' she asked Father Kelly.

'Yes, of course.' The priest made his way to the front of the pews where the runner began. 'I really don't know what to say. I had no idea that Maurice even…'

'Maurice didn't want anyone to know what he was hiding, Father,' Santino reassured him. 'You couldn't have known what he was thinking.'

The priest rolled the runner past Arnya. 'That should do it,' he said, pulling it out of the way.

Santino went around to the other side of the trap door. There was a small metal ring indented into the wood on top. He pulled it hard. Beneath the door it was pitch black. Santino got out his phone. 'My torch isn't very good on this.'

'Hang on, I've got a torch in the back,' Father Kelly said. He headed to his apartment.

When he was gone, Arnya sat on the pew. 'I'm feeling nervous about this, Santino. As much as I want to know what the hell is going on, I'm terrified at the same time.'

Santino moved back, crouched and resting on his haunches. He hadn't even stopped to check how she was doing.

He could see that she was nervous and on edge. The weight of knowing that she might not make it through this was eating away at her. No matter how much she pushed on and focussed on finding out the truth, he knew she was hurting and scared. He wanted to comfort her and assure her that she would be fine, but she was smarter than that. It would be a hollow thing to say. All he could do was acknowledge how she was feeling. 'I'm so sorry that you are in the middle of all of this, Arnya. It's so damn unfair and you don't deserve it.'

A tear ran down her cheek and she wiped it away as fast as it had appeared.

Watching her try to hide her pain wounded him. They needed to see this through, but he also wanted her to have the chance to come to terms with all they had uncovered and what that meant for her. If he'd been in the same position, he wasn't sure he'd be able to hold himself together the way that she was. 'I know there's nothing I can say that will make any of this better, but what I can tell you is that I'll be with you through whatever comes our way, no matter what happens.'

'I'm just not ready to go yet.' She said. Her voice was husky and low. 'I want more time. I want more everything. Kids, a house, maybe even a dog, who knows.'

She laughed at the end, but it was hollow and pained. 'I still can't get my head around why anyone would do something like this, no matter what the reason. There are other ways to make money. Why kill a whole bunch of innocent people?'

Santino tried to answer gently. 'That's the thing, Arnya, you'll never be able to understand such evil. How could you accept any explanation, no matter what it is? For Fitzgerald, there had to be a massive payday somewhere along the line. But I think that the deaths are what went wrong. I don't think they were part of the plan.'

Arnya turned her tear-streaked face from Father Kelly as he appeared with a torch in hand, flicking it on and off to check the batteries. He handed it to Santino.

Santino took it. 'Thanks, Father.'

Arnya wiped her face on her sleeve and knelt at the edge of the opening as Santino turned on the torch. The space was no more than two metres by three metres and about seven feet deep. The sides were crumbling stone and the bottom was a mix of dirt and rubble with a gas valve poking through.

Santino shone the light into the corner and held it there, fixed on something. From where he was, it looked like a bag or case. 'Father, can you come over here?'

Father Kelly came closer. He crouched down and leaned over the opening to look inside.

'Does that look like the item Maurice had with him that night?' Santino asked.

The priest leaned in further and squinted. 'It's hard to tell.'

'I'll go down,' Arnya volunteered. 'I'm the smallest, it'll be easier for me.'

Santino looked over at her. 'You don't have to do that, I can go.'

Arnya cut him off before he could say anything else. 'Santino, I'm doing this. Just let me do it, please.'

Santino held her determined eyes for a moment, before standing up. 'Okay, but take it slow. It's rocky and dusty down there.' He flashed the torch against the far wall. 'There's two metal pegs set into the wall, make sure you use them.'

Arnya moved to the edge of the opening. She put her left foot on one of the rusty pegs and braced her right leg against the other wall. She lowered herself in and then went down to the remaining peg. When she was close enough, she let go and landed on the dirt bottom.

Santino shone the torch at the package in the corner. 'Can you have a look at what that is? Don't pick it up. Just see if you can look inside.'

Arnya gently pulled at the bag. 'Okay, well it looks like an army green canvas rucksack.' She pulled at the top flap and flipped it over. 'Inside, there's a box. It's metal, I think.'

'Okay, can you move it toward you and see how heavy it is?' Santino said.

Reaching for the strap, Arnya gently inched the bag toward her. 'It's not very heavy at all,' she called up to them.

'Can you pick it up and lift it to me?'

Arnya picked up the bag and held it up for Santino to see. 'It's pretty light. I can pass it up to you.'

Santino shifted on his knees and dropped lower, leaning into the cavity. Father Kelly went around to the other side, but stopped. His eyes went to the front of the church and the side entrance.

'What is it, Father?' Santino asked.

The priest was still watching the door. 'I heard something. It sounded like voices.'

Santino turned back to Arnya. 'Okay, ready? We need to hurry.' He reached down and held out his hand to her.

Bracing herself on the sides of the pit, she reached up and took his arm. She placed both feet on one of the two rusty steel pegs and it snapped suddenly. Arnya fell to the ground, her hip landing heavily on the gas main valve.

'Arnya, shit! Are you okay?'

Arnya pulled herself up. 'I'm okay,' she said through gritted teeth.

'Sorry for swearing father,' Santino apologised, but Father Kelly's attention was on the voices outside.

Clutching the canvas bag and grimacing with pain, Arnya again reached for Santino's outstretched hand. With the first peg gone, he leaned in as far as he could reach. He wrapped his hand around her forearm and pulled her towards him.

Santino rose awkwardly to his knees and then his feet, gripping Arnya's arm as she emerged from the darkness.

Father Kelly went to the front of the church and checked the door. He locked it and pressed his ear against it before returning.

Arnya handed the bag to Santino and took out the metal box. Underneath it was a set of three notebooks, bound together with a cotton tie. He set the box on the floor and took the notebooks out, pulling the tie to release them from each other. He opened the first one and scanned the pages. 'It looks like notes and some dated entries.'

Arnya reached over, took the second notebook and flicked through it. 'This one is the same, but there's also a lot of numbers and diagrams. What dates have you got on that one?'

Santino flipped back to the front page. 'Starts at the fifth of April, 1983, and ends,' he flipped through to the final page, 'ends on eighteenth of December, 1987, so just under four years.'

'This one starts at January 1981 and ends '83, so this one's the first one, I'd say.'

Santino picked up the final notebook and checked the entries. 'This one's the last then. 1988 to 1992.'

Santino put down the notebook and took the keys from his pocket. Picking up the box, he hesitated and looked up at Arnya. He gave her a look that reminded her without words that no matter what they found, he would be at her side. He opened the padlock and turned it around for her to see.

Inside was a single item, a mobile phone. He picked it up. 'It's an old-style iPhone. Probably one of the early ones, looking at it.' He looked at Father Kelly. 'Maurice must have placed it here under the church that night, while you were looking for the beads.'

Santino's phone began ringing in his pocket. 'Santino,' he answered.

Robert James was on the other end. 'I think I have something, can you come to my place as soon as you can?'

'What is it?' Santino asked.

'I don't want to talk on the phone, I think someone's been watching me. But it's important. Meet me at my place, I'm heading there now.'

'We're in the middle of something here, Robert, but we'll head over as soon as we can.'

'I'm really starting to get freaked out with all this, Santino,' Robert said. 'Shit's really messed up. Have you got anything new?'

Before Santino could answer, there was a loud noise at the front of the church. Father Kelly hurried to the entrance doors to check.

Santino watched the priest while he spoke to Robert. 'We've found Maurice's stash, all his notes. I think we're finally closing in on the truth. I need to call Harry first, but I'll explain when I get to your place. And try to stay out of sight, Robert.'

'Don't call Harry yet, Santino. What I have involves him too. Just get to my place as soon as you can.'

Santino hung up the phone as Arnya gasped. The doors to the church flew open and Fitzgerald's men entered. Chimney punched Father Kelly hard in the jaw sending him backwards on his feet before crashing to the ground.

'Fuck, get down,' Santino whispered. He pulled her to the floor as Chimney's offsider moved to the back of the church and checked the door.

'Father Kelly's hurt,' Arnya whispered. 'We need to get him help.'

Santino sent Harry Bryant a text message.

Get cars and an ambulance to St Cuthbert's Church. Now!

Arnya quietly put the items back in the bag as Fitzgerald's men searched the church.

'Come out, come out, wherever you are,' Chimney called. 'We know you're in here.'

Santino could see the priest lying on the floor. His face was bleeding and he made eye contact with Santino.

Reaching into his pocket, the priest slowly pulled out a set of keys and placed them beside him. He pointed to the exit door near the altar and mouthed the words, take my car.

Santino nodded. He and Arnya needed to make their move, but the men were close. He wouldn't be able to get to the door without passing them.

'We'll have to go through the front and go around,' Santino whispered.

Arnya closed her eyes and nodded.

'Ready?' Santino asked.

Chimney was checking the confessional boxes, while the other man opened the side door and looked outside.

'Go,' Santino said quietly.

Staying low, they made their way to Father Kelly. His face was bleeding badly and his eye already swelling. 'Help is on the way,' Santino whispered.

'God speed and God bless you both,' Father Kelly replied.

Santino grabbed the keys and headed for the doors with Arnya at his side. He could already hear the loud pounding of the men's feet as they gave chase.

By the time Santino and Arnya reached Father Kelly's car, the men were close. Chimney fired a shot, but it missed. The second shot didn't.

Santino got into the car, his shoulder already streaming blood. He started the engine and took off, leaving Chimney and the other man standing in a haze of churned up dust.

'Jesus, Santino, you're bleeding,' Arnya shouted. She searched the back seat, finding a jacket to drape over his shoulder to soak up the blood.

Santino ignored her concern. 'We need to get an old iPhone charger,' he said. 'Maurice's phone looks like a first-generation iPhone and we need the charger for it.'

'No. We need to get you to a hospital!' Her tone was firm.

Santino turned his eyes on her. 'It's just a graze, I'm telling you. It didn't penetrate muscle or bone. We need to get a charger.'

Arnya's eyes were wide. 'You're bleeding everywhere. You need a doctor.'

Santino accelerated. 'Arnya, I know gunshot wounds and this is not serious. I'll wrap it when we get to Robert's and he can have a look at it too if that makes you feel better, but right now, we need a charger. Those guys will keep coming for us and next time, they might not miss. We got lucky back there.'

Arnya sank back into her seat, accepting his plan. 'Where the hell do we find an old phone charger these days? Do they even still make them?'

'The only place I can think of is a pawn shop. There's one on Range Road, close to Robert's place, we can grab it on the way,' Santino said.

'Why are we even going to Robert's? What did he say?' Arnya asked.

'He said he had something, but he thought he was being watched and didn't want to talk too much on the phone. I'm worried though. He said not to call Harry. That he's somehow involved.'

'Harry Bryant?' She sat forward. 'Do you believe it?'

Santino hesitated. 'I don't want to.' The very thought made him feel ill. 'Why would Harry start this investigation if he was somehow involved?'

Arnya didn't answer. She stared out the window, unsure if her instincts had been off yet again with Harry Bryant. She had been convinced he was one of the good guys.

'But I've been blindsided by people I've trusted before. Where Fitzgerald is concerned, anything is possible. He digs and he digs. Not everyone who works for him is paid off. Some of them are blackmailed or threatened and their families are threatened.'

'He could have it wrong, Santino. Robert could be wrong,' Arnya insisted.

Santino shrugged. He feared he didn't know anything anymore. 'Robert's heading home, so we'll meet him there. It'll be a safer place for us to get the phone plugged in and see what's on it anyway.'

Arnya wrapped her arms around herself. 'I hope Father Kelly is okay.'

'The ambulance will have taken care of him and hopefully Harry sent police.'

'Are we safe anywhere?' Arnya asked. 'It seems like they can find us wherever we go.'

Santino checked his rear-view mirror. 'If we're lucky, we got enough of a head start that they won't know which direction we took.' He pulled into a lane behind a store with a flashing Pawn Shop sign in the window.

'That looks a bit shady,' Arnya said, looking over her shoulder and then out the car windows. 'And it's open at night?'

'Stay here,' Santino said, hopping out. He pulled the jacket from his shoulder and put it on to hide the blood.

As he walked toward the entrance, he could feel blood running from the wound. He checked the street for any sign of Fitzgerald's men, or anyone else that might be looking for them.

Before entering the pawn shop, Santino took the cross from beneath his shirt and kissed it. 'If I ever ask for anything, Lord, this is it. Help us get this bastard.'

CHAPTER

18

While she waited in the darkness of the priest's car in the dimly lit lane behind the pawn shop, Arnya took out her phone and checked her messages. There were at least a dozen from her office and many more from numbers she didn't recognise. As she scrolled through the list, it occurred to her how completely insignificant it all felt now. Sitting outside a pawn shop in the middle of the night, trying to get an old power cable for a secret phone hidden by a murder victim in a church. Her life was completely unrecognisable from what it had been only a few weeks ago, or ever would be again, if she lived that long.

Arnya scrolled down the list of calls until she saw multiple missed calls from a familiar number. She dialled her voicemail and deleted message after message until she again heard the familiar but unsettling voice of her mentor, Arthur.

'Arnya, honey. I'm sorry I was a little short with you when we last spoke, please don't be upset. I need you to return my call. I want to talk and I need to see you. Please call me back as soon as you get this. There are things I need to tell you and I'm worried. Please, call me.'

Arnya hung up as Santino got back in the car, his arrival making her jump, pulling at her injured hip. She winced and made a sound.

Santino held up the charger and smiled. 'What's up? You have a strange look on your face,' he said.

She smiled back, deciding not to tell him about Arthur's message, or the pain. 'Nothing, just feeling jumpy and on edge, that's all.' She looked out her window and then out the back for any sign of Fitzgerald's men.

Santino started the car. 'We'll be careful on the road,' he assured her. 'And we can eat something at Robert's. We could both use some food and a drink. The next 24 hours will probably be even more crazy.'

Arnya tucked her phone back in her bag. Arthur's words replayed in her mind as they drove. What did he need to tell her and why was he trying so hard to speak with her?

She pushed the thoughts away. One battle at a time, she thought.

When they arrived at Robert's apartment building, he buzzed them in. He was waiting for them at the top of the stairs and greeted them with a wave, but even from that distance Arnya could see he was on edge. 'Come on up, I'll pour us a drink. God knows I could use one.'

Santino gestured for Arnya to go first, taking the bag of Maurice's things from her. 'We'd love a drink, Robert,' he said. 'Any chance you've got something to go with it? we're starving.'

They followed Robert inside and watched as he fumbled in his cupboard. 'Yeah, I think so.' He pulled out chips and salsa and a loaf of bread. 'There's some ham in the fridge, I think.'

Arnya took the phone from the bag Santino had put on the kitchen counter. 'Robert, can I plug this in?'

Robert looked up and pointed to a spot beneath a small side table in the living room. Arnya plugged it in and flicked the switch on, willing it to work. She wondered what the hell Maurice had put on it. In spite of the fact that she had no real belief in anything beyond science, she said a little prayer to the universe that whatever Maurice had given them would not only reveal the truth about what he had done but, more importantly, how they could undo it.

Robert fixed them a sandwich and poured some wine.

Santino gingerly checked the wound on his shoulder. It was still bleeding.

'Jesus Christ, Santino, what the fuck?' Robert exclaimed. He came around to have a look at the injury. 'You're lucky it's only a flesh wound, but it looks pretty bad. What happened?'

'Fitzgerald's men,' Santino said.

Robert opened a cupboard and handed Santino a clean bandage and antiseptic. Santino took it and slipped his arm from his shirt to wrap it.

Robert picked up his wine glass and leaned back against the sink.

'What's going on, Robert?' Santino asked as he wound the bandage. He could see Robert's hands were shaking slightly.

Arnya returned to the kitchen, momentarily pulled from her thoughts about the contents of the iPhone. The pain in her hip was radiating down her leg. She touched the spot where she had landed on the gas valve, feeling the swollen skin.

'I've been on edge all day,' Robert said. His brow was furrowed and his lips cracked. 'The office is out of control and I had to get out of there. We've got media camped outside and everyone's breathing down my neck.' He ran his hands through his hair and swallowed a large mouthful of wine.

'Take it easy, Robert' Santino said. 'You're going to give yourself a heart attack.'

Arnya went around to the other side of the kitchen counter. From what she had seen at her apartment, she feared Robert's jumpiness and shakes were being caused by more than just stress. 'It's alright Robert, we're all uneasy, but we're making headway. We're getting close,' she offered.

Santino pulled the notebooks from the bag. 'This is what I was telling you about on the phone. Maurice Stephens had been going to a local church over on Martin Place and the priest there said that, not long before he died, Maurice had paid him a visit late one night. He had a bag with him and he stashed it there under the floor in the church.'

Robert made sandwiches, cutting one in half and sliding it over to Arnya. He listened intently, saying nothing.

Arnya took it from him, looking him in the eyes. 'Thanks Robert, I really appreciate it.'

Robert held her gaze for a moment, but quickly shifted his attention back to finish the other sandwich.

'So, what do the books say? Anything of value?' Robert asked.

Arnya answered. 'That's what we're hoping to find out. We haven't had a chance to go through it all yet and we thought you might be able to help with some of the technical stuff in here. There's a lot of it.'

'Of course, what do you need?'

In spite of Robert's words and his hospitality, Arnya could still sense a building uneasiness about him. He was nervous and shifting on his feet. His phone vibrated on the counter behind him and he stepped away to answer it, apologising awkwardly.

Arnya picked up a notebook and began flicking through the pages. 'Some of these first entries look like university work, maybe while he was still studying or working through something?'

Santino moved closer and looked over her shoulder. 'Maybe. That stuff all looks like another language to me. This one though, this one's a bit later.' He opened another notebook and read from the entry.

'Every day that passes I know that time is drawing closer. People walk by me in the street, going about their days, their lives, with no idea that at any possible minute the unlucky ones will begin to fall. I prayed again last night as I always do. I went back to the church. Father Kelly assures me that God forgives those who repent, no matter what the crime, but I fear that this, what we have done, will not be forgivable, even in his eyes.'

He looked up at both Arnya and Robert, who had returned. Both were fixed on him, listening intently. Santino continued reading.

> 'Parker's making his threats, of course, as if anything that he could do would ever compare to the torture to be endured in eternal damnation. We have sinned, and like all those that we have sinned against and committed to their deaths, we too will pay with our souls, one way or another.'

Santino flicked to another page. 'There's some more like this, but then pages of just rambling. His mind sounds really scattered in some of it.'

Robert poured himself a scotch and downed half in one gulp. 'That's heavy shit. What the hell have they done?' He paced the length of the kitchen, sweat forming at his temples. 'This is too much, I just want out. You dance with the Devil and...'

'But it's exactly what we need, Robert. Proof of Fitzgerald's involvement,' Santino said.

Robert's phone vibrated on the counter in the corner. 'Sorry, I have to get this.' He went down the hallway, leaving Arnya and Santino alone.

'He doesn't look well,' Santino said, keeping his voice low.

'I know. I was going to tell you earlier that he got a call when we were at my apartment and I could hear that he was angry. I also saw him taking something, cocaine I think. There's something going on. His phone is going off all the time.'

Arnya moved over to the side table to see if the old iPhone had turned on yet. It hadn't. It's small, dark screen filled her with dread.

Robert returned from his call, his face flushed and his eyes darting.

'Jesus, Robert, what's going on? What's got you so rattled? And don't tell me it's just work. We know each other better than that,' Santino said.

Robert drank the last of the scotch and put his hands on the kitchen bench. Leaning forward, he rocked back and forth with his head bowed. Santino's gut tensed in response. 'Robert, tell me what's going on.'

'It's completely fucked, Santino. I'm sorry. I totally screwed up and now I'm in it.'

Arnya dropped the notebook she was holding. Her eyes locked first onto Robert and then on the apartment door as footsteps approached outside.

'Jesus, Robert, what have you done?' Santino demanded. 'Tell me!'

Parker Fitzgerald was inside Robert's apartment. He eyed Robert who was now cowering in the corner of the kitchen. A smug smile moved over Fitzgerald's fat, red face before his eyes shifted to Arnya and then Santino.

'Well, Detective, we meet again. We'll have to stop this, or people will start to talk about us.'

Santino moved back, shielding Arnya from Fitzgerald's glare. 'Fuck off, Fitzgerald. The only thing people will be talking about is you being a murdering son of a bitch.'

Arnya wasn't going to stay quiet. 'You've had people following us this whole time. Do you know your men even punched a defenceless priest and left him bleeding on the floor? What do you want from us?'

Parker's smile widened. 'What do I want? I think you know the answer to that.' He moved to the kitchen, going around to where Robert had been standing. He picked up the wine bottle and poured a glass. Lifting it to his nose, he inhaled and took a sip. 'This is really shit wine, Robert. You filthy cheapskate. I don't think the City is paying you enough. Oh wait, maybe it's all those gambling debts that are drying up your resources.' He tapped his chin and grinned. 'Or, maybe it's that little cocaine habit you seem to have lost your hold on. That must be costing you a few bucks too, I suppose.'

Robert's eyes were bloodshot and his jaw clenched tight. He looked like he might lunge at Fitzgerald. His three men who were standing nearby, readied themselves.

Fitzgerald groaned. 'Come on now, Robert, we're all friends here, aren't we? Surely it's better to get all your secrets out in the open. Don't you think it's time? That way you can get the help you need. After all, your friend, Detective Santino here, would have found out sooner or later anyway. He's like that, isn't he? Like a dog with a bone, always snooping around things that are none of his business and making himself a nuisance. He just won't let go.' Fitzgerald winked at Arnya as he made the final remark.

Arnya looked back at Robert. He was staring blankly at the kitchen wall behind them.

Santino moved his hand to his hip, closer to his holster.

The move caused Fitzgerald to laugh. 'Really, Santino? Come on.' He gestured for Chimney to take the gun.

'So, are you here to kill us all now?' Santino spat. 'If you are, then you're even more stupid than I gave you credit for. Not even you could get away with something like that.'

Fitzgerald lit up a cigar, blowing smoke high into the air above them. 'Kill you? What do you take me for? I'm a businessman, not a hitman. I just want what's mine, that's all. Oh, and to make sure that you're dealt with for good. Nothing more and nothing less.' He motioned to one of his men who moved in close behind Arnya.'

Santino pushed the notebooks toward him. 'Here, this is what you came for, isn't it? They're all yours, take them.'

Fitzgerald picked up the books. 'Now, that's what I like to hear.' He turned to Arnya. 'You must mean something to him sweetheart, or perhaps you're great in the sack.'

Arnya narrowed her eyes but didn't give him the satisfaction of making her squirm.

He opened the top notebook and flicked through the pages. 'Fucking Maurice. For a genius, he was literally an imbecile when it came to anything outside of his little bubble.'

'Did you really have to kill him?' Arnya demanded. 'Surely no one would have believed what he was saying anyway. He was a drunk, wasn't he?'

'Yes, well I let it go at first. I warned him again and again and gave him chance after chance, but he harped on about telling the truth, whatever the hell that is, and all this going to Hell bullshit. It's sad really. People consumed by guilt-driven religious crap. In the end, there was nothing else I could do. He really left me no other option.'

'You're not going to let us go, are you? You're a fucking liar and murderer.' Arnya was shouting. She shook her head slowly, mocking him. 'You are a fucking coward.'

Fitzgerald tapped his chin. 'Well now, I'm going to let him go, but not you, that wouldn't work. You see, I need to let him go.' He pointed to Santino. 'I need him, so that then he can be arrested for trying to kill me and for your murder. Robert here will attest to the crime, won't you Robert?'

Robert didn't move.

Fitzgerald leaned in and spoke to Arnya in a low voice. 'He doesn't really have a choice in the matter, but I won't bore you with all the petty details. Basically, Robert will do as I tell him to do. You are the bait, or victim if you like, and Santino here is the Detective turned killer. They're already looking for him after he attacked me. I even have the wounds to prove it.' He lifted his shirt and showed a bandage across his stomach. 'He stabbed me, the crazy son of a bitch.'

Fitzgerald's phone sounded in his pocket. He lifted it to read the message and then gestured to one of his men.

'Just tell me why?' Arnya asked. 'What was it all for? Why are all these people dying?'

Fitzgerald inhaled deeply and let the air out in a rush, as if telling the story was too much effort. 'Now, that's the 50-million-dollar question,' he said. 'However, I have other players yet to enter the game and at least one that I'm expecting soon. You see, they all need to face the consequences of choices made. If you're going to play with the big boys, you better make damn sure that you're all in. No developing a sudden conscience or some higher moral compass just as things get interesting. Isn't that right, Robert?'

Robert stayed silent, his eyes now on the floor.

Fitzgerald blew a heavy stream of smoke into the air. 'Now we wait.'

CHAPTER

19

Robert's apartment was silent. Arnya clenched her teeth, trying to keep the rage inside her at bay as she watched Fitzgerald inhaling his foul cigar. He let slow streams of thick smoke escape through pursed lips and whirl into the air above them. He checked his phone and rested against the kitchen bench, a smug grin across his ruddy face. He pointed his finger at Arnya like she was a game show contestant being chosen to play along.

He had refused to answer her about why people were dying, and even as the question had left her mouth, Arnya wondered why she had bothered to ask it. But now he seemed to want to talk.

'While I wouldn't usually bother answering your trivial and unimportant questions, Professor, I do love a good story, but the truth is, I actually don't have an answer for that. Maurice is the only one who could have answered that question and he's no longer with us, as you know.' He said it as if he had given it great thought.

'The truth?' Arnya spat. 'You wouldn't know the truth if it walked up to you and introduced itself.'

Fitzgerald laughed again, clearly amused by her statement. 'Okay, well then,' he offered. 'Let's just say that what we were doing didn't go the way we originally planned.'

A voice came from behind them in the hallway leading to the apartment's door. 'No, it didn't go to plan. But I can tell you the truth. I want to tell you because you deserve to know.' Arnya swung around, her body stiffening at the sound and at the sight of a familiar face. She felt momentarily faint.

Arthur, her mentor and friend, walked over to her and took her shaking hands. 'I'm so very sorry my darling. I didn't want you having any part in this.'

Arnya's face reddened and her eyes fixed with disbelief on the man she once admired more than anyone else in the world. 'I don't understand, Arthur.' The words came out with a stammer and she pulled away. 'What is this?' She could hear the shaking in her voice, threatening to unleash a flood of shock and emotion.

'I'd like to know that myself,' Fitzgerald interrupted. 'I think you forgot to tell her that you had a hand in this enterprise. I'm so glad you were able to make it to our party so that she could know the truth finally. It was unfair to keep her in the dark right until the end.'

Arthur kept his eyes on Arnya, ignoring Fitzgerald in the background. She looked past his shoulder at Santino who was sitting awkwardly on the other stool, almost half on it and half off as if he might try to launch at any second.

'All of this happened a long time ago, Arnya. It was a lifetime ago. No one could have predicted that this would be the outcome. I had opened my clinic in Boston, you remember the one? Where your mother and father would bring you when you were little.'

Arnya refused to answer. She didn't want to look at him or even acknowledge whatever excuse or explanation he was about to give.

Arthur continued. 'It was early days in IVF research then and I was running my new practice. Your mother and father were very dear to me, you know that. When they confided in me that they were unable to conceive, your father and I decided to do a little research into the new technologies that were available. We contacted the universities that were pioneering the technology, and when IVF really got up and running, I began offering it to my patients, your mother being one of them.'

She turned her eyes to him. 'So, they came to you for the treatment?' she asked.

Arthur's face softened. 'And I was happy to help. There were some failed attempts, and then finally, you, the miracle they had prayed for.'

'But that doesn't explain anything about what's going on now, Arthur.' Arnya couldn't believe he was attempting to paint himself as some kind of miracle maker. 'Why are all these people dying? Did you do something? Please don't tell me that you're actually a part of this.'

Arthur reached for her and tried to squeeze her hand. He looked over at Fitzgerald. 'I didn't know this would happen, Arnya. I was foolish, I admit, but it was never meant to happen this way.'

Arnya snatched her hands away from him. 'Then tell me how it was supposed to happen, God damn you. Tell us the truth, for once, please, just tell us the fucking truth.'

Arthur stepped back and clasped his hands together in front of him. 'He turned from her and took a few steps away. 'My clinic was busy, but financially I had fallen on hard times. I tried my very best. I did everything that I could for the people in my community, my patients, but running a business that way was to my own financial detriment. It was only a matter of time before I would have had to close the doors and…'

'That's where I came in,' Fitzgerald finished. 'I made him an offer he couldn't refuse and he took it. And he wasn't the only one, I can tell you that. Plenty more accepted, but I only invited your friends to this party.'

'An offer?' Santino said. 'An offer to kill millions?'

Fitzgerald scoffed. 'You really are a complete simpleton, aren't you, Santino?' He picked up the notebooks on the counter and held them up. 'Maurice was a fucking genius, you know that much, don't you? He could understand science and the world in ways that no one else could.' He laughed, shaking his head. 'I was in awe of him once. I was actually quite jealous of that gigantic brain that could literally unravel anything you put in front of him. It's funny to think about it now, but we were completely drunk the night we came up with the plan. My old man had threatened to cut me off, again, if I didn't get my act together and Maurice didn't have any real family to speak of, so we figured, what did we really have to lose? We sat up all night working out how we could somehow set in motion a sickness or a disease that we could set loose. The idea, and it was a brilliant one, was to put something out there, wait for people to fall ill and then be ready with the treatment, or even better, a cure. A cure that no one else would have access to.' He smiled again at the memory of their brilliance. 'Maurice thought that if there was an illness that we could create, something that could be triggered by us, we could be at the ready with drugs for the treatment and eventually, when we'd made our money, the cure. It really was genius. Heroes and billionaires and winners of the Nobel prize.'

Arnya stared in disbelief. 'Are you saying that you intentionally created some sort of deadly illness just so that you could make money from drugs to treat it?'

Santino exhaled and closed his eyes. 'That's exactly what he's saying. It was always about the money.'

Fitzgerald shook his head. 'Do you honestly think that this is the first time that something like this has been done by industries to make money? You're all so fucking naive. Every single thing that you buy, from whitegoods to cars, is built to break down so that billions can be made through parts and fixing them. The drugs you buy, the bullshit you buy into, generates billions in revenue every single year. We don't want people to get better or be cured. We don't want them to buy goods that last forever. We want them to keep buying goods and drugs and the *dream* of being cured. And so do you.'

'So do we?' Arnya said. Her tone was venomous.

'Of course you do. Climb down from that high horse. Without money generated from treatments and other drugs, the government purse would fall in a heap. Even you, Professor Sloane, can surely understand that. You participate in it every day.'

'How dare you?' Arnya's words came out through clenched teeth. Her face was red and her eyes wild.

Fitzgerald suddenly pounded both fists on the kitchen bench. 'We didn't set out to kill anyone, let's get that straight. I'm not a fucking monster!'

Arnya and Santino gasped in unison, Arnya's eyes wide with disbelief.

'Whatever you think, I didn't want anyone dead,' Fitzgerald insisted. 'As I said, it was just drunken talk at first, a way to show my father and all the other assholes who thought they were better than us. But over the next few weeks and months, the idea started to really sink in. The timing was perfect because my father was also pushing me to take something on to prove to him that I was getting my act together. He decided that the very small IVF market at the time was a good starting place. And it was. It was also the perfect opportunity to test our idea, and Maurice and I both knew it.'

Tears had begun to fall from Arnya's eyes. 'It doesn't matter how you sugar coat it, or how many excuses you try to make. People are dying you son of a bitch, they're fucking dying.'

Fitzgerald thumped the bench again, the force startling them all, including Robert who was still standing silently in the corner. 'Don't you think I know that, you stupid bitch? I can see what's going on, but that's all on Maurice. He fucked it up and whatever he did,' he pointed to the window, his lips pulled back in a snarl and his eyes narrowed, 'what's happening out there is the result.'

'Then why kill him?' Santino asked. 'Why kill the only man who truly knew what it was that had been done to create this and the only one who might have been able to stop it?'

Arthur cut in. 'Because he was going to expose us all and we couldn't… we can't… take that chance.'

CHAPTER

20

Santino didn't take his eyes from Arnya. He knew that the revelation of Arthur's involvement would have shattered her and he could see she was shaking uncontrollably. But right now, they needed to find a way out of this or they would both be dead.

Arthur was still trying to explain, but it was no use. 'At the time, no one was dying,' he said, his voice almost pleading for understanding. 'There weren't even any signs of illness and none of us truly believed Maurice's dire predictions. He was a drunk and he'd completely lost his grip on reality. We thought he had simply become delusional and irrational. I had wiped my hands of it and bowed out a long time ago.' He turned to Fitzgerald. 'When the plan originally failed, I told you, I told you both that I wanted nothing more to do with it. It was a mistake and I was relieved when it all just fell in a heap.'

Arthur turned his attention back to Arnya. 'I warned you not to involve yourself in this. I tried to keep you out of it. You must understand, Maurice was ranting and incoherent. We had all agreed to keep silent, no matter what the outcome, for the safety of everyone, including those who had been a part of the experiment, but Maurice had broken that pact.'

'Part of the *experiment*?' Santino hissed. 'So, you want us to believe that you were trying to protect who knows how many innocent lives that had been used as an experiment without their knowledge or consent?' He glared at Arthur.

Arthur put his palms together as if he was praying. His tone was desperate. 'We couldn't have known what was coming, dear Arnya, don't you see? I swear it. On your father, God rest his soul, I swear it.' Arthur shook his head and turned toward the window.

'On my father? How dare you even say his name?' Arnya almost spat the words in his direction. 'I'm glad my father isn't here to see this, Arthur, it would have killed him to see you for who you really are. I'm glad he never had to witness it the way that I'm having to.'

'I'm so very sorry, darling. I really am.' Arthur dropped his head, but kept his eyes on Arnya. 'I was stupid and consumed with my own circumstances. I convinced myself that the outcome of being able to stay in business and help many more people would far outweigh what we had done, but it was foolish and greedy.'

Arthur's head was still bowed as he moved his eyes to Santino. 'Maurice eventually realised that whatever he had done - whatever signs he was looking for in these people - didn't unfold as they were meant to. He knew that he had made a mistake and the outcome might be fatal instead of a health condition the company could make money from.'

Santino had no words. To hear it said like that, out loud as if it was somehow reasonable, made his head feel as if it might explode.

'You're all mad men,' Arnya shouted. 'You're actually fucking crazy.'

Arthur moved toward her, reaching out for her again. She pulled back and refused his touch. 'I know that everyone is panicking,' Arthur said, 'but I can assure you, it's only a select few clinics that were used. Some of them knew what was going on and there were a few that didn't. We're talking a few thousand people at the most. Everyone else is completely safe.'

Arnya covered her ears and closed her eyes. She couldn't bear to hear another word or see his face. 'Can you hear yourself? Are you actually listening to what you're saying? Is the fact that thousands of innocent sons, daughters, sisters, brothers or friends, are going to die, supposed to make us feel better?' Her voice was uneven and on the verge of shouting again. 'Does that make *you* feel better about all of this, Arthur?'

Arthur shook his head. 'No, of course not, but I need you to understand. The science was new at the time. We didn't even know if these kids would survive at all, let alone long-term. It was already a human experiment. It didn't seem so far-fetched to add a new element to it. Arnya, you're naive if you think that there aren't already many cures out there for illnesses that are kept secret because the drugs they provide for those illnesses are a multi-billion-dollar industry, as Parker said. If you fixed that problem, then the money goes with it. It's how the world turns.'

Arnya stood up, exasperation filling her. One of Fitzgerald's men stepped closer in response.

Santino clapped his hands together in loud slaps of skin on skin. 'So, you killed off Maurice to shut him up and hoped that it would all go away, did you? Well done. I hope you're not God-fearing men, any of you, because I'd say that your judgement day will be coming. And a burning Hell awaits. I'm sure of that.'

Robert looked up at Arnya, 'I'm so sorry.' He mouthed the words to her, his eyes filling.

'Sorry?' she shouted back. 'You're sorry?' She felt as if there was a fire burning her from the inside out. She stared at Robert, sick to her stomach that only a short time ago she had been contemplating the possibility of reigniting a connection with him, a future even.

She glared at Arthur again. 'You are all pure evil and nothing less.'

Fitzgerald shouted, his voice strained. 'Well, evil or not sweetheart, it is what it is. Maurice fucked up, a few people are dead, and now all of this has to be cleaned up, yet again, by me. Pretty soon they'll stop dying and everything will go back to normal. Santino will be in the big house, and this fucking nightmare will all be over, once and for all. Oh, and I'll make sure to go and piss on Maurice's grave too, just for old time's sake.'

Arthur stepped forward. 'Leave Arnya to me, Parker. I'll make sure she understands and keeps her mouth shut. She won't talk, I can promise you that.'

Arnya felt the heat inside her intensify. She didn't want Arthur speaking for her or pretending to protect her. She would rather die than accept anything from such a murdering, soulless creature. She looked at Santino. He was waiting for Fitzgerald's answer.

'Have I ever struck you as a careless man, Arthur? The kind of man that takes chances and leaves loose ends?' He laughed and pointed at Maurice's notebooks. 'I may have been stupid enough to leave something like that in the past, but I won't make that mistake again.'

Arthur pushed harder, his voice firm. 'Parker, I'll handle it. I've known her since she was born. She knows what's at stake and she'll stay quiet. I'll ship her off to Australia or Germany or somewhere remote, under another name if it'll make you feel better.'

'Just let her go, Parker, for fuck's sake,' Robert spat.

Parker spun around to look at him. 'Oh, so now you've got something to say, have you? Found that gutless tongue that we've all come to know and love?' He pulled a pistol from the back of his pants and pressed it against Robert's forehead.

Robert lifted his hands in defence. 'Okay, okay, I'm sorry. Please!'

Santino launched from his stool, but was quickly caught by two of Fitzgerald's men. 'Don't be a hero, Santino. Jesus, haven't you had enough of playing the good guy?' Fitzgerald said, waving him away.

'That's the difference between us, Fitzgerald. I don't have to play the good guy. You know, I remember your father at your murder trial, talking to the lawyer outside the court. He talked non-stop about what a complete fuck-up and disappointment you were to him and how he wished he'd made your mother get rid of you like he planned to. Said that all her bawling had made him drop his guard, but he should have made sure it was done. You were nothing but an unwanted screw-up then and you're still one now.'

Fitzgerald moved swiftly around to the other side of the counter. 'Is that right, tough little Detective? You know, I have so many contacts on the inside, I'm going to make sure that every day for the rest of your miserable life is filled with pain - unimaginable pain - so even you, the fucking hero, will wish you were dead.'

'Parker, you've got what you came for,' Arthur yelled. He pointed at the notebooks. 'There's no trail left now and nothing that leads back to you. It ends here, I assure you. Arnya will not say anything.'

Fitzgerald moved towards Arnya. 'C'mon Arthur, we both know that's not how this goes. You and the cry baby Medical Examiner over there are in this as deep as I am. Without these two, there's no leverage. He has to kill her. That's the only way and you know it. It's the only way we all get out of here clean.'

Arthur stepped in front of him to shield Arnya. 'I'm not asking for your permission. You will not hurt her, or I will tell the story myself. Find another way.'

'You're not asking?' Fitzgerald's voice was low and guttural like the sound a dog would make when warning off an approaching rival.

Santino pulled against the men holding his arms, wrestling to get free, but Fitzgerald's men held tight.

Fitzgerald put the gun to Arthur's head and cocked it. 'Move out of my fucking way old man.'

Arthur stood firm, his eyes bulging and the veins in his neck throbbing. The room seemed to freeze as if time itself had paused. Heavy breathing and thudding heartbeats were the only sounds. Fitzgerald took a step closer. Arnya flinched, but it was Robert who moved first. He seized the opportunity and lunged across the counter, pulling Fitzgerald to the floor.

As one of Fitzgerald's men rushed to his aid, Arnya dropped to the ground and scrambled into the living room. She could see Santino pulling violently against the arms of the other captor. Santino broke free and grabbed his gun. With two shots, he hit both of Fitzgerald's men. He moved quickly to Arnya, pulling her toward the door. The scuffle continued behind them. When they reached the stairs outside the apartment, there was another gunshot.

Arnya stopped on the first step. 'Arnya, don't!' Santino said, but she moved swiftly and ran back into the apartment. Santino climbed back up, taking two stairs at a time, but ducked to the side of the doorway when another shot rang out.

'Arnya!' he called through the partially open doorway, trying to muffle the sound of his voice. There was movement and voices inside – and then silence. Santino ducked down and peered through the opening. On the other side of the room, near the kitchen, Arthur was lying on the floor. Parker was on top of him, holding him down. Nearby, Robert was face down on the kitchen tiles, limp and bleeding badly from a gunshot wound to his chest. The third man – Parker's muscle - was unmoving beside him but Santino couldn't see Arnya.

'Shit,' he muttered. Santino took a small step into the apartment and pulled the door in front of him. From here, he could see Arnya as she crawled towards the table in the living room. He watched as she quietly disconnected the phone from the power socket and headed towards him.

Fitzgerald also caught sight of her. He stood up awkwardly and swung around in her direction. Lunging like an animal taking its prey, he brought her to the ground.

Santino rushed at them. He grabbed Fitzgerald from behind, yanking him backwards as hard as he could, causing his shoulder wound to rip open. He felt the warmth as it tore and blood gushed down his arm through the bandage.

Fitzgerald groaned and landed heavily on top of Santino. As the pair wrestled, Arnya pulled herself up using the sofa and reached quickly for the gun on the floor beside Arthur. It was almost in her hand when one of Fitzgerald's men wrapped his arm around her neck.

Watching her struggle, Santino let his grip on Fitzgerald loosen. 'Let her go, man,' he demanded, 'just let her go.' His eyes were wide and fixed on the man. 'Let her fucking go!'

Fitzgerald got up, giving Santino a kick to the ribs. 'That's the trouble with you, Santino, you always think you're gonna come out on top, but not this time.' He panted and wiped at the blood running down his chin.

Santino sat up, feeling the burn in his side from the kick. Pain shot through him when he inhaled. 'It doesn't matter what you do, Fitzgerald, or how this plays out, you'll get what's coming to you. I won't stop, you know I won't.'

Fitzgerald laughed. He was breathing heavily and red-faced. 'Tell yourself whatever you need to, Santino. If that helps you sleep at night when you're cowering in the corner of your cold, lonely cell for the next 50 years, say whatever you must to get you through those long nights.'

He left Santino on the floor and went back to the kitchen. Taking in the chaos he had brought about, Parker

Fitzgerald drank the last of the wine from a glass on the kitchen counter.

Arnya pulled against the hands of her captor and kicked backwards, hard. She managed to connect with his shin, causing the man to groan in pain. But Arnya knew she couldn't inflict enough damage to free herself. She looked at Santino on the floor. She knew it was stupid to come back in. She should have left the phone. She had sealed their fate and the fate of many others in one stupid ill-considered move.

'Oh honey.' Fitzgerald came over to stroke her face. 'It'll all be over soon.' He nodded at his henchman who dragged Arnya to the sofa and pushed her down. 'Now this is the fun part. We're going to need you for this, Santino.'

The thug went over to Santino and grabbed him by his bleeding arm. He dragged him over to the sofa to stand over Arnya. 'Now you're going to shoot her,' Fitzgerald said. He pointed the gun at Arnya. 'We'll, actually, I'm going to shoot her, but you're going to put your hand on the gun so we can get some evidence and all that jazz. You know the drill.'

Santino pulled back from the man's clutches, wincing as pain shot through him. Blood from his shoulder had soaked through the bandage and shirt. 'There's another way,' Santino said, breathless with pain. 'You can still have everything you want without killing her. Just hear me out.'

'Do I look like I'm in the mood to negotiate? It's fucking done.' Fitzgerald gestured to his man who had been joined by his sidekick. They were both bleeding. With one on each side, they held Santino steady and forced his hand on top of the gun Fitzgerald was pointing at Arnya.

Santino looked at Arnya's face. She refused to cry or plead. She sat still and rigid. She stared deep into Santino's eyes. The sound of the gun being cocked caused both of them to squeeze their eyes tight.

Tensing against the crippling pain in his shoulder, Santino pushed himself back, hard against the men, but to no avail. He watched as Arnya's eyelids relaxed and she let go. She didn't see the moment that Robert, wounded and enraged, set upon them, stabbing Parker in the shoulder with a kitchen knife and sending him to the ground.

The thugs momentarily loosened their grip enough for Santino to pull free. He hit one of them hard with the pistol grip as Robert plunged the knife into the chest of the other.

In a daze, Arnya felt for the phone in her pocket as Santino led her to the door. When she turned back to look, Robert was on the ground, with both of Fitzgerald's men on top of him. She looked over at Arthur, his vacant eyes stared back at her.

Feeling the urgent tug on her arm, she followed Santino down the stairs and out into the night. Before either of them could say a word, they were in the car, the engine revving, Santino with his foot hard on the accelerator. He gripped the wheel with one hand as his wounded shoulder caused his other arm to hang limp in his lap, still bleeding heavily.

'Are you okay?' he asked as the car sped from the apartment building. He looked over at her. 'Are you hurt?'

She was staring straight ahead. She nodded, holding the phone in her hand. 'I think so. I'm so sorry I went back in. I just needed…'

'It's okay, I know. We need to get somewhere safe and out of sight, and I need to get onto Harry Bryant.'

Arnya held up the phone, the charger still dangling from it. 'We need to find out what's on this. It didn't charge enough to even turn on. Either that or it's broken after all these years.'

'It better not be,' Santino said. 'It's all we have.'

CHAPTER

21

Santino headed away from Robert's apartment at speed. After a few minutes, he turned off the headlights and pulled in behind a darkened building. He checked that no one was following them. 'We need to find a safe place to go, somewhere out of sight,' he said.

Arnya looked out her window. The air outside had cooled and she shivered. 'Go to my office at the university. No one will be able to get in without a key code or a swipe card.'

Santino pulled back out onto the road. 'My phone is in the centre console, can you grab it for me? I need to call Harry.'

Arnya turned carefully, protecting her injured hip. She took out the phone and found Harry's number in the contacts. He answered on the first ring. 'Where the hell have you been, Santino? I've been chasing you down all day, and then that text to send an ambulance to the church. Fucking hell.'

'Harry, listen to me. We've just left Robert James' apartment. He lured us there and then tipped off Parker Fitzgerald and his goons.'

'Hang on, slow down. Robert James the Medical Examiner? Is he a part of this? And Fitzgerald, how do they even know each other?'

'I can't explain everything right now, Harry. Fitzgerald had an insane plan to kill Arnya and pin it on me. We've managed to get away, but they'll be looking for us. Everyone is looking for us by the sound of it. Everything leads back to the Maurice Stephens murder, like I told you, and now we have the proof. Maurice left some notebooks and a phone that was hidden at the local church he used to go to. Fitzgerald has the notebooks and he thinks that's all there is, but we have the phone.'

'What's on it?' Harry asked.

'We don't know yet. It's an old iPhone. We've managed to charge it a little at Robert's but we're in the car now.'

Arnya pressed the button on the phone. She stared at the screen, feeling acid rising to the back of her throat as she waited.

'Jesus, Santino, what the hell is this? Is Fitzgerald behind all of it? All these deaths, including Jason?' Harry demanded.

'Him and a few other players. Arnya's trying to turn the phone on now. I'll call you back as soon as I have more.'

'Where are you headed?'

Santino hesitated. 'I'd rather not say right now, Harry. There are too many people involved and we don't know who could be listening. Fitzgerald has eyes and ears everywhere. Right now, we can't trust anyone. I'll come back to you as soon as I have something solid that we can use.'

'For God's sake, stay safe and get back to me as soon as you can,' Harry urged. 'If this fucker has something to do with Jason's death, I'll kill him myself. I promise you.'

Arnya gestured to Santino. 'Harry, I have to go.' Santino hung up the phone.

'It's showing a little bit of charge, but it's still not turning on.' Arnya held Maurice's phone up for Santino to see, the disappointment etched on her face. 'We'll have to get it plugged back in. I hope to God it still works.'

'So do I,' Santino said. 'It has to.'

Arnya wondered if they would have any useful evidence even with the phone. Given Maurice's confused state at the time of his death, he could have put anything on the phone. Would anything he had to say be understandable and believable when pitted against powerful agencies all denying their involvement and spinning a different story?

She asked the question that neither of them wanted to contemplate. 'What if it doesn't give us anything?'

Santino turned a corner, wincing and exhaling from the pain in his shoulder. 'We cross that bridge when we come to it. If it doesn't work, or if there's nothing on there that's useful, we decide then how to proceed. No matter what, this won't be over. It can't be because Fitzgerald won't stop until we stop him. He won't stop chasing us and trying to destroy us.'

Arnya leaned over and gently pulled the top of his shirt back to look at his shoulder. 'This isn't looking great. There's a lot of blood. You need to see a doctor.'

Santino shrugged his arm to pull the shirt back. 'Right now, we have bigger problems.'

As he said it, they passed a medical clinic where dozens of people were gathered in the carpark and on the street. Some were holding signs and shouting. 'Turn the radio on,' Santino said, looking at his watch.

Within a few minutes, a news bulletin came on.

> 'Tonight, news of more deaths. As hospitals overflow and tensions rise, many are wondering where this is all going to end. As yet, there are no reports of related deaths in other countries, but they are bracing for that possibility. Despite the FBI's assurances that there is no evidence of a connection to IVF, the more than 5-million people conceived using the technology are not feeling any less distraught. Many have been describing this situation as a human experiment gone wrong. FBI Agent Troy Boffa spoke again to media tonight, saying they are convinced the cases relate to a new superbug, possibly out of the Middle East. But many others remain unconvinced.'

Arnya turned the volume down. 'We have to let people know now. We can't wait any longer. Can Harry release a statement or something saying that it is IVF and that not everyone is going to die, that it's only certain clinics that are affected?'

'At this point, I don't think it will do any good. People are in a state of mass hysteria. Nothing that any cop says, without hard evidence to back it up, is going to make a shred of difference and the Feds will block it anyway. There are already people like Boffa making those statements and the only thing that people know right now is that there is something terribly wrong and people are dying. Nothing, except for the truth and concrete evidence to back it up, will convince them now. Nothing.'

Arnya pulled her hair back from her face and rubbed her stinging eyes. 'I hate the thought that parents are sitting at home right now looking at their children and wondering if at any moment they might drop dead in front of them.'

'Right now, our only hope is to see what's on that phone and pray that it's something we can use.' Santino looked out the window at a local mosque. There was an anti-Islamic sign stuck awkwardly into the grass. It was hanging to one side and threatening to topple at any moment. It was on fire. 'We need to bring an end to this madness.'

Arnya thought of Robert and what had just unfolded at the apartment. The reality of it hadn't yet fully sunk in. She had known Robert for years, so had Santino. Both had considered him a friend. To know that he was as easily manipulated as the rest of the others was just too much.

Santino was thinking the same thing. 'I never would have thought that Robert…' he stopped short and she could tell that he was trying to find the words to sum up his feelings.

Arnya could sense the depth of his hurt. She picked up where he left off to save him from having to find the words. 'Robert's involvement was a terrible shock. Thank God we walked away from each other all those years ago. If that's the kind of man he has become, I'm thankful to have gotten out early. But Arthur, that's something else.' She was on the verge of tears. 'Arthur has been like a second father to me. I've known my whole life, Santino. And now, to find out that he was never the man that I thought he was, I can't even begin to take that in.'

'It must be such a shock, I'm so sorry,' he said, shaking his head.

She could feel the sadness in his words and knew that he meant it.

'So, Arthur had the clinic that did IVF treatment in the early years, but your father wasn't a part of that, was he? Santino asked.

Arnya was sure he wasn't. 'Arthur and my father were best friends. They were both doctors, but Arthur was always far more ambitious. My father was happy with his small local practice and long-term patients.' She smiled at the memory. 'He literally had a few dozen patients that were like family. Dad knew all their kids by name. He didn't even need a file because he knew them so well. Arthur's clinic, from what I can remember, started out small but got bigger. At one stage it expanded to another location but then I think he closed that and just kept the one clinic. I guess that expansion was undertaken in anticipation of a payoff that never came to fruition. At the time, growing up, Arthur was my hero and my parents thought the world of him.'

Santino stared out into the darkness and chaos. 'People do all sorts of things for all sorts of reasons. I don't think it's possible to ever truly know anyone. I can honestly say that I didn't have a clue that Robert had gambling problems or drug debts, or that he'd ever turn on us like that.'

Arnya reached out to touch his arm to offer reassurance. 'I think I'm disappointed by him more than anything. And ashamed.'

Santino gave her a questioning look. 'Ashamed?'

Arnya closed her eyes. 'I honestly don't know what I'm doing anymore. I feel as if I've lost any sense of myself and what I want for my life. When I was younger, I remember feeling determined. Not for anything in particular, just determined in everything; in forging a career, keeping fit, being good at whatever I set my mind to, the usual things. But here I am, with absolutely no clue who I am or what I want. These last few weeks have made me realise how little I was interacting with people and how distant I had become from every facet of life other than my office and my work. Seeing Robert again, and getting caught up in all of this, stirred me up. It made me feel again, to the point of even contemplating the *what if* with Robert. I feel ashamed of how much I've given up on my dreams and how easily I could have fallen back into something with Robert just because I'm lonely.'

Arnya's sad eyes remained on the road ahead.

'I think that's understandable given the circumstances,' Santino said. 'Something like this would give anyone cause to re-evaluate their life. We all think about the *what ifs*, believe me.'

'Yes, but I feel as if I let myself become desperate for connection. I'm not in love with Robert, definitely not now and maybe I never was, but I was so quick to think about him like that again for no other reason than feeling so alone.'

Santino could hear the hurt and the self-doubt in her words. He wasn't sure what to offer other than to listen and try to understand.

'And while I'm bearing my soul,' Arnya said, changing he subject, 'what are your *what if* moments? Sounds like you've had your fair share.'

Santino shrugged. 'A few, I suppose. The closest I came to anything of significance was being engaged once.'

'Really?' She paused. 'I would never have guessed that.'

Santino let out a long sigh that seemed to bring with it something that softened him. 'It feels like another life now, one I didn't live, or wish I hadn't lived. We were high school sweethearts, totally in love. We always told each other we'd get married and have a big family, all that usual stuff. She went off to college and I joined the LAPD and we went our separate ways, the way that most people do during those years. But then we re-connected when I was in my twenties and it was as if we had never been apart, you know?'

'That's the best kind of love. The kind that keeps finding its way back,' Arnya said.

'That's what I thought too, but it didn't work out that way. We were happy, really happy, and planning a future together. My family loved her and I thought everything was perfect. I asked her to marry me and she accepted, but two months out from the wedding she told me she was pregnant and it wasn't mine. There was a guy, someone she had been seeing through college, and she thought she might still be in love with him.'

'I'm so sorry, Santino. I can't even...' Her heart ached for him.

'It was a long time ago now. I haven't even thought about it in years. That's life though, isn't it? You never really know people, even when you think you do.' Santino pulled up outside Arnya's office building. He parked the car under the darkness of a large tree. The entrance door was only a short walk across a grass verge.

Arnya got out and scanned the area as they walked to the building entrance. She checked behind her numerous times before punching the code into the keypad on the door. Inside the dark building she hit the light switch on the wall and headed to the elevator with Santino behind her. 'Let's get the phone plugged in and see what we've got. If there's something of value, do we go straight to Harry?' she asked.

'It'll depend on what it is. No matter what, we'll keep Harry in the loop, but if there's cold, hard, irrefutable evidence on there, then we take it straight to the top.'

'Boffa?' Arnya asked, hitting the lights on her office wall.

Santino scoffed. 'Definitely not Boffa. We'll go above him. It'll be good to put him back in his box at the same time. I don't trust any of them. We go straight to the DA.'

'Let's hope that Maurice has delivered.' Arnya plugged the phone into the wall. She got some Cokes from the fridge and crackers from her drawer. 'Here,' she said, handing a can to Santino. 'It's not much, but we both need to eat something.'

She went to the cupboard and got out a bandage and pain killers. She handed the bandage to Santino and took two tablets from the packaging for herself.

Santino undid the bandage. 'After all this time, knowing in my gut that there was more to all of this, I just want to know the whole truth. Not Fitzgerald's version, but Maurice's truth, the whole truth.'

Arnya stared at the floor, fear and sadness etched on her face. 'Too many people have already lost their lives. What scares me the most is that, no matter what the truth is, we may not be able to stop people from dying. What if a cure can't be found? People will continue to die and there will be nothing we, or anyone else, can do about it. How do you tell people that?'

There was a strain in her voice. Santino finished wrapping his shoulder and pulled her in close to him with his good arm. She immediately eased into his embrace. 'We've done everything we possibly can,' he said. 'That's all anyone can do. And if we can't save them, if that fate is already sealed, then at least they'll know why and who is to blame. We can only try, Arnya. It's all we've got.'

Arnya pulled away and wiped her eyes. She didn't want to let herself get too comfortable in Santino's arms. 'I'm sorry to get emotional. I know we need clear heads right now, but this is too much to comprehend.'

The phone screen lit up on the bench. Santino rushed over and picked it up. 'Thank God, it's not pin-coded,' he said. Relief washed over him, a welcome feeling from the constant adrenaline coursing through his veins.

Arnya moved in close at his side so she could see.

Santino clicked into the apps. 'There's three videos.' He turned to Arnya and pursed his lips, exhaling slowly. 'Okay, here goes.'

Arnya craned her neck to watch as Maurice Stephens face appeared on the screen. His eyes were bloodshot and his hair looked oily and unwashed. 'That's his apartment,' Santino said. They watched as Maurice tried to stand the phone up against something on his desk. It fell a few times, shaking the camera before he stabilised it. He sat down, facing the screen.

'If you're watching this, then I'm dead. I just hope that whoever has this will do with it what I couldn't.'

Maurice's eyes darted back and forth and he turned several times to look behind him.

'I don't know how this happened. Any of this. All I know is that it all went wrong and now people are going to die. I need you all to know that hurting them was not my intention. When Parker and I first thought about this, it seemed simple and it had the potential to make a lot of money. Shit, I was so stupid.'

He placed his face in his hands and then ran them up through his matted hair.

'We should never have done it, I know that now. But Parker won't let me stop it. Hell, I don't even know if I can, but he doesn't want to intervene. They don't believe me. They don't believe that it's going to happen, but it will. I don't know when, but when it does, it will unravel fast.'

He bit down hard on his lip and seemed to fight back tears.

'I can't let this happen without warning people. How can we just let them die? I think he's going to kill me.'

Maurice turned back toward the door and snatched up the phone. The screen went black. There was only muffled audio before the recording stopped.

'Play the next one.' Arnya's said. Her hands were shaking. She leaned on Santino for support.

Santino pressed play on the next video. 'That's his apartment again. It's just a different angle.' He leaned in to look at the figure in the background. 'Shit, that's Fitzgerald near the door, look.'

'He must have had the camera hidden before Fitzgerald arrived.'

Maurice was standing near the sofa, looking over at the man he had once considered to be his best friend.

'Parker, c'mon, please. This is eating me up inside and it will eat you up too. We can't let this be, we can't hide from what we've done.'

Parker walked toward the sofa and leaned down to the coffee table. He held up a bottle.

'This is what's eating you up. It's not your conscience, or God, or anything else. Get off the booze, Maurice. You don't even know what's going to happen. This was always going to be a long game. Maybe longer than we anticipated, but it's not over. You're guessing.'

Maurice was shaking his head vigorously.

'You don't understand. You never understand. All you do is bark orders and tell me to make things happen. Well, I can't this time.'

Fitzgerald's face hardened, his jaw clenching.

'You listen to me. I had to do a lot of ass covering with a lot of people when this crap didn't play out when it was supposed to.

You spouting this shit now is going to stir up a hornet's nest of trouble. You need to keep your mouth shut or I will have to shut it for you.'

'I can't, don't you understand?'

Maurice was pleading. He walked back and forth and tapped his forehead.

'These people didn't develop the condition they were supposed to because I made a mistake. I didn't know back then what I know now. The science has moved forward and I've had time to research. What I did then isn't good, Parker, I'm telling you. We didn't intervene in the process the right way.'

Fitzgerald's voice was low. He spoke slowly, almost melodically.

'You said it would be simple, like a planned obsolete, and that we'd be ready with treatments. You were fucking sure, Maurice. Why are you now so sure that they'll die?'

Maurice interrupted.

'It's planned obsolescence.'

Parker stiffened at the correction.

'I don't give a shit what it is. My point is, maybe it's only delayed somehow. Just because it didn't happen at the time you thought it would, doesn't mean everyone is suddenly going to die. You were wrong the first time and you're probably wrong

again. You're being paranoid and ridiculous. You have to understand the fire you're playing with here, Maurice. I'm trying to help you. This has the potential to ruin us both.'

Maurice was shaking his head.

'I didn't do it right somehow. They should have begun showing signs years ago. And I waited it out Parker, you know I did. I rechecked everything and I went over every single step. That's how I know. Don't you get it? I fucked up. Instead of setting off a sickness that we can treat, it's going to act like an expiry. When they reach that point, whenever that is, that's it. There won't even be any warning signs.'

Fitzgerald's face reddened. With one swift swipe of his hand, he pushed the contents of the coffee table onto the floor.

'We were supposed to make millions from this, you fucking idiot. Do something to fix it, Maurice, there must be a way. I put years into waiting for this and now you're telling me there will never be any kind of payday? Not ever? This was my one chance to stick it to that son of a bitch!'

'We fucked up, Park. It's not just about the money anymore, people will die. We have to come clean and warn people.'

Parker moved closer and grabbed Maurice's arm.

'I get it Maurice, don't worry about that. The situation is this. You fucked this up. You lost us millions and now you're going to find a way to fix it.'

His voice boomed so loud the recording distorted.

'Fucking fix it and keep your mouth shut!'

Santino pressed the pause button. They both needed a moment to comprehend what they had just witnessed.

Arnya straightened and looked at him. 'Jesus. I feel sick.' She walked over to the armchair and sat down. 'He didn't have a hope in hell of getting Parker to come clean, did he? He must have known that pushing for it would be dangerous, but he did it anyway. I'd almost feel sorry for Maurice, if he wasn't such a monster. He may have been a part of the disgusting plan from the start, but at least he found his way to understanding that what he had done was wrong. Even if it was too late to save anyone.'

Santino unplugged the phone and sat on the chair beside her.

Arnya moved closer to watch. When he pressed play again, Arthur appeared in Maurice's apartment. He had entered through the front door and was standing beside Maurice. Arnya could feel her heart growing heavy with the weight of what she was seeing.

Arthur sat down beside Maurice on the sofa. Arthur seemed calm, his voice even and controlled, the way he might speak to one of his patients.

'Maurice, please think about what you're saying. Think about the implications here, for all of us. What you're imagining might happen could very well never come to pass. If you really care about people, why would you even consider putting them

*through the trauma and pain of wondering what might possibly
happen to them? Surely you can see that?'*

Maurice was shaking his head and shouting.

*'You don't get it, none of you do. It's not a matter of IF, it's
WHEN. I know it!'*

He slammed his fist into is chest.

*'I know it in here. This is going to happen and no matter how
much you try to hide from it, it's going to come out. It's better
to tell people now so at least there's some time for them.'*

Fitzgerald was standing in the background, leaning
against the wall between the front door and the living
room. Arthur exchanged a look with him and Arnya turned
her head away. She knew that very look signalled plans to
get rid of Maurice.

Arnya covered her face with her hands. Arthur had been
a part of the whole thing. 'I can't watch anymore, Santino.
I'm sorry, I can't.'

Santino pressed stop and put the phone on the table.

'Fucking hell. I'm sorry you had to see that,' he said. His
eyes were wide and he raked his fingers through his hair. 'I
can't fucking believe this, Arnya. I knew. Even back then I
knew, but to see what actually happened on video like this
is… insane.'

'I know.' Arnya met his eyes. 'But when it's someone
that you loved and trusted… I trusted Arthur like I would
my own father. I just can't even begin to…'

Santino got up. His nerves were wired and adrenaline was pumping through his veins. 'I know how it feels to be betrayed by people you trust. It hurts so badly and it messes with you in ways that stay with you forever.'

Arnya sighed. It did hurt. Her parents were gone. She had no one in her life that felt like family, other than Arthur, and now that had been taken from her too. It was more than hurt. It wounded her beyond words.

Santino carefully lifted his shirt to check his shoulder. The bleeding had slowed, but his shirt was soaked and sticking to him. He looked up at Arnya. 'I never thought I'd get the whole story, you know? After everything that happened with the Fitzgerald trial and all the corruption and people that blamed me, I never thought I'd get definitive proof like this. Something that would completely vindicate me.'

Arnya squeezed his hand and looked deep into his eyes. 'The truth will come out, Santino.'

Before he could respond, she turned her attention to the third video file on the phone and pressed play. Maurice's face again appeared. He looked worse than he had in the other two videos. His hair was matted and his eyes sunken. He held the phone in front of him while recording.

'That's the church, Saint Cuthbert's, look,' Santino said. 'You can see the pews behind him.'

Maurice's voice was low and desperate.

'As I sit here before God, I ask for not only his forgiveness, but yours. I've done a terrible thing and for that I must pay my penance. They're coming for me, I know that. My life has not been a good one. I was blessed with the kind of mind that could do good in this world and yet, tainted by a wolf in sheep's

clothing, I chose to take the darker path. I own that and I'm so very sorry. I'm not afraid to be judged. It's time that I paid for what I've done, but before I meet my maker, I need to be sure that the truth is recorded and I pray that the right person will eventually come looking for the answers.'

Maurice straightened and inhaled, long and steady. He let it out, looking upward and then began.

'My name is Maurice Stephens and I am guilty of murder. Actually, mass-murders that will occur some time in the future. I cannot say when. This is my confession. When I first met Parker Fitzgerald we were in college. He was a rich brat but I liked him. He was charismatic and he took the time to get to know me. In hindsight it was likely because he thought I could do his work for him, but I didn't see that then. He loved partying, girls and drugs, which he freely sourced from his father's company, Alpha Pharmaceuticals. We shared a dorm room and, although I was shy and naive, he took me under his wing and we became inseparable.'

Maurice paused, lifting a flask to take a drink before continuing.

'Parker was smart in life, but not when it came to study and he used me to get himself through.'

He let out a stifled laugh imbued with the heaviness of regret.

'I was a willing participant, mind you. The perks of being his friend were too good to pass up. I was weak and pathetic. Parker's old man was getting fed-up though.'

He leaned back and shook his head at the memory.

'Park was an embarrassment to his family with his antics and troublemaking, so his father put him in charge of a new section of the business to keep him busy and get him out of the way. That new section was IVF. It was pretty much brand new then and it was already being met with massive backlash from religious groups and some political players. At that time, it wasn't yet a big market, but after a while, many more IVF clinics began to open as the technology took off. Babies were born and those who opposed the technology seemed to give up, or at least quieten down. But in his father's eyes, Park was still a screw up. He definitely was, don't get me wrong, but his old man, the way he treated Park, I wouldn't wish that on anyone. That's when we came up with what we thought was a brilliant plan. We could get out from under that old bastard once and for all and forge our own way.'

Maurice took another swig from the flask and looked around him. When he looked back at the camera there were tears in his eyes.

'I was drinking heavily and we were both using drugs. We thought that we could do anything. What we came up with was an idea to engineer particular flaws in the normal development of an embryo that would only begin to appear at a certain time in the individual's life. I remember trying to explain it to him because he could never really understand the science. He really

wasn't that clever. Basically, we could use IVF to deliberately program the human body to become ill at a point in the future, requiring new drugs and radical new therapeutic treatments, all of which could be designed in advance, by us, and released at the most opportune moment.'

Maurice shook his head slowly from side to side before closing his eyes and bowing his head.

Santino looked over at Arnya, her eyes were glued to the phone, wide and sad.

'We had access to all of it. The clinics, the products, the embryos, it was unlimited. We estimated that about eight to ten years would give us enough time to be at the ready with treatment options and we'd be in the perfect position to reap massive rewards. But Park pushed hard and, no matter how many times I told him we weren't ready to begin, he refused to hear it. After about two years we began distributing IVF supplies to some clinics and everything progressed as planned. IVF grew and grew and Alpha became a big player in that field. Park wanted to push it out everywhere, but I insisted we limit the number of clinics so we could manage our operations and our record keeping. I kept detailed records of all distribution.'

He picked up his notebooks from the seat beside him and faced them toward the camera.

'Everything you will ever need to know about what we did is in these books, including those involved and the clinics. I kept detailed notes, just in case.'

'Shit!' Santino shouted. Fitzgerald has them. If he destroys them, it's all gone forever.'

Arnya closed her eyes tightly. She could feel a numbness working its way through her body.

Arnya's entire view of life, and the world she lived in, had shifted. She needed to fight for herself and for all of those innocent victims who were simply going about their days never knowing they were being played like pieces in a giant game of chess.

On the video, Maurice continued.

> 'No matter how much Alpha made from their IVF products, Park hated being under his father's control. He focussed on our approaching pay day, making me work day and night on treatment plans for when the conditions began to show. And that's where it all started to fall apart. I was ready, but ten years came and went, and nothing happened. The people showed no signs of illness and I knew then that there was a chance I'd made a huge mistake. At the time, I was sure I'd done everything right, but when I went back over my methods, it became clear. I'd made a grave error, an error that would probably cost many innocent people their lives. Instead of illnesses we could make money providing drugs for, we were going to kill people. Park was enraged, of course, but the more I researched, the more I became sure that what I did would be fatal for those affected. I've pleaded again and again with Park and the others to come clean. Because it's over. There's not going to be a pay day, but they refuse to hear me and I know that I'm now a liability to him and to them. Maybe he doesn't believe me, or maybe he just doesn't care, but it's coming. I know it is, I know it in my soul.'

Maurice's head jerked upward and another voice could be heard further away. 'That's Father Kelly,' Arnya said, 'he's speaking to Maurice.'

The screen went black as Maurice put the camera down on his lap, and then it went silent. The recording had stopped.

'It's enough,' Santino said. 'We've got enough to take it to the top and bring that bastard down once and for all.'

Arnya felt some relief wash over her, but the sick feeling in her stomach remained. 'Thank God Maurice made the videos. It's still bothering me though about Robert's involvement. Was he a part of the whole thing or was he just another pawn in Fitzgerald's game?'

Santino had already drawn his own conclusions about that. 'I'm pretty sure that Fitzgerald would have been controlling Robert by buying his drug and gambling debts and then using them to blackmail him. It happened with a cop I knew during Maurice's murder case. Fitzgerald made sure that he got intel on everyone he could. Everyone that he could exploit and use to his advantage. People that had a lot to lose. He found those that had weaknesses - like gambling or drugs like Robert - and he bought the debts from whoever they owed. From then on, he owned them. If they didn't do what he wanted...' he was mid-sentence when Arnya placed her finger on her lips and shook her head.

'The elevator. Someone's inside the building.' Her ashen face reflected the gravity of their situation. While they finally had the proof they had sought, Arnya feared they were now trapped like rats in a cage.

Santino put the phone in his pocket and moved toward the office door. He opened it just a crack and peered into the waiting area before closing it. 'There's two of them that I can see,' he whispered. 'Could be more. How do we get out of here?'

Fighting against a wave of fear and rising panic, Arnya moved toward the laboratory door behind her desk. 'Follow me. We can get to the ground floor, but then we have to go out through the front entrance. It's the only way out after the building's been locked-up.'

Santino followed, quietly pulling the laboratory door shut and locking it behind him. He followed Arnya down the stairs and into the building's foyer. She hovered in the alcove adjacent to the elevator, scanning the area.

The light above the elevator lit up. 'They're coming down. Come on,' Santino said. He gestured for her to follow him, crossing the foyer to the front door. Through the window, he spotted another man on the grass in the distance, near the car park. 'Shit, there's another one.'

'What now?' Arnya said, holding her hand to her thudding chest.

'When I open the door, run as fast as you can to the car. When he turns to go for you, I'll take him from behind.'

Arnya's eyes were wide. 'You will get him, won't you? What about your shoulder?"

'I'll get him, I promise,' he assured her. 'Go!' He flung the door open.

Arnya raced out, crossing the lawn toward the car as fast as she could manage with pain searing through her hip. Santino waited for the doors of the elevator to open, then set off as soon as the man turned on his heels in Arnya's direction. Santino reached the pair just as the man grabbed the back of her shirt. She elbowed him hard, causing him to lurch forward and giving Santino the opportunity to land a blow at the base of the man's neck. 'Go!' he yelled.

Arnya took off again for the car. She made it to the driver's seat and started the engine. 'C'mon, c'mon!' she shouted, willing Santino to break free from the man's hold.

The other men, dressed all in black and with balaclava's covering their faces, emerged from the building and sprinted toward Santino and the other man as they wrestled on the ground. One of them had a gun and held it in front of him as he charged toward Santino. Arnya threw the car into gear and mounted the curb, crossing the grass at speed. Barely missing Santino and the man, she braked hard beside Santino. He clambered from the ground and into the passenger seat, clutching his bloody shoulder. Arnya slammed her foot on the gas, the tyres spinning on the grass, flicking up turf as the car took off.

As bullets hit the back windscreen of the car, shattering it, Santino and Arnya ducked low in their seats. She pressed harder on the gas and gripped the wheel, feeling Father Kelly's small car sway and jerk.

Santino was panting heavily and trying to catch his breath. He looked out of the back, checking if Fitzgerald's men were in pursuit. 'Are you okay?' he asked, looking her over for signs of injury.

'I'm okay.' She looked back at him. There was a gash on his forehead and she could see he was holding his shoulder. 'But you're not.'

Santino checked his head in the mirror. 'We need to get Downtown, to police headquarters,' Santino said, his chest heaving. 'Now that we have the videos, no one will be able to refute our claims. I'll call Harry on the way.' He pulled his phone out and dialled Harry's number. 'Shit, he's not picking up. I'll leave a message.' When he heard the beep, he spoke quickly. 'Harry, we've got Maurice Stephens' phone and on it he confesses everything. He and Fitzgerald concocted a plan to make billions by causing IVF children to be affected by some kind of condition.' He paused, again trying to catch his breath. 'They were going to make sure that when the kids got sick, they would be the only ones ready with a treatment and drugs, but something went wrong. Maurice said that everything is in the notebooks he left, but Fitzgerald has them. We have the videos though and Fitzgerald makes an appearance in them. We've finally got him, Harry. We're coming in, but Fitzgerald's goons are on our tail. When you get this, get a squad to come in our direction. We'll be coming along Bluestone Road. I'm sure Fitzgerald's not far behind, so send them to meet us. And send an ambulance…I'm bleeding pretty bad.'

'Fuck, Santino! They're behind us,' Arnya shouted. She straightened in the seat, watching the SUV approaching behind them. It came close and backed off several times. 'They're going to hit us, Jesus! I'm not sure I can outrun them in this piece of shit.'

'Just keep driving,' Santino said. 'Harry should have squad cars heading in our direction soon. We just have to stay in front of them long enough for the others to reach us.'

'Are we handing this over to Harry then? I thought you wanted to take it higher, just in case.'

'Now that we know we have the video evidence, we'll go to Harry first. He was the one who set this whole thing in motion for his nephew and he deserves the credit for bringing the truth to the public.'

Santino's speech had slowed and his eyes were rolling back into their sockets. His shoulder wound was bleeding heavily. He got out Maurice's phone and held it in his hand.

Arnya gripped the steering wheel. 'Just in case anything happens, I want you to know that I am so grateful for all you've done. You're a good human being, Santino, and there aren't too many of them in this world. I really want you to know that.'

Santino looked over to her and smiled, struggling to speak due to the pain and loss of blood. He was fading fast. 'You're a good human being yourself, Arnya Sloane. And that's why I want you to be prepared for what comes next. The media, the players in this game who will be panicked, and the public demanding answers, will all be striking hard and causing chaos. It won't be easy to handle and I've seen much lesser things break people. I got you into this, Arnya and I want to be there for you. We're in this together, no matter what. I promise you that.'

Just as the words left his lips there was a loud bang. The car launched forward pushing them both back, hard against their seats. A feeling of weightlessness took over. The car careened through the road barrier. Santino said a silent prayer and reached for Arnya's hand. The sound of her scream rang out in his ears. He felt her skin touch his and closed his eyes before the impact. The car hit the ground and rolled.

There was nothing but silence.

CHAPTER

22

Arnya felt an intense pain searing across her forehead before any other senses returned. There was something warm running down her face and dripping from her ear. The sensation felt odd as the drops fell from her cheek to her earlobe. She was lying sideways, she knew that much. She willed her heavy eyes to open.

The car had gone off the road. They had been hit hard from behind and pushed through the roadside barrier before the car crashed. Her memories were returning in pieces. In front of her, she could see the windshield, badly broken, with only shards clinging in place. There seemed to be trees and darkness beyond it, lit only by the moon. The air in the car felt cold and the smell of fuel was burning her nostrils.

Arnya turned her head painfully to the right, looking for Santino. He was slumped forward, his head resting on the shattered side window. 'Santino,' she called out to him. Her voice was hoarse. 'Santino, wake up.'

The fogginess of her thoughts was slowly lifting and she could see that the car had landed partially on its right side. Arnya couldn't feel her hands and her right arm was pinned at her side. She tugged hard from her shoulder, slowly pulling it free with her other hand. The pain made her wince as she reached out to Santino, pushing his chest. 'Santino, please, wake up!' Her voice didn't sound like her own.

As the ringing in her ears lessened, she started to make out voices. Male voices. Outside, among the dense trees, she could see torch lights dancing beyond the pieces of glass that clung to the edges of the windscreen. 'Shit!' she gasped, tilting her head back. *The phone.*

Pulling herself up, she checked on Santino. His head was badly gashed and his right arm pinned against the door. His breathing was shallow and irregular.

As she tried to move closer to him, the car creaked and moved. Arnya grabbed hold of the seat as it rolled back to land on all four wheels.

Maurice's phone had been on Santino's lap, and Santino's phone was now wedged awkwardly between the passenger seat and the middle console. Arnya placed one throbbing hand on the dash for support before unbuckling her seatbelt with the other. She turned herself in the seat to face the headrest and then pulled her knees up to kneel on the seat. Leaning over, she thought she could make out the shape of Maurice's phone on the floor at Santino's feet.

Somewhere outside, the voices were getting louder as the lights roamed in the darkness. Arnya stretched over, resting her arms on Santino's legs. She reached down, feeling for the phone as pain shot through her back and hip. She moved her hands around, squinting as blood ran into her eyes, clouding her vision. The voices grew louder.

'Please, please.' She managed to get her other hand down into the space, reaching further toward the front of the footwell until she felt Maurice's phone. She pulled herself back to her seat and pressed the buttons on both of the phones. Santino's phone had service and Maurice's still had some charge.

'Santino.' She pushed his arm again and firmly tapped his cheek with her fingers. 'Wake up. Please. They're coming.'

Santino remained unresponsive and the smell of fuel grew stronger.

'Shit.' Arnya scanned the area outside. If she tried to run, they'd surely catch her. She could already feel that her left leg was bleeding and she didn't know if she would be able put weight on it. Holding the phones in her hands, she could hear the voices drawing closer. She swiped to open Santino's phone and played the video on Maurice's device simultaneously.

Within minutes the voices were around the car. She turned the phones off, hid Maurice's underneath her and buckled her seat belt. She placed Santino's phone in the console and waited. When the voices were at the window, she closed her eyes and held her breath.

With one blow, the back passenger window shattered. She winced, but tried to remain still. Outside she could hear people moving. One went around to Santino's side and the other came around to hers. Slowly they circled the vehicle and met at the front. She could sense them in front of her, leaning in over the hood.

'Drag her out of there. Fitzgerald wants nothing left behind.'

Arnya could feel the sensation of the man leaning in, the heat emanating from his body.

'I'll have to pull her through the window, she's out cold and her door is jammed. What are we supposed to do with him? He looks dead.'

'Get them both out. We'll find out what he wants us to do later.'

Arnya could feel the car move as the man leaned on the hood and moved closer to her. She thought she might throw up and her heart was pounding fast. It was hard to hear through the thudding it caused in her ears and inside her head. In her mind, she made a plan. Once the man got her out and onto the ground, she would continue to pretend to be unconscious. When he went back for Santino, she would test her foot to make sure she could put weight on it. If she could, she would run. She didn't want to think about the scenario if she couldn't.

Beside her, she heard Santino make a low groan. He was coming to. She willed him to be quiet. If they thought he was already dead, they might not kill him. 'Stay down,' she breathed in a barely audible whisper, hoping Santino might hear her and understand what she was telling him.

She felt the man's hand grab her arm. A jolt of fear raced from one end of her to the other, burning like hot water in her veins and kicking her into a fight or flight response. She wanted to kick and scream and yell and get away, but she willed herself to stay silent. It was the only way. After everything they had been through, and all of the lives that were hanging in the balance, she had to stay calm and unresponsive.

When a phone rang, the man let go of her and slid down the hood onto the ground. She jumped slightly at the ringing and wondered if he had noticed. The man stood up, turning his focus to his partner.

'What? Are you fucking kidding me?' There was a mix of anger and exasperation in the man's tone.

Arnya opened her eyes to slits. The man on the phone turned back to the other who was still at the car. 'It's blown up, we have to go.'

'What do you mean it's blown up? Fitzgerald will kill us if we don't finish this.'

'It's all over the TV. Fitzgerald is finished. We need to get the fuck out of here.'

'And what about these two?' The other man gestured towards Arnya and Santino.

The first man shrugged. 'Burn it? I dunno, but do it quick.'

Arnya's eyes shot open. They were going to burn them alive.

'Jesus Christ, this is fucked up. Are we even gonna get paid to burn two people in a car?'

'Just fuckin' burn it and let's get the hell out of here. I'm not going down with him. If you're smart, you'll get as far from here as possible after this, that's what I'm doin'. Apparently, some video that fingers Fitzgerald is all over the news. The heat will be all over him. I'm getting as far from him as fucking possible.'

Arnya could smell the fuel. It was closer to her, maybe even on her clothes, but she couldn't be sure. She looked over to Santino who was stirring slightly. 'Santino, come on. I need you. I need you,' she whispered.

Outside, the men moved to a position where they could see the road above. The first man made another call and the other waited beside him for further instructions.

Santino turned his head toward Arnya and tried to open his eyes. Blood was running from the gash in his head. 'I'm here,' he groaned, barely audible.

'They're going to burn us alive. We have to get out,' she said.

Squinting, Santino looked around. 'Where are they? How many?' His speech was slurred and he was pale.

'Two I think, that's all I saw. They're at the back. We're going to have to go out the front window, it's the only way.'

Arnya turned slowly in her seat as she had before and climbed up on top of it. Turning back to face the front, she carefully put her hands on the dashboard.

'Be careful of the broken glass,' Santino warned. 'Climb out and, if they see you, just roll. Roll right off the hood and onto the ground. If you can get to your feet, take off and keep running, I mean it.'

'I won't leave you, not like this.' The words caught in her throat as the terror threatened to overwhelm her. 'I don't care what happens, I'm not going to let you be… burnt alive.'

Santino's voice was soft but stern. 'Arnya, go, I mean it. If you don't go now, we'll both die here tonight and I don't want that on my conscience. Promise me. Someone has to make sure this story is told and that those bastards pay for what they've done. Call 911 as soon as you can.'

Arnya hesitated, but then nodded. She leaned over and kissed his lips. She cupped his face in her hands as tears ran down her cheeks. 'We're not going to die here. Do you hear me? We're not.'

Santino smiled. 'Go, now!'

Arnya pulled herself up and through the window and onto the hood of the car, the noise alerting the men who were still figuring out what to do. She rolled, just as Santino had instructed, and felt the grass beneath her when she landed heavily. She got to her knees and quickly crawled around to the side of the car. Within seconds, hands were on her shoulders and gripping her hair, dragging her to a standing position. The man walked her back to the front of the car and wrapped one arm around her neck. He stared into the wreckage at Santino. 'Do it Billy, burn this fucking pig.' His offsider reached into his jacket pocket.

Arnya and Santino's eyes were firmly locked on each other. The large man with the cigarette lighter hovered, momentarily halted by the sound of approaching sirens. He turned on his heels and took off into the darkness.

Arnya felt a hard shove from behind as the other man reached into his pants and pulled out a gun. She lunged to the side of the car and hid, her chest exploding with pain as a single shot rang out. For the second time that night, darkness and silence engulfed her.

—\|⌣\|—

Arnya's whole body felt heavy. From her toes to the hair on her head, there didn't seem to be a single piece of her that didn't ache. When she opened her eyes, she realised she was in a hospital bed.

She turned her head slightly, feeling the burn in her shoulder and neck. Santino was at her side. He was clean shaven and dressed in a shirt and pants. The gash on his head had been sown up with visible stitches. 'How are you?' he asked, smiling. He leaned in closer to the bed, close enough for her to see the bruising on his face and the stitches that started at his forehead and disappeared beneath his hair.

Arnya felt her dry lips as she tried to speak. She licked them, causing the cracks to sting. She blinked to re-focus her eyes. Behind Santino and, in fact, all around her, were flowers, cards, and baskets filled with food and wine. There were even stuffed animals strewn about, hiding on top of the cupboard and poking out from behind wafts of cellophane.

Santino stood back, his right arm pinned to his chest with a sling. He handed her a cup of water and then helped to lift her head enough to drink. Every move caused pain to surge through her like a wildfire. 'You'll need to go slow, you've been out for a while.'

Arnya took a sip of the water, letting it soothe her lips and ease her throat. She let it sit in her mouth for a moment, grateful for the moisture. She thought how crazy it was for something as simple as water, and the sensation of that liquid, to feel so good.

'How long?' she rasped. Laying her head back down, she winced again. She could feel the intensity of the pain pushing out from her chest and abdomen to other parts of her body.

'A few days. You went straight into surgery and you've been unconscious since then.' He sat at her side. Leaning in, he held her hand and looked at her weary face with a smile that lit up his eyes. 'We nearly lost you.'

'Surgery?' It felt as if her mind was somehow behind the rest of her and was scrambling to catch up. Pieces of what had happened were filtering in, but not all of it. She could remember being at Robert's apartment and later going off the road, but then it got hazy. There was an accident and strange sounds that swam about in her head. They were mixed up and coming to her in a disjointed order.

'You were shot, Arnya. In the chest, by one of Fitzgerald's men. Do you remember?'

She closed her eyes trying to grab the fragments and images that floated around in a jumble as she tried to take hold of them. Memories of being in the car with Santino and hearing the men around her. And then the sound of the gunshot.

'Jesus, Santino, what about the video?' She tried to pull herself to a sitting position, but pain tore through her. She grabbed at her ribs, 'Ugh, no.'

Santino stood up and quickly eased her back to the pillow.

'What about Fitzgerald? Tell me what happened?' she pleaded. Tears were filling her bloodshot eyes.

Santino sat on the edge of the bed beside her. 'Hang on, one thing at a time, you need to stay rested. There's a pain relief pump here you can press.'

Santino handed her the button. She pressed and waited for the pain to ease.

When she was settled, Santino explained what happened. 'After you were shot, they airlifted you here. There was a team waiting and you went straight into surgery. It was touch and go. They lost you several times.

The surgeon said that it was as if you refused to give up on that table.' He rubbed his eyes with the back of his wrist.

Arnya squeezed his hand. She wiped a tear from his cheek as her own eyes continued to fill. 'How did you get out?' she asked him. 'I thought you were going to die there in the car. I thought we both were.'

'The team Harry sent arrived just after you were shot. The medivac helicopter was on its way already, thanks to you, and they got me out too. I'm alive because of you, you know that? Because of what you did.'

'What I did?' she asked.

Santino smiled. 'Yes, the video. Don't you remember?'

She remembered holding Santino's phone in her hand and Maurice's video on the other device as the men were approaching.

'Streaming the video live was genius. You told them where we were and to send help and then played the last of Maurice's videos for the whole world to see. Within minutes the news sites had all picked it up. Fitzgerald was done, they all were.'

The news was like a bolt of electricity coursing throughout Arnya's battered body. Not once had she let herself really feel the true depth of her fear. And now that it was over, every ounce of hurt, fear and sadness came crashing down on her. She closed her eyes and let the knowledge that Fitzgerald was behind bars sink in.

She held her face in her hands and cried harder than she had ever cried before. She had died. Several times, she had died, and yet here she was, sitting up in bed talking to Santino. He was telling her that she was a hero. She had come so close to never fulfilling any of her dreams. Never finding love or having a family. She had barely made it through, and now that she was through, she couldn't face losing it all again.

She lifted her face from her hands. She wanted to look at Santino when she asked her next question. She needed to be able to read the truth in his expression, regardless of the answer. She wanted to ask it. She needed to know, but she didn't want to hear herself say it out loud.

'And the people dying? Is there anything that can be done?'

Santino reached out to touch her arm. He kept his eyes firmly on hers, long enough for her to know the answer. 'There's nothing that can be done. I'm so sorry, Arnya. Whatever they did just can't be undone, not by anyone, at least that's what I've been told.'

Arnya could feel her body turning cold from the inside out. After all the hard work to find the answers so they could save the lives of innocent people. There was nothing that could be done?

A deep sound found its way to her throat. A sound that mirrored the pain of the burning inside her. The inevitability of her own fate settled on her and a feeling of acceptance began to slowly seep in, weaving its way through her skin and into her bones.

Santino held her tighter. 'You're going to be okay, Arnya. Arthur was injured, but he didn't die. I've already been to see him, and he has assured me that you were not part of the experiment.' He gave her a gentle smile. 'He said that only he dealt with your parents' embryo. He gave me his word.'

Arnya sobbed into Santino's chest. A wave of relief sweeping over her before the guilt set in. The room spun and her eyes lost focus.

'Lie back, please. This is all too much. You need to rest.' Santino helped her back to the pillow and offered her some more water.

'I don't even have the words to say how I'm feeling, Santino. Hearing that from Arthur is like a death sentence being lifted, and yet at the same time…' She was finding it hard to put the words together through heaving sobs. 'I feel so horribly sad that others are not going to get that. They deserve to be told this too. They deserve to be told that they will be okay.'

'I know. And I'm sure this must be so conflicting for you, but you have to allow yourself to work through the feelings. You died Arnya, multiple times, fighting for all of them. And then you woke up not knowing if you were still on that death list. But you're not. You're going to live and you're allowed to feel happy about that. You've done everything you possibly can, and more, to uncover the truth and save those people.'

Arnya knew he was right, but the knowledge that others would continue to lose their loved ones was too horrific to contemplate.

Santino could see the pain in her eyes as she stared at the ceiling. He wished there was something he could say to ease her sorrow. 'Those who are affected will die no matter what we do, but based on Maurice's notes of the clinics and locations, we can at least allow them the dignity and opportunity to say goodbye to their loved ones and get their affairs in order. That has to be better than nothing, Arnya. Giving them some time is everything.'

Arnya could feel the warmth of tears trailing down her cheeks. 'It's just not fair, Santino. It's unfair and tragic and it should never have happened. I can't - and I never will -

come to terms with how anyone could have done such a thing to innocent people. These are people in positions of power and trust and they use that for their own gain. There are monsters out there walking around as human beings and fooling us all. They disguise themselves as influential and important people who are acting in our best interests, while they smile and slowly kill us for financial gain. I just can't...' She winced, the pain returning with the exertion.

'I know, Arnya. It's impossible to understand or even come to terms with, but right now, you need to take one step at a time and heal. We might not be able to bring down every bad guy, but this time, we got some of them. They'll pay for what they've done, but you have just been shot and your recovery needs to take priority. I don't want to lose you - again. I couldn't.' His eyes were wide and pleading.

Arnya's chest ached and so did her heart. 'We make a pretty good team, don't we?' she said. 'Thank you for staying with me.'

Santino smiled. 'You saved my life. I'll never forget that. And you helped me put Fitzgerald behind bars. Thank you, Arnya Sloane.'

'Well, I hope he rots in Hell, I really do.'

'If it's any consolation, Alpha Pharmaceuticals is being completely shut down. The FBI and CDC have already gone in and closed all of its operations. Its billions in holdings will likely be placed into a victims' compensation fund for the families, and Fitzgerald will never see the light of day again. You're a hero.'

Arnya scoffed. 'A hero? I'm sure the Feds have spun some story to swing the credit to them.'

Santino shook his head. 'Not this time. Thanks to the video, they had no choice but to give you - both of us - the credit for unravelling the whole thing. Boffa was in the middle of a press conference about their virus theory when the video went viral. They're red-faced and backpedalling of course, but they'll cover that up pretty easily.'

'And Kathryn? Is she safe?'

Santino could see the worry on Arnya's face. 'She's safe and well and she even came in to see you. So did Father Kelly. You're quite popular.'

Arnya began to laugh, slowly giving way to a sob. 'I'm sorry,' she whispered. 'It's all just too much, isn't it? I don't know how the hell I got here or how this all happened.'

Santino leaned forward and embraced her. 'You're in shock, Arnya. It's okay and it's normal. I'm here for you and I'm not going anywhere.' He pulled back slightly to look at her. 'You should be so proud of yourself. I am.'

Arnya closed her eyes and let herself fall completely into his embrace. Arthur, Robert, the innocent lives, all of it. It all felt surreal. The only real thing she could understand was the feeling of Santino holding onto her tightly. When her tears finally subsided, she rested back against the pillow.

'I think I might be falling in love with you, Professor,' Santino said. He put his hand to her face and gently wiped her cheeks.

'Good,' she grinned.

Santino leaned in and kissed her gently. 'I'm going to grab some coffees. Can I get you anything?'

'Coffee sounds good,' she smiled.

Santino headed to the cafeteria, calling Harry on the way.

'Hey, Santino. How is she?' Harry asked.

'She's good. She's awake and sore, but she's going to be okay.'

Harry was quiet. 'I'm at the cemetery,' he said. 'My sister and I are here and we're raising a glass of whiskey to Jason – and to you and Arnya.'

'It was you who started all this Harry. You were the one who set it in motion.'

Harry laughed. 'Well, thank you, but my sister is telling me to pass on her deepest thanks.'

Santino hung up with a sense of contentment. It had been years since he felt as if there wasn't something hanging over his head, unfinished.

He took the coffees and headed back to Arnya. The thanks from Harry and his sister would certainly brighten her spirits.

When he got to her ward there was a flurry of doctors and nurses at the end of the corridor. At Arnya's room.

The coffees fell from his hands and landed on the ground, splattering their contents in front of him.

He knew she was gone.

Also by this author

Confetti Confidential: They Do, I Don't
Confetti Confidential: Annabel's Wedding
Aloha Love
A Moonta Bay Christmas

Manufactured by Amazon.com.au
Sydney, New South Wales, Australia